Before We Drowned

Book One

Ashley Rae

Before We Drowned, by Ashley Rae
Utterback

Book design by Ashley Rae Utterback
Editing by Roxana Coumans

Author's Note

Before We Drowned is intended for mature, adult audiences only. This novel covers some heavy topics that may be triggering for some readers. Please read at your own risk.

Trigger warnings are listed on the back of this page. If you want to avoid spoilers, feel free to skip.

Trigger Warnings

This book contains triggering matters for some readers, including but not limited to: alcohol, alcoholism, substance abuse, addiction, blood, cheating, death, depression, drugs, needles, profanity, PTSD, sexually explicit scenes, suicide, violence.

Before We Drowned Playlist

1. Yellowcard "Ocean Avenue"
2. Sublime "Badfish"
3. Rolling Stones "Sympathy for the Devil"
4. Iration "Summer Nights"
5. MGMT "Kids"
6. Kid Cudi "Pursuit of Happiness"
7. Tyler Childers "Whitehouse Road"
8. The 502s "Just a Little While"
9. Børns "Electric Love"
10. The Lumineers "Flowers In Your Hair"
11. Aurora "Runaway"
12. Tyler Childers "Feathered Indians"
13. Miley Cyrus "Angels Like You"
14. Billie Eilish "Ocean Eyes"
15. Lady Gaga & Bradley Cooper "Shallow"

Table of Contents

17. Jordan	139
18. Adrian	143
19. Jordan	149
20. Adrian	152
21. Jordan	160
22. Adrian	163
23. Jordan	167
24. Adrian	172
25. Jordan	175
26. Jordan	180
27. Adrian	195
28. Jordan	198
29. Adrian	211
30. Jordan	215
31. Jordan	227
32. Jordan	236
33. Adrian	241
34. Adrian	245
35. Jordan	256
36. Adrian	259

If the world goes up in flames around you,
you might as well join the party.

Prologue

Adrian

The eyes of the body on the floor were lifeless, serving as an invisible border between the broken and the absent.

Her eyes were filled with tears.

Mine were hollow.

Blood staining the carpet below us was my biggest concern. A dark red pool that large would surely take a while to clean from our beige carpet. I watched as it seeped deeper into the fibers below my feet, my mind blank.

This pain was too much to fathom. Instead, I pushed it away. I didn't allow myself to process what had happened so that the heart wrenching, selfish betrayal could go unnoticed.

I felt nothing. It was easier that way.

Thick air filled the surrounding room, drowning out screams that desperately tried to ring into my ears. I stood unblinking, watching as the room's lighting changed from golden to red and blue hues. Sirens surely disrupted the quiet evening in our neighborhood, but their sound never became audible, either.

The gaping hole in our once tight-knit family, I could turn a blind eye to.

Losing my childhood hero and confidant? Something I would surely recover from eventually if I played my cards right and made sure it didn't break me.

Taking away the power of the situation was a sure path to survival. As long as I remained numb, the crumbling world around me held no relevance.

From that moment forward, I would do anything to remain disconnected to anything that could threaten my steadfast ability to survive.

My mother's hands gripped her forehead as she gasped for air between sobs and screams. Tears streamed down her reddened face, filled with sorrow and despair. The face of a broken woman should have been powerful enough to make the world stop for a moment.

Only it didn't. It kept spinning. Air kept continued, waves crashed, and birds continued to fucking sing. People kept pouring into our house to assess the situation. To look for a way to fix this.

Too late.

I remained motionless, watching her fall apart at the seams. As soon as she found his body, lying in a bloodbath on her bedroom floor, the screams she let out told me all I needed to, before I saw for myself. Urgency and fear dissipated quickly once his empty eyes met mine, sideways as the lifeless body looked at me from the floor.

There was no changing what he had done.

No fixing this.

No waking up from this bad dream.

The only thing I was in control of was my reaction to his decision. If one of us was going to disintegrate in anguish, the other had to be there to pick up the pieces.

Death wouldn't be what broke me, as it had my mother.

What happened next would be what led to my demise.

Avoiding the turbulence, which was barreling towards us like a freight train, was the only way I would keep my head above water. Staying numb was essential now. I would do anything in my power to ensure I didn't collapse, along with the rest of my family.

5 Years Later

1. Adrian

I rolled to the side of the bed and placed my feet on the carpeted floor below. The pounding headache – that always greeted me each morning – had revealed itself once again to accompany me throughout my day.

Just what I needed, another form of punishment for last night's actions.

My phone had a blank, dead screen when I went to check the time. I plugged it in and left it on my dark brown wooden nightstand, along with any concern for who might have been trying to contact me.

Odds were, no one was.

I flipped on the bathroom light as it blinded me like someone who had never seen the goddamn sun. My eyes squinted in the mirror, trying to focus on the image in the reflection.

Did my eyes look as clouded as they felt?

Who fucking knew.

Living alone in a country you weren't born in was isolating. FaceTime calls with your family back home, longing for but also dreading the day you return was unusual too, but you get used to it after a few years.

When my mom had moved back home, I chose not to go with her. I stayed in California because it was hard to fathom being back in a country I hardly remembered. I couldn't imagine saying goodbye to the life I had always known.

It was paradise, rich with culture and adventure. That didn't make it any more inviting to pack up my life and just move back to Honduras. To act like everything about Long Beach, and California, and the United States had never mattered.

Though sometimes, I wished I could erase the fucking immeasurable damage that had occurred while living in the states. My need to survive here had pushed me to do things I was less than proud of.

But it was all a drop in the bucket now.

Now that I had not only chosen to stay – I had scraped by for almost five years since my family left – I was questioning my decision. Sure, holidays were great when they flew back here to visit, but how many days out of the year was that? Since they moved back home, we had only spent about three or four weeks together.

I didn't really need anyone to replace my family.

Only one of them was fucking gone forever, the rest only a phone call away, and the alone time had become almost enjoyable.

Expected.

It was easier to keep my mind off of the tormented aspects of my life with no fucking baggage.

My eyes struggled to stay open as I dug through my drawer for a fresh shirt, tossing it over my head.

I tried to shake the minimal memories of the night before that lingered in my brain. It was in the past.

The past and the future were equally unimportant.

Right now, the only thing that mattered was the current moment. It was the only component of time that couldn't be expected or regretted.

After working late – and waking up to puke in the middle of my slumber – I pounded two bottles of water. Then I moved myself from the cold, tile bathroom floor back into the comfort of my bed, where I slept until nearly 2 P.M.

Overall, I had gotten my full eight hours – and then some – plus I was a few steps ahead in the hydration game compared to usual, thanks to the water I had chugged between vomiting spells.

I put on a fresh pair of black jeans, shaking my hand through the brown curls that sat on top of my head, and walked to the kitchen.

Before Trevor, my roommate, went to his shift, he left a bottle of Pedialyte and a joint on the counter, which I snatched up on my way to the patio. Trevor was the more responsible member of the household, always taking care of everyone around him. Leaving a free leftover joint from the dispensary was just one way of helping me out when he knew I was, once again, dying from a self-inflicted hangover caused by my unique form of self-punishment.

I trudged out onto our second-story balcony and lit the joint, inhaling the smoke deeply so it burnt the inside of my ribs. I rested on the outdoor couch and kicked my feet up onto the glass coffee table.

It was July, meaning that it was fucking hot. Especially in the afternoon sun that cascaded down onto our balcony.

After one last puff, I was back inside, feeling leveled out from the influx of cannabis into my system. I ate a semi-stale donut from the day-old dozen on our countertop, along with two benzos and a gulp of OJ. After snatching my surfboard from the living room floor, I stepped out into the bright, warm summer afternoon and locked the front door to our second-story apartment.

An empty spot was waiting in the parking lot that overlooked the cliffs in Huntington Beach when I arrived. The beach was exactly how I'd hoped it would be: not super crowded yet, warm and breezy, with pumping waves.

Late summer and early fall were the best times of the year to surf, when the water was warm and the weather was perfect.

The sand burnt the soles of my feet as I hurried across the beach and straight into the water. I ran until waist deep and threw my board in front of me, gaining momentum, before lying down on the waxy, rough surface and drifting deeper into the water. My arms paddled steadily, duck diving under the crashing waves and eventually past the shore break. Sun rays warmed my back as I floated on the surface of the water.

Another thing I loved about surfing this time of year – no need for a wetsuit.

After catching my breath, a set that was worth riding made its way past the dark blue horizon. My board turned towards the beach and I began paddling in rhythm with the rushing current. As a barreling wave caught up to me and began carrying my board, I stood up and allowed myself to float on top of the surfboard weightlessly. The edges of my surfboard carved into the water with each turn as it glided toward the sand, finding the closest feeling to zero gravity I could get without going to the actual moon.

I would give anything for that thirty-second rush.

It was something to make me feel alive again.

Something to fucking feel again in general – it had been months, or years, since I had felt anything at all.

Not just a desire and passion, but an essential part of life.

A burst of adrenaline pulsed through my veins, as I rode out the last of the wave before it inevitably turned into white wash. When it finally did, I dove off my board, falling into the silence of the ocean and letting her swallow me up whole.

2. Jordan

The wooden dock creaked beneath my feet, swaying with each step, as we walked towards the fishing boat.

I followed behind Jake, who wore the same Ray-Ban style sunglasses he did every day. His glasses and shaggy blonde hair always hid his dark blue eyes, which I knew was because they were bloodshot as hell from being stoned out of his mind ninety-nine percent of the time.

"Welllll, look who showed up." Camilla, my best friend, mocked us from one of the boat benches and gulped a McDonald's sweet tea the size of her face. The large sweet teas were on sale for a dollar, and we were all on the verge of type 2 diabetes from drinking them so damn much.

"I know. We were just going to get an acai bowl, but here we are. I'll blame the warm weather on my lack of motivation." I smiled, grabbing the sweet tea from her and taking a drink myself.
"Then I guess the weather must always be warm with how long we always wait for you guys." She winked at me and snatched the Styrofoam cup back into her hands, taking a long sip.

"Hey, Anthony." I nodded to my brother's friend, sitting on the bow of the boat with a beer in one hand and a joint in the other. "Care to share?"

He looked up at me with a smile, lifting the beer can to his lips. "I can share, but only with you, *princessa*."

Jake smacked him on the back of the head before returning to whatever cleat he was untying. For only being a few months older than me, Jake took being an overprotective brother to a new level. Especially for both of us being older than twelve.

I blocked the sun rays reflecting off the ocean from my eyes with my hand, and watched Jake as he maneuvered around the boat, untying dock lines and tossing them in the hull.

"You need any help?" I asked.

He kept his eyes fixed on the rope as he untwisted it from the cleat. "Nice of you to ask." Sarcasm laced his voice as he threw the final rope into the hull.

I rolled my eyes. Jake always had a stick up his ass, and I was used to being on the receiving end of his snarky attitude.

"Any plans for the night?" I asked, turning my attention to Camilla as I took a spot next to her on the edge of the boat. We bobbed lightly on the water as sunlight warmed my bare shoulders.

"Nothing yet. Kaylee said we can all meet up at hers around 8 and go from there, see what happens," she said before she clicked her tongue.

"Are you down to go out with us tonight?" Camilla shouted back to Jake as he pushed off the dock with his foot, gaining space between the wooden planks and the boat.

"Of course he's down to come," I muttered to her under my breath. Jake gave the engine throttle, steering us towards the exit to the harbor.

"How many times do I have to tell you guys not to talk to me while I'm docking?" Jake mumbled, keeping his eyes fixed on the reflecting sun ahead.

"I just figured that rule no longer applied since you're such a pro," she teased.

"I *am* a fucking pro, but I still don't want to listen to you when I'm trying to focus. Yes, I'll go out with you guys. Come on, have I ever let you down?"

Camilla leaned back on her palms, shaking her long black curls behind her shoulders as she tilted her head up towards the sun, rays dancing across her skin. "There's the fun Jake. Thought you had gone cold on me for a minute." Her eyelids slid shut. "I hope we can catch something decent today."

Jake scoffed. "Doubt it. We only have a few hours before we have to drop Jo off at work."

Camilla's lips turned down into a pouty expression. "Well, at least we can come back out while she's on her shift."

Anthony snapped, pointing his finger at Camilla. "We better. It's been months and we haven't caught jack shit."

Wind picked up around us as the boat began picking up speed, barrelling out of the safety of the harbor and into open waters.

"Time to catch us some fish!" Anthony's face housed a wide grin as he stared into the open water ahead of him. "Shotgun, shall we?" He flung the cooler lid open, bouncing with each wave we crossed, and dug inside of the ice.

"And some for you, ladies." Anthony passed two seltzers in our direction. We popped open the cans and my head swung back, letting the cool, carbonated liquid slide down my throat. Bubbles burnt with each gulp, chugging until I drained the can completely and tears pricked the corners of my eyes.

The ocean had forever been my sanctuary. It was always there, ebbing and flowing, careless to whatever was happening in my small world. Large enough to get lost in a hundred times over. The ultimate escape from anything that I was running from.

Anthony placed a cool can in my lap, his fingers bushing over my thigh as he pulled away.

"Thanks." I smiled at him, popping it open and taking another drink. The sun glistened over the rippling water before we plunged through it, the boat's wake creating a hurricane in the water below.

Our family had always been avid water lovers. My dad owned a yacht – large enough to sleep fifteen comfortably – and Jake and I had learned to wakeboard behind our ski boat by the time we turned four. Once we graduated high school, our dad bought us a thirty-foot whaler and told us to get after it. We spent our summer days with a cooler full of beer and hours of floating in the harbor, letting our skin change shades and fingers prune in the ocean. Every week we would cast our rods and fish, using whatever we caught for some fresh poke or filet.

After plummeting over rolling waves, we reached deep enough waters to turn the motor off and throw some lines in. Jake swung the pole over his head and let the lure fly through the warm summer air, sinking beneath the surface of the ocean. Anthony did the same before placing both poles into the holder and sinking into the seat next to me.

"I'm gonna miss this shit." Anthony relaxed into the cushion, spreading his legs in front of him.

"Oh shut up, quit talking about summer ending. It's only July. We've got like two months left, at least." I grumbled.

"We do, but it's going to go by fucking fast, always does."

After being skunked for hours, my shift approached, along with our empty boat. Camilla was lying on one of the cushioned benches, her eyes closed as we maneuvered slowly through the harbor, towards the yacht club. I yanked a white blouse over my head and ran my fingers through my dirty blonde hair as we slowly drifted closer.

Attending a yacht club would be exciting for most, but I was indifferent at the thought of stepping foot in the building. The luxurious, brag-worthy lifestyle a certain percentage of the Southern California population enjoyed, including my family, was less than impressive. Their hollow personalities and greater-than thou attitude made me loathe most of them even more. All that most of them had going for them was some inherited wealth and a drinking problem to go along with it.

Jake positioned the bow of the boat near the dock, and I leaped over the foot of water separating me and the wooden slabs.

"Don't forget I'm off at 10! Please don't be late!" I shouted to the boat as it slowly reversed away from me, turning back towards the open water. As badly as I longed to drink beer while floating on the ocean, watching the vibrant sunset with Camilla, Jake, and Anthony, that would have to wait for another day. My job at the yacht club was too stable to risk losing, especially just to have the chance of catching a couple of fish.

The night breezed by like any other. I bounced from table to table, schmoozing a bunch of yuppies as they tried to make small talk, all while I was simply hoping for a few good tips. I snuck into the break room for a few champagne flutes whenever I got the chance to do so.

With each one gulped down, I remembered the resemblance that I shared with my mother.

But it was a resemblance that didn't expand past that, just a moment.

Not a lifestyle.

Jake, Kaylee and Camilla came during my break, and we inhaled dinner on the boat, tied to the dock, bobbing up and down with each small wake that passed. We laughed about Anthony's inability to catch a single fish during the last month and snuck White Claws from the cooler. Once my break was over, I returned to the outdoor patio to soak in the ocean view and salty air for the last few hours of my shift.

3. Adrian

Cold water pounded against my back as I rinsed off in one of the outdoor showers that were scattered along the boardwalk.

A mixture of sand and salt water ran off my legs and feet, into the drain below. Dark blue waves continued to crash onto the shore and slowly roll back into the stomach of the ocean, and I stared into the sunset behind them as I continued to rinse, begging my eyes to stay open.

Everyone back home had always spoken of California as a dream. The United States was one thing, but Southern California, the home of Los Angeles, was entirely different. People spoke of it like a land made of gold, sunshine, and celebrities.

Once you got past the initial excitement of it, most of Southern California was just burnt out musicians and wanna-be actors, miserable 9-5 workers who sat on the freeway for hours every day, and young surfers and skaters who smoked weed more often than they got an actual board. My identity somewhat belonged to the third group, since surfing was a natural activity for me.

Rush hour had begun and the drive home was getting crowded, so after what felt like years of fighting crammed lanes, I hurried into my apartment and changed into my black work clothes. Trevor sat on the couch as I plopped myself down beside him and chugged a water bottle.

"I think I'm gonna come by Hansen's tonight," he announced without making eye contact or missing a beat on his video game.

"You are? Why?"

He shot me a sideways look, to which I shrugged in response. Trevor never went out to bars, especially not Hansen's. That was my type of scene. Chaos, loud noise, stuffy air. He had only come by maybe twice in my two years of working there.

"Jake and Anthony want to meet up tonight and I figured we could go to Hansen's. If you're chill with getting them in." He continued playing his game.

"That's fine. Just don't come before eleven, so I can be at the door for sure. Is Macy coming?"

"Hell no." He chuckled. "That's half the reason I'm going. She's up in NorCal visiting her family."

I slapped my hand on my leg and stood up from the couch.

Of course, she wasn't going.

That was the only reason he could step foot in that fucking building.

I went into the kitchen and opened the cabinet above our fridge. After a swig from the bottle of orange juice, I popped three pills in my mouth. The only way I was continuing on anymore was these capsules of joy and misery twisted together.

Trevor shot me another glare, which I mindlessly ignored.

It was easier to continue on autopilot than to do some self-reflecting when I was in a fucking time crunch.

I opened the front door to the comforting reality that was Long Beach during summer. Hot, even after dark, and especially outside of the protection and luxury of an air conditioner. I threw on my baseball cap to hide the wild beast that was my hair, and hurried down the stairs, not touching the black metal railing that had burnt me about twenty goddamn times already this summer.

4. Jordan

Jake shook his head when he noticed the apprehension plastered across my face. Rolling his eyes, he waved off my concern.

"Relax, Jo. My friends I used to surf with can get you in."

I looked young for my age, but not too young to make it into a bar. In a year, I would be a legal patron anyway. Camilla was the one I was worried about sticking out.

She had a type of youth that she just couldn't shake, or hide with a pound of makeup. Flawless light brown skin was framed by black curls, which hung all the way to the top of her jeans, and I envied tremendously. Especially compared to my textureless hair that lingered somewhere between brunette and blonde.

Jake had convinced us to go to a bar on 2nd Street, despite none of us being of legal drinking age, or having fake IDs that said we were. I bit my lip nervously as I stared at him.

As we walked around the corner onto 2nd Street, we ran right into the back of whoever stood at the end of the line for Hansen's, which was almost half a block.

"Well, looks like we'll be here a while," Camilla sighed.

"Do you always just complain?" Jake sneered.

"Only when I'm around you, Jakey." She winked and looked back at her phone, chewing her gum.

The line inched forward every five minutes until we finally reached the front, where Jake's friend was supposed to come and let us in. As we reached the red ropes that told us we were next to enter, someone called to us from inside.

Trevor greeted us with half hugs before he moved past us and followed Jake deeper into the bar. Behind him, green eyes swallowed my gaze as Jake's friend moved towards me.

"I'm Adrian." A half smile danced across his pink lips.

"Jordan."

Adrian's soft green eyes melted the ice that filled mine. "It's very nice to meet you, Jordan."

His Hispanic accent decorated my name, and I pulled my eyes away from his magnetic force. Colorful tattoos decorated his arm above the hand that still cradled my own, showing off a rose tattoo between his index finger and thumb.

My grip released, and I let Camilla take my place.

With each word she said, Adrian's head tilted back when he let out a laugh at whatever comedic comment Camilla had made. He lifted his black baseball cap for a moment, running his fingers through a brown wave of hair on top of his head.

I silently turned away from the two of them and trudged towards the bar, slipping onto the stool to Jake.

I felt small in Camilla's shadow, but I was thankful for it. In reality, I felt small all the time, but usually by choice. It was easier to keep my guard up when no one noticed me or wanted to get past it, anyway.

5. Adrian

Hours dragged on as I checked ID's and wandered around the crowded bar. By the time the rush slowed down enough for me to go grab another drink, it was nearly 1 A.M. I stopped by the bar top to chug a Jack and coke, grabbed a refill, and headed off to find Trevor.

Blood slowly moved through my veins, thickening with each heartbeat, engulfed with prescription toxins close to a lethal level. Placing one foot in front of the other, I swayed my way through the bar and towards the dancefloor, where I noticed Jake and the others. My eyes hung low as they trailed over Jordan's body.

Her dirty blonde hair trailed down her back, pouty lips sat below deep blue eyes, which were outlined by dark lashes. Light freckles decorated her nose and cheeks, and she stood about six inches shorter than the rest of the group.

Jordan's existence was fucking intoxicating.

As intoxicating as all the benzos, narcotics, and opiates I had ever taken combined. Her hips swayed as she leaned her head back and sang the lyrics to each song, hand lying on her chest right above her breasts, which peeked out of her black tank top, taunting me. I licked my lips, taking in each of

35

her curves individually. Her smile lit up her face, emitting enough light to brighten the grungy fucking room. As I watched her, cravings stormed my cloudy mind.

I wanted her.

Wanted her clothes ripping in my hands.

A fistful of her hair, as she screamed my name into my pillow.

Just because I didn't want to drag anyone down along with me, didn't mean I couldn't enjoy one night with her. Drunk hookups, one-night stands, you name it; they fucking happened.

A lot.

It wasn't a rarity, especially in the scummy bar scene. Someone who could fill a void, even for one night, was a temptation nearly impossible to pass up.

One-night stands kept my closed off heart from stopping. One way to further distract myself from my current situation, and from who I had fucking become.

Trevor asked Camilla if he could use her phone to call his girlfriend, Macy, and they both headed to the back patio. I turned to see Jordan walking towards the bar and lightly grabbed her hand to turn her around.

"The bar's going to be packed since it's almost last call. Want me to get you another?" I flashed a lazy half smile and kept her soft hand in mine, running my thumb along her knuckles.

She studied me for a moment before speaking. "No, that's fine. Thanks."

"Wanna dance before they come back?"

Surely, I sounded like an asshole looking for a one-night stand, which was exactly what I was at the moment, but I didn't care. I squeezed her hand, hoping to give her a bit of reassurance.

"Sure, I guess."

My grip found the arch of her back and I followed her to the dancefloor before pulling her towards me. She was timid, keeping a small distance between us, before slowly inching back until her body met mine. Her ass planted firmly against me, sending heat up my spine and my eyes shut for a second. I clutched her waist with one arm and my drink with another.

Even with my steadfast numbness and lack of reality, dancing with her caused me to feel human again.

Only for a moment.

Music faded and lights dimmed as her hips pressed into mine.

"So, how do you know Trevor? Did you go to school with him?" My words went directly into her ear as I leaned into her shoulder. The faint smell of roses took over my senses, lingering and driving my desires for more.

"I did."

"Were you on surf team with them?"

"No. Jake just hung out with him a lot, so I got to know him." Her responses were short and quiet. Like she was doing me a favor by allowing me to be near her.

I took a deep breath, letting the warm air against her neck bring goosebumps to the surface.

And with that sight, I knew I would win.

She spun around to face me as my hand rested on her hip, pulling her closer.

My focus fell on her eyes. I struggled to make out the blending colors circling the room; the world shifting around me. Dark blue with specks of gold, like tile at the bottom of a pool. The only things noticeable in the frenzy of lights and sounds that were flashing every direction.

"I'm surprised I've never met you since you know him. If you want to come back to our place tonight, we can Uber together."

She took the corner of her bottom lip nervously between her teeth. "If Jake and Camilla come, sure." Her words were hardly audible above the music.

I leaned in so she could hear me easier than I could hear her. "How do you know Jake?" The words fell from my lips to her bare neck as her heat radiated against my skin.

She chuckled. "He's my brother."
Jake had a fucking sister?

I had known Jake for years and never once had he mentioned having a sister. That I could remember.

My hand fell as I took a step back. Of course, the girl I had my eye on all night was Jake's fucking sister. Out of all the girls in the bar that I could have wanted. It didn't matter how badly I wanted to fuck her, or how far from sober I was. She was off limits. Despite how desperately I wanted to take her home, my past was no secret to Jake. He wasn't delusional enough to let someone like me go near his sister.

She leaned back on her heels, looking around the crowded bar.

I scratched my cheek, searching my brain for something to say. Any fucking words. "Want to go find him?"

Jordan sighed, moving her gaze to the wall behind me. "He's in the bathroom. I should go find Camilla, though."

I took her hand back into my grasp, sure not to interlock our fingers, and pushed through the crowded dance floor.

6. Jordan

Trevor paced the back wall of the patio with the phone pressed to his ear as he ran his hand through his straight, dirty blonde hair. Camila sat slouched over on a bench attached to a picnic style table, smoking a nicotine vape and picking at her split ends.

"Hey!" she called to me as she stood up. "Where's Jake? We should go soon. Uber prices are going to get insane if we don't."

"I'll text him to meet us out front."

She chewed her gum as she talked to Adrian, and I tuned out of the conversation, focusing on pressing the right keys to compose a text to Jake.

I waited for him to find us, watching various people argue or laugh or sit drunkenly on the patio. My mind couldn't focus on anything but trying to get away from Adrian.

It was flattering to be flirted with by someone I didn't know, even if just briefly. Sometimes a self-esteem boost is necessary in one way or another, and this definitely did the job temporarily. With how outgoing Camilla was and Kaylee's head turning looks, I was the friend who went to bed while they made out with their pick of the night.

I knew the only reason he asked me to dance was because he felt sorry for me when I was alone, or because his chance with Camilla walked out the back door to the patio when Trevor did.

Which was why I needed to leave.

Never to be seen again.

After a short Uber ride home, Jake, Camilla and I walked into the front door of my mom's house. Still smoke filled the air, coating the dim lights in the kitchen and dining room.

"What the fuck happened in here?" Jake mumbled, making his way towards the living room.

I stumbled over to the oven, turning it off and opening the oven door. Smoke billowed out, cascading from a frozen pizza that had been burnt to a crisp. It resembled a black frisbee more than it did anything that had been even close to edible.

"Just the oven." I sighed, opening the door that led to the patio from the kitchen. Slipping my black booties off, I joined Jake in the living room. My mom slept on the couch, Louboutin heels still strapped around her ankles, like she had just walked in and became unconscious within moments.

"Mom." Jake shook her shoulder, her limp body swaying back and forth. Her eyes blinked slowly, bloodshot from another night of mixing alcohol like she was fifteen.
"Let's go upstairs."

Struggling to make out who she was looking at, she chewed her cheek, unaware of what Jake was saying to her.

"Get up. I'll carry you."

She swatted away his outreached hand, slowly sitting upright and unstrapping her shoes. Once she was barefoot, she lifted herself from the couch and regained her balance. "I don't need you to carry me."

"Jesus Christ," Jake grumbled as he took a step backwards. His hand slid down his face as he watched her wobble towards the stairs, staying close behind her.

Jake had a much shorter fuse than I did with my mom. What I had expected, and learned to ignore, still got under his skin and made a home in his mind, taunting him throughout his day.

Camilla had turned on the fan above the stove, opening all the windows that weren't already. She stood in front of the open fridge, scanning for anything that was worth sinking her teeth into. "That pizza would have come in handy."

I leaned my back against the pantry door beside her, pulling my phone out. Seven new texts from my ex, Alec, lit up my screen.

"I wish In n Out was open. I'm hungry," I muttered, scrolling through the messages.

"I am starving, not just hungry. Want some cereal?" Camilla asked.

"Uh yeah, sure, thanks."

Drunkenness covered Alec's last message, with words spelled wrong and a charming attitude put on for show.

"Alec wants me to come over."

Camilla didn't look up at me, pouring milk into two bowls now full of cocoa puffs. "I take it that's what you're going to do?"

I sighed, stepping towards the counter and resting my elbows on the cool granite. Supporting my chin with my hands, I watched as she got two spoons from the drawer and plopped them inside of our cereal before pushing one bowl towards me.

"Thanks," I muttered, stirring the cereal with my spoon. "I don't know. I know I shouldn't, but a demonic voice inside of my head wants to."

"Have you forgiven him?" She asked around a full bite, fishing into her bowl with her spoon.

"No. I don't know if I ever will. I guess I just miss him. What I thought we had."

"Are you still mad at him?"

"Yeah, I'm pissed. I think I'll always be mad about what he did, though some days I'm more mad than others."

She nodded, eyes fixed on her cereal. "Well, I can't tell you what he did. I'm not going to tell you that you're stupid for even entertaining a guy who cheated on you and that he's a piece of shit, even though I really want to, because you already know that. I'm not going to rub it in. So it's up to you, but I would advise against going over there tonight."

"I know." Sighing, I took another bite of the creamy chocolate cereal. "I'm just going to turn my phone off." Sliding my thumb across the screen, I powered my phone down, tucking it in the back pocket of my jeans. Camilla made her way to the sink, rinsing her dish and leaving it on the drying rack.

"Good idea," she confirmed, taking my dish and emptying it for me. "Now we can go watch a movie and smoke a joint on the balcony to celebrate your good decision." She winked at me, her knowing smile flashing in my direction.

Camilla was my backbone. The one who let me do what I wanted, no matter how stupid, and told anyone to fuck off who made me the slightest bit upset. I had good friends; Jake, Ryan, Anthony, and Kaylee, but Camilla was my best friend. Like two souls who had traveled through lifetimes beside each other.

We trudged upstairs, Camilla knocking on Jake's door, as I slipped into pajamas in my room. She followed shortly after, a joint and lighter in her hands and Jake close behind her. He rolled his eyes, walking to my balcony door. "Let's get this over with."

"Why did you come if you're going to have an attitude? Go to bed," I mumbled, close behind him as we walked outside.

"If you guys are going to smoke my weed, I'm at least going to partake." He held the joint between his lips and lifted the lighter to the tip, the flame lighting up his tan face. I lowered onto the patio chair beside him, Camilla sitting on the floor and looking out towards the ocean. My balcony had a partial ocean view, down the side of the house. My mom's room, the kitchen, and the downstairs patio all were waterfront. Our house had the perfect views of the harbor on one side and the sunset on the other.

Tonight, the air and water were calm, without a wake or breeze to pass by. Lights twinkled off of the surface of the bay, the early hours of sunlight not far off.

"Don't use the hall bathroom," Jake said as he sunk deeper into the cushions.

"Why?" Camilla asked, holding the smoke in her lungs and joint in between her fingers. She passed it in my direction as she blew the smoke out, her brown eyes fixed on Jake.

"Smells like vomit. I'll have the maids come tomorrow and clean it."

She nodded silently, turning back toward the ocean. I inhaled slowly, smoke grabbing my lungs and clouding my already tired mind. I leaned my head back against the chair, my eyes heavy as I watched small ripples of water tickle the sand. By the time we finished the last of the joint, limbs sank into my mattress, falling asleep before I even took my makeup off.

7. Jordan

The fire grew higher as Jake poured gasoline onto wooden logs, towering the blaze towards the sky.

I watched silently, studying the way the flames danced with one another, as conversations rang out around me. Orange and yellow hues danced across Camilla and Kaylee's skin, taking sips of vodka lemonade as the flames engulfed my vision.

Bonfires were the norm during summer months – warm nights by the ocean, dancing and drinking around the open flames. The moon was full and bright above us, providing the perfect natural light, as my toes wiggled in the sand, soaking in the August evening. I was hardly ever one to be dancing through the sand around the fire pit, flirting and doing lines of coke as all of my friends did. A beach chair along the cement ring always found me somehow.

"What are you doing over here all by yourself?"

My eyes landed on Adrian, sitting in the previously vacant folding chair next to me. I looked back towards the flames and pulled my blue beanie further down my forehead.

"I'm not by myself."

The corner of his mouth lifted, revealing the same white smile I had seen weeks ago. "Sure looks like it."

My eyes fell over the surrounding crowd, talking and drinking without the slightest notice of our conversation. I lifted my red cup with a shrug and let the bitter liquid take over my tongue.

He nodded silently. "I feel you. I'm not much of one for these things either."

"Then why are you here?"

Adrian pulled a joint from behind his ear and lit it, inhaling the smoke deep into his lungs. "I could ask you the same thing. You smoke?"

I nodded, taking the joint between my fingertips and lifting it to my lips. With each inhale, my lungs burnt, relieved with each exhale. Relaxing against the chair, I melted into the fabric and kept my eyes fixed on the fire pit.

Orange and yellow battled with one another in the form of individual flames.

Rising and falling.

Rising and falling.

As I passed the joint back to Adrian, he shook his head with a chuckle. "I probably shouldn't have offered you that. Now you'll be even more quiet than before."

My shoulders shrugged as I took another sip of my drink. I substituted times that I should have been socializing with something that could give me a head change.

With Alec on my ass, one of the most attractive guys I knew sitting next to me, and nearly a hundred wasted people surrounding the firepit, it was easier to be an observer than a participant.

And observing was not nearly as fun to do when I was sober.

"I totally respect your liking of being alone, hell I love my alone time too. But you're at a damn bonfire. You'd think you would liven up a bit. You've got to be one of the quietest fucking people I've ever met."

Bringing my bottom lip between my teeth, I let my eyes find his. I had to give him credit. Most people would have walked away after a few seconds of sitting next to me, let alone minutes. Personal skills weren't exactly my forte.

"And you, one of the most blunt."

His face grew into a sexy ass half smile, green eyes laced red with smoke. "I guess you've got me there. Opposites attract, don't they?"

"Sometimes."

"Who you here with?"

"My brother and some friends."

He kept his eyes focused on the joint, leading another cloud of smoke in and out of his chest. "Which one's your brother?"

My eyebrows drew together on my forehead. Had he been that drunk when I met him? If he was, he never let it show.

"Jake?"

"My bad, didn't know he was your brother. You guys getting ready to head out of here?"

I sent the rest of my drink down my throat. "I doubt it."

My feet stepped onto the cement fire pit, lifting me high enough to see through the crowd. My eyes scanned each head for shaggy, dirty blonde hair, though finding him seemed impossible.

"You good?" He asked.

"Yeah."

"Then what the fuck are you doing?"
I scrunched my eyebrows together, my eyes fixed on the crowd in front of me. "Looking for Jake so I can make another drink."

"I'll give you some of my vodka. Just get your ass down from there." Adrian said plainly from his chair, continually filling his veins with weed.

"Why? This is the easiest way to find him."

"What are you going to do if you catch on fucking fire?"

I turned to face him, Adrian's eyes trailing up my body to meet mine. I tried to hide my smile, pointing towards the ocean only yards away from us. "Jump in the water?"

"Burnt, wet, and sandy sounds like a shitty way to spend the night." His tongue wet his lips as he allowed his eyes to get caught on my body once again, this time without a care if I saw him. "Well, besides the wet part."

Heat rose through my cheeks as I turned away, lifting myself onto my toes and searching through each person in the growing crowd.

After minutes of no success, I stepped down onto the sand and dropped back into the beach chair. My skin was warm from where the fire's heat had snuck through the holes in my jeans. My cropped white tank top was hot to the touch from standing over the fire, along with my stomach from the vodka.

"As promised." Adrian placed the glass vodka bottle to his lips, the bump in his throat bobbing with each gulp. He dropped the bottle into my lap along with a bottle of sprite. "We're almost out of chaser, so no mixed drinks."

"Cheers," I nearly whispered before lifting the bottle to my lips. The liquid burnt my throat, making me scrunch my nose as I chased it down with soda. "Who'd you come with?"

Adrian took one last puff of smoke, flicking the finished joint into the sand and stepping on it. Another one waited to be lit, tucked behind his ear. His black Dodgers hat hid it almost completely. "Trevor. I'm sure he's off arguing with his girlfriend somewhere. You know him?"

I nodded silently, fidgeting with my ring. "He's been friends with Jake for a while. I'm surprised I haven't seen you much before."

He let out a sad smile, keeping his eyes locked onto mine. "Yeah. I haven't been around in a while."

An hour passed with minimal words and plenty of shots, making me warm and fuzzy from the inside out. Adrian spent the entire time by my side, making comments about the surrounding crowd and mostly sitting in comfortable silence with me. Whether my warmth was from the fire, the alcohol, or Adrian's leg rubbing up against the fabric of my jeans, it was hard to tell.

Suddenly, hands were lightly gripping my shoulders from behind, while the voice of whoever was grabbing me rang out. "No wonder you've been holding her hostage, Adrian. She *is* hot!"

My eyebrows lifted as I bit my lip, trying to hide my drunken smile. Adrian stared back at me, unamused by whatever girl had just called him out. As I shifted in my chair to turn around, my eyes fell on a beautiful Latina girl with long brown hair. Camilla stood next to her, tapping her on the shoulder.

"I told you," Camilla taunted as she circled around to sit on my lap. "One of the biggest babes I know." She planted a kiss on my cheek and grabbed the vodka bottle from my hand, taking a swig for herself. "Haven't moved from this spot all night, huh?"

"No, squeezing through the crowd to find you wasn't on the top of my to do list," I breathed, my eyelids heavy.

"Are you *drunk?*" Camilla laughed, looking at Adrian with an accusatory look. "You got her *drunk?*

I hate to break it to you, but that's my job and my job only."

I plucked the glass bottle from her hand and pressed my lips to it before passing it to Adrian. He put his palm towards me in rejection, keeping his eyes trained on the three of us. His jaw was tense and his shoulders were rigid. Whatever relaxation and carefree attitude that had oozed out of him only moments ago was now gone. "Keep it."

"I'm Analyn, by the way," the girl informed me, slipping the vodka bottle from my fingertips. "And I'm sure he won't mind if I finish this off." She smirked in Adrian's direction before sending the vodka bottle upside down, draining any remaining liquid from it. Her caramel eyes locked onto mine, full of something that I couldn't read.

"Come have some fun. You can't just sit here all damn night." Camilla reached her hand towards me and pulled me out of my chair.

"What do you mean I can't? I can, and I will." My hands found her shoulders to steady myself as I begged my feet to cooperate.

"Jesus, you're hammered."

Analyn circled around behind me and began swaying with me to the music, belting out the lyrics to *Bad Fish* by Sublime. Her hands found Camilla's shoulders as they yell-sang in unison, closing their eyes to the rhythm of the guitar strings.

"I swim, but I wish I never learned." Their words rang into the air along with Bradley's, finding their way from the speaker into the summer night air.

Camilla held her hands out to me, interlacing her fingers with mine, as I fell victim to the Long Beach anthem, along with the rest of the crowd. Hips swaying, my free hand made its way down my chest as my other raised above my head, pulling Camilla towards me.

"Lord knows I'm weak, won't somebody get me off of this reef?"

We yelled inches away from one another, falling into a drunken fit of laughter. Analyn joined in, leaning her body against mine as she passed me her beer. I downed the cool liquid, my eyes meeting with Adrian's that remained pinned to me. Leaning back in his chair with his ankle resting on his knee, his expression remained unreadable. I dragged my eyes away from him, his gaze holding steady on me.

Could a gaze be powerful enough to not just be seen, but also felt?

Kaylee approached with a bottle of Jack Daniel's Honey, and I tilted it backwards. Spice and sugar stung my tongue as I continued to gulp before Kaylee swiped the bottle from my hands. "Who the fuck got her wasted?"

Camilla laughed as she rested her head on my shoulder. "I think she got herself wasted. That's what happens when you leave Jo alone with a bottle of vodka, I guess."

My chest tightened as I shot Camilla an expressionless look. "Oh fuck, I'm sorry. You know I didn't mean it like that."

I shook my head, grabbing for the glass bottle and pressing it to my lips once again. Chills ran up my spine as the ice-cold liquor made its way into my stomach, covering my arms with goosebumps. I continued to chug despite the sudden drop in body temperature, desperate for some liquid warmth that alcohol brought.

"It's fine. I know."

I knew she didn't mean it like that. And even if she had, I was too drunk to care.

"I'm freezing," I breathed to Camilla between gritted teeth. "Have you seen Jake?"

"You look cold, poor thing. How about this to warm us up?" Analyn dragged a small plastic from her jacket pockets, the same smirk dancing across her face. She took a long drawl of the whiskey and threw a pill into her mouth, passing the bag in my direction. "Here. You guys want to stay at my place tonight?"

Before I had a chance to grab it, warm fabric wrapped around my shoulders as a firm grip turned my body in the other direction. I struggled to keep up with the light force leading me back towards my designated spot next to the firepit.

"She's not into that stuff." I heard Camilla giggle as the distance between us grew.

Adrian sunk into the chair he had been sitting in, leading me onto his lap where I surprisingly, and willingly, fell into. His hand pulled the jacket that was resting on my shoulders and helped my arms through the sleeves. I hopelessly fought with the fabric to get it on correctly.

My blinks were slow as I pushed my hands through the sleeve openings, soaking in the warmth against my skin. A cedar scent mixed with mint and marijuana teased my nose. Grabbing a half empty beer from the chair cup holder, I invited the liquid into my stomach and finished the rest of it off.

"What the hell did Camilla mean? I'm not into that type of stuff? It's not like it was meth." I pouted, struggling to make it past each syllable without an obnoxious slur.

Adrian leaned back into the chair once again, his hand draping around my back and finding my hip. "I don't think that's what she meant."

"How would you know?"

"I just do."

"And you care why?" I hiccuped as the words left my mouth.

"I never said that I did."

"You cared enough to listen to our conversation and come get me."

A slight smile lit up his face once again as his thumb ran lightly against my skin. "No, I came to offer you my jacket until I saw what she was up to."

Green eyes bore into mine as I begged my brain to come up with any words and spit them out of my mouth. Instead of my words, Jake's came next.

"Jo. We're going." His voice was flat as he stood next to Ryan on the other side of the firepit. They both stared coldly at Adrian, who dropped his hand from my waist.

"Right," I breathed, struggling to get to my feet without toppling over. Adrian steadied me for a moment before turning around and leaving without a word.

I trudged through the crowd, grabbing Camilla and Kaylee on the way. Ryan crouched in front of me as I approached, signaling to jump on his back. I hopped up slightly and wrapped my legs around his waist, resting my cheek on his shoulder blade.

"What's gotten into you?" He laughed, hiking me up his back.

"Whiskey, vodka, beer, weed.." Camilla answered for me, her eyes meeting me with a wink. I hiccuped back, resting my eyelids and staring into the darkness. With each step Ryan took, my world rocked a little more, like I was sleeping on the boat anchored to the ocean floor.

"Be careful with him, Jo. I don't want to see you get hurt."

"With who?" I mumbled, my words laced with liquor and sleep. I inhaled his familiar scent, sinking deeper into his back as we walked forward.

"With Adrian. You are two of my best friends, which is why I'm telling you he's no good for you."

I laughed, my eyes opening, as Ryan stepped onto the concrete sidewalk and began trudging down Ocean Blvd., towards my house. Jake walked in front of us with Camilla and Kaylee, not bothering to look back and check on me.

He knew Ryan would handle me, as he had for so many years now.

"I've only met him twice. He doesn't even know my name." I slurred, wading through the sand as Ryan walked.

"The way he's looking at me right now for carrying you would say otherwise."

I lifted my head and looked over my shoulder, back towards the crowd of people gathered around the glowing flames on the sand. Adrian was sitting back in the chair that he had been in all night, Analyn in the chair next to him, running her fingers up and down the tattoo on the inside of his forearm. His dark eyes glared at Ryan as his head tilted up, resting on the back of the chair. When he finally looked at me, his expression never changed. Subtle anger stormed behind his eyes.

I rested my head back on Ryan's maroon t-shirt, surrendering to the drunken slumber that had been begging me to give in.

8. Jordan

Two weeks crawled by, full of homework and yacht club events and Netflix. My math test was a flunk, but the rest came out to be reasonably easy. The beauty of going to Long Beach Community College was the ability to nap during between my classes.

Ryan was throwing a huge party on Friday, as he always did when his parents were gone. They were gone about ninety-five percent of the time. The only reason he had moved out was because he needed to watch their pets when they were gone, and because he practically lived on his own in a waterfront mansion already with their travel habits.

On the way, Anthony picked Camilla, Kaylee and me up and we drove together to a shitty part of town to pick up some ecstasy. Going before Jake got off work was the only way to avoid being scolded.

Hiding in the car's shelter, we watched Anthony trudge up to the porch of a small house, make the exchange, and head back towards us. He sat back in the driver's seat and reached his hand into his front pocket.

"Fuck…" his fingers fished through his other pocket, pulling back out empty.

"What?" Concern coated Camilla's words.

"I can't find them."

Kaylee leaned forward from the middle bench and rested her hands on the seats in front of her, speaking in a low tone. "What do you *mean* you can't find them?"

"You just had them!" Camilla yelled.

Before we even pulled away from the sketchy neighborhood, we couldn't find what we had come here for in the first place. We silently looked all over the dark car with no luck. Anthony shut the door and retraced his steps back to the porch of the dealer's house, where he and some friends were sitting in green plastic chairs, drinking tall cans and smoking backwoods. Immediately, one of them was standing tall, pointing something at Anthony's head.

A gun.

They were pointing a gun at Anthony's head.

He threw his palms up and slowly stepped back, as the guy questioned what the hell he was doing.

"What the fuck!" Kaylee whisper-shouted as we ducked behind the seats.

My heart pounded against my chest. I peeked through the crack of the headrest and seat in front of me, waiting to see them blow Anthony's head off right in front of us. To see one of our best friends get murdered.

And this was why your parents said to stay away from drugs, I scolded myself, clenching my hands into fists.

Slowly, the guy lowered his arm. Anthony's shoulders were rigid as another guy stood between them, yelling at the one who had just had Anthony staring down the barrel of his shotgun. He grabbed the back of Anthony's neck and began looking through the lawn with his phone's flashlight, scouring the nearby area. I held my breath as my eyes stayed fixed on them.

"He put the gun down," I mumbled beneath my breath.

"Well, thank fucking God. Is he coming here yet?" Kaylee didn't lift her head as she spoke.

I swallowed, trying to subdue my fear. "Yes. With one of them."

"Fuck, get down." Kaylee whisper-shouted.

I tucked my head and squeezed my eyes shut, waiting for the inevitable opening of the car door. My breathing stopped as the door swung open, fresh air filling the car.

"Thanks again man, I really appreciate it. I'll hit you up soon." Anthony slid into the driver's seat and shut the door, locking it immediately.

"No. One. Move." He spoke through his gritted teeth, sticking the keys in the ignition and shifting into drive, before slowly pulling away from the neighborhood.

After a few turns, we slowly gained speed. Anthony let out a deep breath. "Okay, we're good. Buckle your seat belts. We cannot get pulled over right now with these pills. I don't want a fucking felony."

We slowly lifted our heads, creeping our way into our seats. Kaylee consistently looked over our shoulders and out each window from the middle seat. My eyes found the ceiling as I tilted my head against the headrest, trying to steady my heart rate.

Camilla was the first to break the silence.

"What the hell was that, Anthony? You could have had us killed," she sneered, leaning forward and grabbing the back of his chair.

"He wasn't going to do anything. I sketched them out when I came back up to the house, and then we just had some shit to talk about."

"Shit to talk about that required a gun to your head?"

Kaylee and I remained quiet.

"Cam, relax. They wanted to test my trustworthiness, see if I'm able to sell for them."

"You're a fucking idiot, you know that?" She retorted.

"No, I'm not, which is why I told you to keep hiding, because I didn't want them to think I was lying already, not because I was worried about your safety."

"I'm gonna be sick," Camilla replied apprehensively, as she rolled her eyes at him through the rear-view mirror.

The rest of the ride was without conversation, my throat still constricted with fear.

We parked in Ryan's driveway and swallowed our first pills in the car before walking inside.

YG blared through the car speakers, then through the speakers at Ryan's house as Camilla, Kaylee, and I took shots of watermelon Smirnoff straight from the bottle. The taste was high school parties and regret, chased with sprite.

Thirty minutes later, butterflies grew in our stomachs, and the lights throughout the house grew a soft, fluorescent aura. Every song that played on the stereo also ran through my veins and body. Bass rang against my bones, individual lyrics inside my heart and chest. Kaylee, Camila and I chewed gum and sat on the couch in the backyard, talking about our families, and old stories, and things we loved, as fast as we could get the words out and in the most specific detail possible.

"What is your favorite childhood memory?"

"Do you wish your brother were still alive?"

"Don't we all just die, anyway?"

Questions flung around like ones regarding our favorite type of sandwich.

I took a deep breath, tiny ballerinas dancing across the inside of my skull. "I think it's going away."

"I don't think it'll ever go away," Camilla confessed, her eyes watching a plane, deep in the night sky.

Being lost on ecstasy was the only way I could talk about my stupid feelings, when it wasn't physically possible for me to feel an ounce of sadness, thanks to the influx of serotonin and dopamine that ran through my veins. When I was willing to confess my worries and fears into a world that felt liquid and new.

My mom had been halfway absent for nearly five years, since I was a sophomore in high school. She had one day decided she lost her will to live, locking her door with nothing but a bottle of liquor and dwindling hope for the future.

Room littered with empty bottles, no one was sure how much longer she could go on like this, if she chose to. That much alcohol every day surely had to take a toll on your body. Some days she was great, but typically by the afternoon, she was past the point of having a normal conversation.

Yet here she was, three years later, still sealing her fate before considering any other options. Drinking had cost her many trips to the hospital, a few DUIs, and her ability to take part in the final years of her kid's childhood. Whatever had caused her to fall into addiction had a powerful grip on her, and she was gripping back just as hard.

Sometimes, anger is easier to cling to than hope.

*1 A.M. A room full of familiar faces. When did he get here? Another game of cards. First King's Cup, then Bullshit. Ace of spades. Fuck. My turn to take a shot. His hand on my back. Another game of cards. Another round of shots. Bullshit. More shots. Kaylee's text: **Ecstasy?** One pill. Two more pills. Ten shots*

later. Some of vodka, some of whiskey. 2 A.M.
Another text.

Kaylee was the only person who would continuously text you when you were in the same room as her, rather than pulling you to the bathroom to discuss whatever she just had to talk to you about at that exact moment.

Except this time when my phone vibrated, it wasn't Kaylee. It was Alec, texting me from the other side of the party. All night he had been on my heels, flirting with me and trying to win me back once again, as he had so many times before. If I hadn't been in another world of my own, filled with ecstasy and bliss, I would have used him to fill the void. Even he couldn't pull me back from a world that pulsated with colors and rang out with melodies everywhere I went.

Alec: My place?

My racing mind allowed considerate thoughts. It was a ten-minute drive to his apartment. I could go over there, like many times before. Waking up in the morning, filled with regret and self-hate, I would vow that I would never take part in this stupidity, or even text him back, ever again.

That, of course, wouldn't last.

The cycle of being less than, being a second choice, would continue.

Me: I'm staying at Kaylee's tonight.

My eyes shook rapidly, making the bright screen blurry and wavy in my trembling grip. My hands tensed as I tried to type and read the messages on my screen.

Water. That was what I needed.

Camilla and I stumbled inside to find Jake and some more alcohol, or water, whatever appeared first, while Kaylee stayed in the backyard.

I took a deep breath, trying to calm the pounding against the inside of my ribcage. My head continued to spin as my heartbeat sat in my throat. A weird sense of euphoria and disconnect, tangled together as one, clouded my mind as I tried to decipher what was happening in a room that was moving so fast in slow motion. Faces blended together before their features came into focus, one by one.

Immediately, the fog thickened when I realized Adrian was next to Jake. I stared at him for a moment, or an hour, trying to decide if he was real or a figment of my imagination.

I hadn't even noticed he was here.

All night I had been so consumed by heaven pulsing through my veins, and Alec, and chaos.

Why the hell was magically appearing everywhere I was, when he had never been there before?

We had all known each other for years. He claimed the same, yet he had just started showing face.

A whirlwind swallowed me whole, every feeling amplified and unignorable. The only things moving were my pupils as they shook back and forth, all other muscles in my body frozen in uncertainty. Or possibly they were all moving together, involuntarily and unnoticeably.

"Where have you been all night?" Jake studied me as the words left his mouth.

"Just in the backyard." My voice struggled as Adrian locked his eyes with mine. My shaking pupils struggled to lose the grasp of his, soaking in the warmth and coldness tied together as one.

"Where have you been, Jakey?" Camilla chewed her gum audibly, staring at him for a response.

"Right where I need to be, Camilla."

"Good." She reached past Jake for a vodka bottle and a red cup. I could feel Adrian's eyes pinned to me as I watched Camilla's every move.

"Now what we really came for." She gave her signature wink and rocked back on her heels.

Camilla and I were too content and happy to care if Jake was judging us. That was really the only reason I faulted to drugs in these situations. They made parties more bearable, with a false sense of confidence.

It was relieving to come out of my shell and not worry about what anyone thought of me, even if it was only temporary. In the morning, I could face all the things I hated about myself, and a horrible come down to accompany my negative thoughts. Tonight, I could pretend I actually liked the person I was for a few hours.

After stealing the bottle, we locked ourselves in the bathroom to breathe for a second. Seeing Adrian again in this state of mind was dangerous. It made my heart pump even faster than it had been before, and I swear I could hear it through my chest, that everyone else in the room could as well. My jaw already hurt, and my cheeks were close to bleeding from biting my teeth together just from the drugs, let alone his presence.

It had been an hour since we took our last pill, or ten, or two days, or twenty minutes. Did time still work when you were on ecstasy? It was kind of a liquid thing, with no beginning or end, or differentiation from one moment to the next.

My phone vibrated again with a message from Alec, which I deleted before reading. I needed to cut him off completely so that he would leave me alone, but trying to do so when everything made me happy and forgiving wasn't an option.

Avoiding the memories was my best bet.

In the calmness of the empty bathroom, Camilla and I each took a shot, and I immediately vomited it back up.

"Fuck me." I flushed the toilet and stuck my open mouth under the running sink, gurgling the refreshing washer and spitting it down the drain. I stood back up, leaning my hands on the counter, as the stomach acid continued to burn my throat, "I'm rolling so hard."

Camilla chewed her gum with wide eyes as she looked through me, concerned, but in her own disconnected world. "Are you okay? Do you need water? Should we go outside?"

I took a deep breath before speaking. "I'm fine. I just need a second. Give me some gum."

I sprayed myself with my perfume before popping the stick of minty gum into my dry mouth, losing myself in the cool sensation as it took over my being. Adrenaline and contentment rushed through my veins.

How could two such powerful feelings coexist so perfectly?

I looked up at the mirror and studied myself once again, focusing on every pore, every fly away hair. Every imperfection in my skin, and teeth, and facial structure, and body, shouted at me. My eyes were so large, pupils so big, I could see the universe staring back at me in the black round disks. I was pale, and sunken in, and unhealthily thin, and glowing, and flawless, and perfect. My eyes darted away from the mirror, begging to stop the conflicting image from reflecting.

I slid down the wall and sat on the tile in front of Camila's feet, placing my hands over my face to stop the over stimulating world from existing for a moment. Letting pleasure swallow me whole, eating at my mind, and running through my veins like the strongest sensation that life could offer.

9. Adrian

When Jake reintroduced Jordan and Camilla after they walked away, I wanted to say that I knew who they were, that I had wanted to take Jordan home and fucking devour her when we met, that I still did, but I kept my stupid ass mouth shut.

We both knew he saw her on my lap the last time we were together. We could both act like it never happened, for his benefit and mine, but we both still fucking knew.

Anything past about 1 A.M. from the night at Hansen's, when we met, were just sporadic clips tangled in my mind, like scenes from a movie I had never watched. All I hoped was that one of those clips didn't include me making a complete fucking ass out of myself.

Jake's jaw clenched, his grip tighter on the bottle in his hand, as they grabbed a bottle of vodka and some chaser, then disappeared back into the crowded house.

"She's so fucked up." Jake sipped his beer and leaned his elbow on the white tiles of the kitchen counter behind him.

I could see it in their faces as they talked to Jake that they were lost in another fucking dimension. Not the same dimension I was in – where my eyes hung low and I sunk into myself – as I leaned my back against the kitchen counter. I struggled to get words out quick enough to participate in conversation – if I even got them out at all.

My comprehension level was practically nonexistent, but most people thought I was just stoned off my ass – not an observer of the room, while I was in a benzo and opiate-induced dream state. People were so used to this behavior that most just took me as a dick rather than someone high off their ass all the time – though I had proven to be both.

Camilla and Jordan's eyes were wide, pupils the size of dimes. They chewed gum with tense jaws as they looked around, trying to understand everything going on around them, hyper focused on everything and everyone.

I could tell they were on some type of upper; ecstasy, coke, meth, whatever. Uppers were never my go-to because they were too obvious, and nearly impossible to function on when using. Especially on a day-to-day basis.

Uppers created anxiety, not cured it, which was what I was searching for. I had my fun with coke for a few years, when I was living a much different, more impulsive life than my current one – though my present life was still very impulsive in itself. That was as far as my upper love affair went.

I understood why Jake was upset – given it was his sister on drugs and not some random chick – but he needed to look at the reality of the situation. She was at Ryan's with him, where everyone was altered in some way; drunk, stoned, rolling, high as hell, or a combination thereof, including me.

Plus, from the way it looked at the last bonfire, Ryan and Jordan were pretty damn close. I was sure that he was keeping an eye on her as well.

"What do you think, Adrian?" Jake's hand tapped me on the shoulder.

I blinked. Jake, Trevor, and Anthony all stared at me as they waited for a response.

I took a sip of my beer. "Think about what?"

"What do you think they're on?"

"The girls?" I tilted my beer in the direction they had just walked, raising an eyebrow.

Jake tsked and shook his head with a chuckle. "No, Trevor and Anthony. Yes, the chicks, you stoney."

"Pshhh. Ecstasy or coke, for sure."

"No shit. Probably both with the way Jordan's been partying the last couple of years."

He tapped his finger repetitively on his beer can, keeping his eyes fixed on a different group across the room. Concern etched through his face and posture as he tried to shake it off.

"Just let her be, dude. She's fine. Neither of us are gonna let anything happen to her."

A guy appeared suddenly next to us, speaking to Jake confidently before taking a long drawl of his beer.

He was stalky and looked to be of Pacific islander ethnicity. Jake narrowed his eyes in the guy's direction before snarling. "*I* won't let anything happen to *my* sister without your help."

"Hey, if she's going home with anyone, wouldn't you prefer it be with me? Not like it hasn't happened before," he taunted, leaning against the counter.

"Alec, I would *prefer* you get the fuck out of my face by choice rather than force, but that's up to you," Jake retorted.

"You want me to get out of your face? If you think you're going to force me out, why don't we take that up with the owner of the house, shall we? I think we know who he'll fucking side with."

"Jake," I stated plainly, before locking eyes with Alec. "He'll side with Jake. I can fucking guarantee that."

He looked at me with wide eyes before leaning on the counter next to me, silently challenging me with his proximity.

My jaw tightened as I watched the hallway Jordan had walked down, waiting for her to reappear. Each moment that she was absent from my view, my fists clenched, fingernails digging into the skin of my palm. Whatever I was feeling about her and this guy, I fucking hated.

This should be fun.

An hour had passed since Jordan had left and this prick had joined our group, lighting every fiber of my being on fire with his arrogance. Not able to take a moment more of uncertainty, or of being near the cocky asshole acting like he owned Jordan, I pushed past the guys and stalked down the hallway. Jake called out for me as I gained distance between us, but I failed to turn around.

I hoped the asshole, who Jake was also ready to pounce on, would follow me so I could knock him into his fucking place.

I would put him on his ass so hard he would wake up next week.

Had he given me a reason to act this way?

Probably not, but that didn't matter.

Fire burned inside my chest, making me see red. I needed something to pound my fucking fist into until it bled, and if he had been willing to challenge me and become my victim of the night, I was more than willing to accept.

I tapped on the closed door with my knuckle before it swung open, making me face to face with Jordan and Camilla. Jordan licked her pink lips and looked to the floor as my eyes stayed glued to her, Camilla wrapping her arms around me.

"Adrian! I hadn't even realized you were here. Where have you been?" She released me and looked up with a sparkle in her giant, dilated brown eyes.

I let out a long breath, my anger slightly dissipating with the exhale. Jordan was the only thing stopping my rage. Had she not been the face I saw when the door opened, I would have been onto the next fucker to release my pent-up wrath.

"I was standing right next to Jake when you talked to him, ya stoney." I ruffled Camilla's hair like I did with my little sister, as I tried to get myself in check. Desire to make my way back to the kitchen and beat that fucker's teeth out ate at me.

He was a fucking fool if he really wanted to believe that Ryan would side with anyone besides Jake and Jordan. No matter what the situation was.

She chuckled. "Stoney, usually yes, but not right now. Right now I'm anything but stoney. What are you guys doing after this?" Camilla blew a bubble with her pink gum as she stared right at me.

"Probably just going home and sleeping, babe, which I doubt you'll be doing much of." I winked at Camilla and gave her a half smile, pushing my hands into my front pockets.

"Yeah, I don't see much of that in our future. Well, if you end up doing anything after this, hit my line. Or Jake's, since I don't have your number, and he follows us around like a puppy dog, anyway."

I chuckled at her bluntness. "More like an overprotective father, which you both seem to need, but I'll let you know." My eyes glanced at Jordan as

Camilla smiled and gave me a high five before slipping out of the room.

Jordan stood in the bathroom, absorbed by whatever text message sprawled across her screen, unaware that Camilla had abandoned her. I waited a few moments for her to look up and follow Camilla. When she didn't, I walked inside and grabbed her bent elbow. Her phone slipped out from her hand and as I held it above my head.

"You okay?"

"Are you okay? You look kinda pissed." She questioned.

"Quit avoiding my question."

She lifted onto her toes, trying to reach for her phone, with little luck.

"Um, yeah, I'm fine, sorry. Now give me my phone." She laughed.

"There's nothing to be sorry for. Jake seems worried about you, so figured might as well check. I'll give it back when you answer me honestly. You sure you're good?"

"I'm just dealing with someone. It's nothing, really. Jake is just overprotective. Now give me my phone." She held onto my shoulder to lift herself higher, her fingers waving beneath my outstretched hand. I reached further up, savoring her touch.

This fucking girl.

My free fingers shifted her chin, causing her gaze to lock onto mine. Deeply potent sapphire, as blue and pure as untouched arctic waters, bore into me. Oceans I could surely drown in, if I weren't already drowning in my own unfortunate ways.

"That's because he has something worth protecting." I rubbed my thumb over her cheek, resting her face in my palm. "If it's about the guy making half-assed moves on you all night, I promise you're better than him."

Jordan smiled slightly and looked back at the floor, breaking my trance. I pulled her phone down and glanced at the screen, where messages from Alec flashed across.

"Alec, right? The fucking prick who thinks he has a chance with you?" I placed the phone back in her palm.

"I don't think his name matters to share, but I'll try not to let him get to me."

My stomach churned, thinking of his hands all over her tonight. Women came and went often within my life without more than a second thought on my part, but I currently wanted what I knew I couldn't have.

"Baby girl, you're much better than anyone I've ever fucking met. If he gives you trouble, you know where to find Jake, or Ryan, or me if you need me. Want a ride home?"

I waited patiently, silently begging for her to give me more of herself. To give me another glimpse inside, to trust me with whoever she was hiding behind that silent exterior. I could have stayed in that room with only her for hours, letting myself submerge in her ocean eyes. To lie in the bed of her lush rose scent.

"Sure, let me grab Camilla," she breathed. Her jaw was tense as she studied the surrounding room, drifting through the air that filled it.

I kissed the top of her blonde head, squeezing her shoulder to guide her out of the bathroom before shutting the door behind her. My fingers pinched the bridge of my nose, trying to mentally justify abandoning her in a moment of need. I should have gone with her and made sure Alec didn't look in her fucking direction, rather than staying behind and letting her fend for herself.

It was impulsive, but it was necessary. Locking myself away from her was the only way to keep my head above water, by reminding myself I could never have her. She was my friend's sister, and I would ruin her right in front of his eyes.

Jake and Camilla could take care of her in her time of desperation and defeat, as they surely had before.

I had nothing left to give.

That was what I told myself, preaching it internally.

Yet I still chased after her and helped her into the passenger seat of my SUV.

Taking in the quiet neighborhood outside her window, Jordan chewed her cheek continuously.

"Why didn't Camilla come with you?" I turned to face her, studying the way her skin glowed beneath the streetlights. How her blonde hair framed her face and tickled the tops of her shoulders.

"She wanted to stay with everyone, I guess."

"And you didn't?" I pushed my car into reverse, my hand finding the back of her seat as I glanced over my shoulder. "My offer was good all night. I can give you a ride later, if you want."

"No, I would rather go now. I need to get out of that house."

I looked over my shoulder and began pulling out of the driveway, focusing on steering straight. I was less fucked up than usual for a night out, given the sobering distraction of Jordan, and the anger and lust that seeing her tonight had caused, and given my attempt to control my drinking once I spotted her from across the room. Though that still didn't counteract the drowsiness, and the slipping grip on reality, that I had.

"Not to sound crazy, but make sure no one follows us, please," she whispered.

Heart sinking, I put her worries to bed.

"If anyone sees us, I'll make sure it's known this isn't what it looks like. Don't stress."

"I'm not talking about what people think. I just don't want him to follow us to my house."

My brows furrowed as I pressed on the brakes, stopping us in the middle of the neighborhood street. "*What?* You're worried Alec's going to follow us back to your fucking house?"

Jordan's eyes finally met mine, confusion and fear spiraling within them between rapid blinks, brows furrowed. "How did you know I was talking about Alec?"

I scoffed at her obliviousness, but quickly reeled in my judgment. She was fucked up, and I couldn't scold her for not catching onto the world for how it really was. But god, did I want to.

"I saw the way he was acting, and the effect that he had on you, babe. I'm not dumb." My grasp on the steering wheel loosened, trying to remove some tension from my shoulders. "Listen, I'm not taking you home by yourself if you're worried about him showing up there. So we can either both go back inside, and I will take you home later with Camilla or Jake, or you can come to my house."

She began chewing on her cheek again, staring at the floorboards.

"I don't want to intrude. You can drop me back off and I'll go home with them later."

I shook my head silently, trying to calm my frustration with her. Tonight was the most talking I had ever gotten out of her, but of course it had to be when she was somewhere between present and not. I softened my voice and put my hand on her smooth thigh, which earned me some desperately desired eye contact.

"I told you, either we both go back in there, or you're coming over. Not to sound fucking pushy, but if you're worried about Alec, even slightly, which obviously you are, then you're staying with me the rest of the night. I'll be fucking pushy. Everyone else in that house is beyond blacked out by now, and I don't trust them to be tuned in enough to notice what's going on. I love Jake, but I won't be able to sleep tonight while wondering if you are alright."

"I could just give you my number and text you when I get home," she muttered.

"Nope, not going to cut it, mija. I'm not your mom, waiting for the 'I'm okay' text, when I could have just made sure on my own."

"No, you're not my mom, considering she has never gotten that text, but okay." Jordan took a deep breath, moving her eyes to my hand that was still resting on her soft skin. "And how do I know I can trust you? What if you're worse than him and kill me in my sleep or something crazy?" A small smile danced across her lips, her blue eyes torturing me as they bore into mine.

A laugh left my lips as I took my hand from her, digging it into my pocket.

"Here," I said, placing my folded pocket knife onto her lap. "If I give you a reason to be uneasy, you have some sort of defense. You should really carry pepper spray or something anyway, so just keep it. Now, hopefully I can trust *you* not to kill me for no fucking reason."

A genuine smile danced across her face, the first one I had ever seen from her, where dimples grew on each cheek as she focused on the silver metal in her lap.

"And you can sleep in my room with the door locked so you know I won't choke you out in the middle of the night or some shit." I removed my foot from the brake and began driving down the street.

"Jake's going to kill you." Jordan laughed as she relaxed into the seat. "He's bat shit crazy, you know that, right? He's going to kill you for being near me, then kill me, too."

"Not if you kill me first, that is." I looked at her playfully, focusing on each of her blue eyes individually, before staring back in front of me. I mentally noted each white line as it passed. A DUI was the last thing I needed tonight, and to avoid one, I had to keep my eyes on the damn road.

The rest of the ride was silent, aside from whatever reggae songs played quietly through the stereo. After I shifted my car into park, Jordan unbuckled her seatbelt and hopped out of the car.

"Sorry if it's a mess. Haven't been home much to stay on top of shit." I glanced at her, turning my key in the lock, as she chewed on her fingernails. Whatever she was on had rocked her fucking world, but she seemed to be less scattered than before.

The lights flicked on as I trudged inside, kicking my shoes off, and throwing my keys onto the kitchen counter. Absorbed by the silence of the apartment, I turned to Jordan, who was sitting on the couch after the door slammed shut.

"Do you need something to sleep in?"

My eyes trailed down her tight red crop top and jean shorts, which highlighted her hips, and teased me, once again, with the thought of seeing her with nothing fucking on.

"That's alright, there's no way I'll fall asleep tonight with how hard I'm rolling."

I nodded at her confession, acknowledging how beyond gone off of ecstasy she was.

Ecstasy. She was on fucking ecstasy. The only reason that she was saying more than a word to me. Allowing glimpses at her humor and personality.

A rejection worth ignoring, I decided, before I made my way to Trevor's room and dug through Macy's drawer in his dresser. Fishing out a pair of purple sweats, I brought them back out to Jordan.

She raised one brow, focusing on the lavender fabric I was holding out in front of her.

"Did you actually buy a pair of sweats for the girls you have over here? Or are these left over from someone else?"

I shook my head, walking to the kitchen to hide my smile at her openness.

When I had wanted to bring her home with me, I had never imagined it would be because she was out of her mind on fucking ecstasy, and needed somewhere to go.

Beggars can't be choosers, I guess.

"They're Trevor's girlfriend's. I never bring girls here."

"Bullshit," she called to me, earning a shrug in return.

"It's true. Unless they're chicks rolling at a party, who also happen to be my friend's sister, though I must say that this is a first."

I grabbed two glasses from the cabinet and began pouring vodka into them, mixing it with apple and cranberry juice.

"I can't say I've ever gone home with one of my brother's friends while rolling either, so I guess there's a first for everything." She bit her lip nervously and traced the room with her eyes. "If Jake lived on his own, it would practically be a whorehouse. That's pretty much why I haven't moved out with him yet."

"You live with your folks?"

"My mom, but that doesn't count for much."

With one swig, I popped three benzos in my mouth and sent them down my throat, before sitting next to her on the couch, pulling my shirt over my head and placing it in her lap.

"Trying to get on my level or what?" She laughed, taking one of the full glasses from the table.

"I would have to be insane to take that shit this late. Just sleeping pills so I won't be up all night." My throat was dry as I tried to make my lie seem natural.

I was an amazing liar. Truly skilled.

"When did you take it last?" I tried to change the subject.

"When you interrupted Camilla and I in the bathroom, however fucking long ago that was. But I won't be asleep for a while. You can go to bed whenever. I can fend for myself."

A chuckle escaped my lips. "First off, I did not interrupt you, you had been in there a damn hour. Second, I told you to sleep in my room." I took a sip of my drink, savoring the alcohol against my tongue. "Is Jake your only sibling?"

She stood up and began walking towards the bathroom, finding it on her own, and shut the door. She reappeared with my shirt and Macy's sweatpants hanging loosely on her body as she returned to the spot next to me.

I had done plenty with plenty of women sexually, everything in the goddamn book. Never had one of them worn my damn shirt. Yet here she was, a girl I had done nothing sexually with, giving me a first. I savored how she looked in fabrics that belonged to me.

"No, he's not my only sibling," she stated plainly, pulling me from my trance as her glass tilted against her lips. "I have an older sister who has a full family, so I barely see her. And twin brothers, but they're only half."

"Only half? Then they're still siblings." I bumped my shoulder into hers, earning a grin. "He's the oldest?"

"By three months." She placed the glass to her lips again.

"So he's a half sibling too, then?"

"No, he's adopted. But I've lived with him since we were like a year old."

"Jake is adopted?" I enunciated. "You guys are almost identical."

Both Jake and Jordan had matching dirty blonde hair with blue eyes, the same tan skin tone, and closed off personalities.

"Yeah, he was a family friend and his mom died drunk driving. My mom was her best friend, and he had no other family. So she just took custody to avoid having him go into foster care." She spoke matter-of-factly, placing her glass on the table in front of us after she finished it, leaning her head back onto the cushion.

"That's fucking nuts."

With a sigh, she squeezed her eyes shut.

"Don't tell Jake you know any of this. It's not right for me to be telling his business when I'm fucked up. Not many of people remember when we adopted him, and if they do, they don't share it, so please don't."

"I won't tell him shit. There's no reason for me to, and it's not my place."

She nodded silently, taking one last swig from her drink.

"What the fuck was Alec's problem, anyway?"

Her eyes shut lightly, her chest moving slowly with controlled breaths. Like I had brought up the last fucking thing she wanted to talk about, which was my goal.

Moments of honesty and openness seemed rare with her, and I was going to take all that I could get.

She waved me off, a false sense of nonchalance. "He's just crazy."

"I'll fucking say, I've never seen a guy be that possessive over a hookup."

"Oh, he's my ex. But he cheated on me and still wants to act like we're together." She shrugged, twisting the Tiffany & Co. ring that was wrapped around her middle finger.

"That must have fucking sucked. I'm sorry. I'm surprised Ryan still lets him come around."

Her sweet laugh filled the air, rolling her eyes. "Ryan was too busy with Kaylee to have known if the president would have shown up tonight, let alone Alec."

My jaw clenched at the sound of his name leaving her lips. At the fact that he had gotten to see this side of Jordan for longer than I had. That he had what I wanted and threw her away once he got fucking bored.

Laying down, I grabbed her arm and gently pulled her towards me, our chests pressed against one another. Her blue eyes darted around my face.

"I'm not going to kiss you," she said, inches from my face, her sweet breath dancing on my lips.

I backed away slightly, gaining distance between us as my hands raised innocently to my shoulders. "I never asked you to, nor did I plan on it, babe."

"Why?" Her eyebrows furrowed.

A look that had so much thought behind it. One of my favorite expressions of hers. Aside from the smile driven dimples.

"Why what?" I matched her confused expression, along with a slight smile.

"Why weren't you planning to kiss me?"

I shook my head slightly, running my hand through my hair. "Because you're fucked up and that wouldn't be right. I didn't bring you here to make a move on you. I brought you here because you needed to get out of that house, and not be by yourself when you left."

"But you just made a move on me. That's why I'm laying here." A mischievous smile crept across her lips.

I smiled back, squinting my eyes. "Not sexually."

"Emotionally?" Her eyebrows shot up playfully.

"Sure, we'll call it that, I guess. I don't know." I wrapped my arms around her shoulders as she snuggled her head into my chest, speaking into my skin.

"I don't do emotionally, so don't get too excited."

My fingers ran through her blonde hair, my eyes closing as they begged to rest.

"And why is that?"

"I just don't."

"Well, I don't either, but one day you'll find someone who will change that." My words were lazy and slurred with sleep.

I opened one eye and peeked at her texting, her phone on my chest.

Jake: Where are you?

Jordan: Adrian's.

Jake: Wtf.

Once again, I slipped her phone from her fingers, typing to Jake before she could steal it back.

Me: I'm holding her hostage. Better come get her before I keep her. -Dre

She laughed, reaching for her phone as she spoke. "Dre?"

I opened her contacts and put my number in, saving my name with a heart next to it.

"It's an old nickname." I locked her phone and placed it back in her open palm, closing my eyes for the last time that night.

When I woke up, she was gone.

10. Jordan

Sometimes you do stupid shit when you're on drugs. Like really stupid shit. And especially when that drug happens to be ecstasy.

Going to my brother's friend's house, who I didn't fucking know, and my best friend told me to stay away from, was said stupid shit.

Jake and I pulled into the crowded alley behind our house, and I grabbed my purse before unbuckling my seatbelt. The ride home had been tense, but it was likely because of the comedown that had hit me like a freight train.

"Why did you go there last night?" Jake asked in a serious tone.

"He offered, and I didn't want to be rude." I dismissed the conversation and swung the car door open.

"Don't be hanging out with Adrian all the time. He's bad news. I don't want you getting involved with him. I've told him to stay away from you. He fucking knew better than to take you to his house."

"All the time? I hung out with him once, and it was unintentional. What's *so* horrible about him, Jake?"

He remained unaffected, his only focus on winning me into believing his opinion. "He's involved with shit you don't need to be involved in."

"I can handle my own. Being around Anthony has never corrupted me, and I doubt Adrian's any worse."

Jake narrowed his eyes in my direction. "I'm not just talking about selling pills like Anthony. It's a lot more than that. You shouldn't have gone over there. He's just not the type of person you need to be involved with. Trust me on this, okay?"

I rolled my eyes obnoxiously and clicked my tongue. "It's your guys' fault I got stuck there when none of you would leave with me."

Jake sighed and opened his car door before hopping out onto the concrete alley.

I had gotten used to Jake's overprotective tendencies. I knew he cared about me, but sometimes it felt like he just didn't want me to ruin his reputation.

This time hit a nerve more than most. Usually, he didn't blatantly tell me who he did and didn't want me to hang out with. It was difficult to understand how Adrian could be bad news, when he was the only one looking out for me the night before. Jake was full of bullshit, and I wouldn't let him get in my head without a decent explanation.

As I walked to the garage, Jake punching in the code, I scrolled through my new notifications. 'Adrianjiminez' followed you on Instagram.

I tried to hide my stupid, meaningless smile. The only smile that had shown all day.

It had been so easy to care only about a few people. I had been let down and disappointed enough by my mother, and the only guy I ever seriously cared for, to know most people wouldn't ever supply what I needed from them.

Until now.

Until someone took some interest in me, my problems, and what made me tick, who hadn't already known these things for years.

Until ecstasy had caused me to let in someone new, before I could convince myself not to.

It was futile thinking that someone would waltz into my life and take an interest in me. That my already very low expectations would ever be met.

The garage door opened, Jake walking inside as he spoke to me over his shoulder. "Get your suit on. Ryan will be here in 20."

I threw my board down on the sand next to Camilla, who was dozing on her beach towel, with a white bucket hat covering her face. She never was one for surfing, but watching from afar while we were in the water wasn't too big of a chore for her.

"Hey," I said between pants, wringing out my hair, letting the cold drops of ocean water trail down my body. When all I got in response was a snore, I knew that her wax pen had gotten the best of her – once again.

Dropping to my knees, I sprawled out on the towel in front of me and rested my head on my bent elbows. Sunrays warmed my back and evaporated the remaining droplets from my skin, as I listened to *Summer Nights* by Iration ring out from the speaker by my feet.

Last night had been a trip, to say the least. If I hadn't gotten out into the sun, I would have been spiraling into depression, thanks to all the excess dopamine draining from my brain.

Now, all it left me was some anxiety and an existential crisis. But I supposed that was better than the overwhelming despair that comedowns typically caused.

I punched my passcode into my phone when it denied my Face ID, thanks to the beaming sun behind me.

No new notifications.

What was I expecting? No one was at home waiting for me, and I knew that. But it wasn't enough to stop the sinking in my chest that a blank screen brought.

"What a fucking swell," Ryan said as he fell onto his back on the towel next to me. "Offshore winds are really doing us a favor today."

Water glistened on his chest as he covered his eyes with his hand, staring at the blue sky overhead. Ryan was like family to me. I had known him as long as I had known Jake. Our moms all grew up together, so we did too, but that didn't mean I was oblivious to how perfect he looked. Caramel eyes contrasted his light brown skin, and he always kept his hair short on the sides, with some extra length on the top.

"What?" He smiled, looking down at his chest. "Do I have some fucking seaweed on me or something?"

I shook my head, pulling my sunglasses off the sand and weaving them between the wet strands on top of my head.

"No. I just love you."

"I love you too, Jo." He lifted his arms, resting the back of his head on his open hands. "What's up with you?"

I let out an audible breath, focusing on the palm tree in front of me. "Jake and I got into it this morning."

"Did you? And why is that?"

"It's a long story."

"Well, it's a good thing he and Kaylee will still be out there for a while. I've got time."

I shook my head, biting my lip with a slight smile. Jake was harsh, with good reason. With Ryan, our relationship was by choice, not family. That made him a little easier on me than Jake was.

"I... uh, I stayed the night at Adrian's last night."

My eyes slowly moved to find his, a smile breaking through completely. All the shit he was going to give me didn't stop me from smiling.

"You punk." He reached out his hand and pushed my shoulder, my head swinging to one side dramatically. "I told you to stay away from him, *stupid*."

"Yeah, and Jake reiterated that this morning, a little more harshly than you did."

"As he always does."

"Both of you have warned me to stay away from him with no explanation of why."

Ryan sighed, the deep muscles of his chest and abs expanding and deflating. "Adrian is a great guy, honestly. He's one of my best friends. But he's been wrapped up in some shit for the last few years that you don't need, or want, to be wrapped up in. And I'm not sure when he's going to get out of it."

"Like what?"

"Just stupid shit. He's been through a lot, and I mean a *lot*, just since I've known him. I understand why he is the way he is, but I miss how he used to be more." Another sigh. "Anyway, I've seen the way he looks at you and acts around you, which I've never seen from him before. So part of me thinks the right person could get him to change, but a bigger part of me is scared to be wrong about that, and having you be the victim of my mistake."

"Is he like Anthony?"

"Kind of."

I paused. I didn't tell Jake a lot in fear of him getting mad or fighting with me. With Ryan, it was a fine line. He wouldn't fight with me, but he would tell Jake when he thought I was acting like an idiot.

Twisting my ring around my finger, my eyes stayed focused on the grains of sand in front of me. "Anthony almost got shot."

"I know."

"You do?" I asked.

"Yes. How do you know that?"

"I was there."

"I know." He confirmed.

"How do you know?"

"They knew you were there too, even if Anthony said that they didn't. They know everything, Jo Jo. And they did that to remind everyone that knows you, and whoever else was in the car, that they're in charge."

I gulped, twisting my ring in the opposite direction, as my eyebrows scrunched together. "Is that the same stuff that Adrian is involved in?"

I had known that Anthony had connections to a world I wasn't part of, but I always took him for a small street dealer. Never someone who was part of something organized, or bigger than he was.

"Yes and no, kind of. Let's just say that lifestyle has a stronger personal hold on Adrian than it does on Anthony."

11. Jordan

Camilla came over in the afternoon, when we finally dragged our exhausted bodies off of the beach. Her jet-black hair went from puffy to empty as she dipped her head back under the running shower water. "So, where did you run off to last night? Alec's?"

I let out a sigh, my shoulders slumping as I sat on the closed toilet seat.

Whatever ecstasy made me feel, the comedown was the opposite. Content turned to discontent, fulfillment to emptiness, loved to alone. Surfing had softened the blow, but I would need some sleep and weed to finally rid myself of a comedown.

"Adrian's. He asked me if I needed a ride home and I ended up just staying at his house."

"Jo!" She opened the curtain and looked at me, before rinsing the white suds from her head. "Did you fuck?"

I rolled my eyes at her, trying to hide a conflicted smile. "No, obviously we didn't fuck, we didn't even kiss. I left before he woke up."

"Damn. Did you at least cuddle or *something*?" She enunciated the last word with expectation and annoyance.

"Yes, but don't tell Jake. It's not that big of a deal."

"Are you into him?".

"I don't know him well enough to be into him, but it's too soon to think about that, anyway."

"Too soon?!" She stepped out of the shower, and I dropped my clothes onto the floor, before taking her vacant spot beneath the hot water.

"Yes, too soon, Cam. I barely know him. I don't have the time to waste on anyone new," I said in an annoyed tone.

"You should. You barely let anyone new in Jo, and you could use some more people to support you. This is like the most unexpected thing to happen in your life in years."

My eyes fixed on the ceiling, fighting back tears that wanted to mix with the hot shower water, which was dripping from my lashes. The last person I did trust enough to soften up for took my heart out and played it like a violin.

I knew I was never anyone's first choice. The night Alec slept with another girl in front of me, laughing at my pain as I watched him come from a bedroom with his hair ruffled and belt half buckled, reminded me of everything I was lacking.

When my mom chose her addiction over her own child, the proof was in the pudding.

Last choice was just one of my qualities.

"He doesn't see me like that. He was just being nice," I breathed as water trickled down my skin.

"There's only one way to find out, girl," Camilla argued.

Voices rang out in the distance as I floated between awake and asleep. Trying to pull me from a dream, I couldn't focus on who they were, or what they said.

"No shit!" The words swirled around my head, unclear if they were from an internal or external world.

"You've got to be kidding me."

Those were the ones that caused me to come to.

My eyes parted slowly, begging to return to my slumber with each blink. I glanced around the golden room, glowing in the day's wake of final sun rays.

Camilla's legs remained draped over me as we lay in my bed, napping for an unknown amount of hours. My high from our afternoon joint was yet to dissipate as I dragged myself out of bed, looking through my window to find whoever had awoken me, if it was even anyone at all.

Jake was around the unlit fireplace, Adrian and Trevor on either side of him as they passed a joint, Ryan across from them. My fingers hit Jake's name on my phone, ringing once before he spoke.

"Why are you calling me? I'm in the backyard." Jake said jokingly, a mocking attitude lacing his words.

"Because you're loud as hell and woke me up, dipshit."

He huffed. "Get over it. Do you know how many times you have woken me up?"

I rolled my eyes, yawning into the phone. "What are you doing tonight?"

"Don't you have plans of your own?"

"Obviously not or I wouldn't be asking you this right now, would I?"

"I don't know, Jordan. We might go to Hansen's. Why aren't you at Kaylee's?"

"She's working."

"Well, that's not my problem."

Like the jackass my brother could be sometimes, he hung up the phone.

Immediately, chatter started up on the patio below, right outside my bedroom window. I walked over, studying the small sliver of ocean that I could see, as Camilla slowly stirred in my bed.

"What are they up to tonight?" Trevor asked casually.

"Nothing besides being a pain in my ass I guess," Jake grumbled.

Adrian leaned back in his chair, resting his black Vans on the stone firepit. "Do they want to go to Hansen's?"

"I can ask them," Jake muttered.

"Up to you."

Jake reluctantly picked up his phone. Moments later, mine rang loudly. I waited a second before sliding my thumb across the screen. "What?"

"We're going to Hansen's. Do you want to go?" Irritation lined Jake's voice that was surely only recognized by the two of us.

"Sure. I just got up. I'm gonna need a bit to be ready."

"Let me know when you're ready, and don't take a fucking hour," Jake said before he hung up.

Camilla moaned as her arms stretched overhead. "What the hell was his problem?"

"Who knows. Get up, we're going to Hansen's." I threw her vape to her, which she lifted to her lips as soon as she caught it.

"Hansen's?" Her words struggled out as she held the nicotine in her lungs. "Why are we going to Hansen's?"

I turned to my closet and pulled a black dress from the hanger, standing on my toes to get my shoes off the shelf above.

"Because Adrian is out there and suggested it. I refuse to sit here and let Jake tell me who I can and can't hang out with if he doesn't practice what he preaches."

Slipping on my tight black dress, the shortest dress I owned, I turned the curling iron on, and began running mascara through my lashes in the bathroom mirror.

"Look at you, dressing to impress," Camilla taunted as she slapped my ass and walked to the sink next to me.

"I'm going to fucking kill Jake." I dipped the brush back into the tube of mascara and began wrapping my hair around the hot metal.

"He pissed you off that bad, huh?"

I took a deep breath, letting a now curly section of blonde hair fall back over my shoulders. "Yes, I'm just sick of being left in the dark, but whatever. I'll just get drunk."

Camilla smiled at me in the mirror, beating her face with a makeup sponge. "That's my girl."

I still pulled out all the tricks up my sleeve to feel, and look, my best for the night. Not out of spite for Jake, but for subconscious reasons I wasn't willing to let myself accept. Ones that had no validation or meaning, yet were still floating around the dark back corners of my mind.

I was weak. I knew it. Not allowing other people to know about my weakness was the key to not being taken advantage of. The only people who knew were the ones who had earned trust years ago. There wasn't room for any more.

Music poured out of Hansen's onto the sidewalk, bass shaking the cement. Adrian led us to the front of the long line, past a bunch of pissed off college kids who had surely been waiting for hours. Talking into the ear of the bouncer, Adrian patted him on the back and led us inside. My eyes constantly avoided his, trying to become invisible amongst the crowd.

Camilla and I walked to the other side of the bar, shouting our drink orders over the music, and singing along to the songs we knew, while we waited. Hansen's was always busy, with a DJ at the back of the dance floor, and oversized booths lining the walls on either side of a bar in the center of the room. Bartenders moved in rhythm behind the bar, making drinks, and swiping cards, and doing a mindless process, glass after glass.

Ryan walked up behind me, his hands grabbing my shoulders and massaging them. I leaned into his grip, Camilla smiling at me when she saw him. My eyes rolled as I shook my head, blowing off her assumption. She had always wanted there to be something between Ryan and I. But no matter how gorgeous he was, our relationship was rooted in a lifelong friendship.

Neither of us wanted to take it past that.

I would never risk losing him over horniness and stupidity.

Ryan pulled me closer to him, hooking one arm over my shoulders with his elbow bent below my chin.

The entire time, Adrian's eyes were pinned on us.

Now that he had gotten a peek past the brick walls that I held onto like a lifeline, he was making it known that he wouldn't let me take that place from him.

Little did he know that avoiding, hiding, denying?

I was a professional. No task was too big when I was keeping things buried that needed to be.

Ryan kissed my head, squeezing me against his solid chest. I looked up at him with furrowed brows, confused about his affection. Ryan and I were close, but he never made a physical move on me. It was an unspoken understanding.

"Just go with it," he whispered into my ear, glancing quickly in Adrian's direction. "Just want to see how serious he is about you."

A devious wind coming through my head. I leaned back into him, wrapping my hands around the forearm and bicep that was still clinging to my shoulders.

The whole time we waited, his eyes stayed pinned on us. I didn't need to look to know that.

I could feel them burning into my skin. Ryan's continued affection and subtle chuckles confirmed just that.

He was fucking looking.

But I wasn't sure that I wanted him to be.

Apprehensively, I ran my fingers up and down Ryan's forearms, avoiding looking anywhere but at the bottles behind the bar.

Once our drinks were in hand, Camilla plopped down in a booth on the opposite side of me.

Ryan pulled me onto his lap, keeping his hands off of my skin. Text messages from Alec during the last 24 hours littered my phone, and I scrolled through them all, trying to fight the urge to reply to him.

Come over, I miss you.

It's time to stop playing these games.

We can make this work.

All empty words to rope me back in.

My fingers hovered over the keyboard as I tried to decide on a reply.

"If you text him back, I will shatter your phone into a million tiny pieces," Ryan said from behind me, picking up his drink and taking a long drawl.

"Ryan!" I moaned around a laugh, trying to hide my embarrassment. It had been one thing to look at my phone, but another to call me out in front of other people.

"Just remember, my name is the only one that your girl is moaning." Ryan winked across the booth, a mischievous smile dancing across his lips. Adrian lifted an eyebrow, his low eyes trained on Ryan. My gaze bounced between the two of them, waiting silently for who would speak first.

Crap.

He really had to make this awkward.

Ryan slapped his hand on my hip, grabbing me and leading me to stand. "I'll be back, babe." He smirked at me, shuffling out from behind me and towards the bar.

I looked away from him to Camilla, who slowly slid out of the booth. "*I* have to pee," she lied, with a mischievous smile plastered on her face.

12. Adrian

I *was* going to talk to Jake before even looking at or talking to Jordan, or just stay the hell away from her like I should have been, but that was already out the window now that I had taken her home with me the night before.

And now that I had seen fucking Ryan dangling her in front of me. His hands on her hips were enough to abandon my concerns about how Jake would feel, right in the middle of the fucking bar.

Another downside of my fixation: lack of impulse control and consideration for others.

Just like my father.

I shook my head and tried to stop my thoughts from going down that path. Sliding into the booth across from Jordan, I leaned my head back against the cushions and swirled my drink, taking a long drawl of whiskey.

I knew what Ryan was doing. I wasn't fucking stupid.

He cared about Jordan, and he knew I wasn't up for a chase. If he had stood between us, even for a moment, I would leave her alone.

That is, if she had been any other girl.

With her, it lit a fucking fire in me. Seeing him anywhere near her got under my damn skin.

"So, you and Ryan?" I said coolly, studying her from across the table. He may be one for games, but she wasn't. She was far too fucking innocent for that.

"What? No. We're just friends."

"I can see that."

She swirled her drink with her straw, her eyes fixed on the spiraling red liquid. "I don't know why it would matter anyway," she whispered.

I leaned forward, coaxing her into looking at me.

"What's up with you?"

She glanced my way. "Nothing is up with me."

"You sure about that?"

"Yup."

"Are you lying?"

"Nope."

With a sigh, I gulped down my drink. "You're avoiding me."

"I'm not avoiding you, Adrian. I have no reason to be."

My eyes pinned to her with a knowing look while I kept my tone flat. "You're acting different."

"I just am not on ecstasy, which is the only way you really know me. No one is the same when they're sober as they are when they're on drugs," she muttered.

A knot formed in my throat.

"I liked you better that way."

Insulted, her brows furrowed in my direction, "You like me better fucked up? Wow, thank you." She rolled ocean blue eyes as she flipped her hair over her shoulder.

I laughed, tapping my finger on the cool glass in my hand. She sure was a spitfire when she wanted to be. I would take that over apathetic and reserved.

"No mija, I liked you better when you weren't so closed off and quiet."

Frustrated, she let out a sigh. "I'm sorry about last night. I appreciate it and won't bother you again."

"Don't apologize. I'm the one who kidnapped you." I leaned forward, pushing a strand of blonde hair behind her ear. "I would actually love it if you bothered me again."

Being around her took all my logic and threw it out the window. I knew I should run the other way, full fucking sprint, that I was absolutely no fucking good for her, but I still wanted to do anything in my power to be near her.

Her big blue eyes looked up at me, taking a small sip of her drink. "I don't do sexual."

Despite her serious expression, playfulness still made its way to the surface.

"Emotional?"

She shook her head as her lips took the black plastic straw between them. "No, I don't do that either."

"Then let me take you out. Nothing sexual or emotional, let's just go surf, or eat, or something."

Her teeth sunk into her bottom lip. She looked at her drink as she twirled it with her straw once again. Each passing moment, my doubt and regret grew.

She was sunlight in a dark room. Ocean air in a stuffy, crowded bar. Drown worthy eyes in the middle of a desert.

I was the fucking cancer of a healthy society. The scum that my community wished to rid itself of.

She looked at me with a hint of a smile after what felt like a fucking eternity. "It's not a date."

"It's not a date," I confirmed confidently. "Does tomorrow work?"

"For surfing or eating?"

"How about both?"

She paused again and looked back at her drink.

"Sure. What time?"

I took a deep breath. It felt like the room had disappeared around us, and all I saw was just me and her, despite the sea of drunk people and overwhelming music. "Let me see how my day goes. I'll let you know in the morning."

She nodded lightly. "I don't work, so I'm free all day. Just text me in the morning if you still want to go."

I chuckled at her doubt in me before leaning a little closer to her. "I don't have your number. You never texted me after I gave you mine."

"I'll send it to you."

"Where do you work?"

"Long Beach Yacht Club."

"I didn't take you as a yacht club type of person," I exclaimed.

She bit her lip playfully, resting her elbow on the table. "I'm not a yacht club type of person. My dad got me the job since he's a member. It pays well enough to provide me with some spending money and I can show up after being on the boat easily, so I couldn't pass it up."

I bit my lip at the thought of her in short skirts, exposing her smooth, sun kissed legs, and escorting rich assholes to their tables. Jealousy and attraction scrambled together, taking over my head.

As she pulled out her phone, Jake and Trevor approached our table. The people I had been hoping to avoid all fucking night.

I ran my hand through my curls as I stared at them.

I was playing an internal game of tug of war with wrong and right. I wanted to believe what I was doing was right – that maybe she could be the life ring that I needed to keep my head above water.

But a bigger part of me knew I was far too fucking gone to have hopes like that. Even the smallest of ones.

"What are you guys up to?" Jake slurred slowly, his bloodshot blue eyes pinned on me, directing his question.

Jordan spoke before I had the chance to, placing her phone face down on the table. "Nothing. Just waiting for Camilla to get back from the bathroom."

Camilla reappeared and sat on the other side of the booth next to Jordan. She smiled, eyes darting from me to Jordan, before telling Trevor to come sit with her and patting the bench cushion. As he slid into the booth, I stood up and pulled Jake away to the bar.

I had never been apprehensive about any girl before. They had always been unworthy of any emotion, serving no purpose other than a drunk hook up I would never think of again. A momentary release.

If they came around more than once, which was rare, the circumstances were the same as before. No wiggle room on that policy within my life.

Why was I bending my own rules for her?

Fucking stirring up trouble I knew I wouldn't be able to get out of?

Because I lacked the self-control to stop myself from doing so.

Jake leaned his elbows against the bar, Ryan walking up next to him, with a girl on his heels. The one from the bonfire.

What the fuck was her name again?

"Kaylee." She held her hand out to me, and I shook it softly.

"Adrian. Nice to meet you."

I pinned my eyes to Ryan, annoyance plastered across my face. Fucker really thought he would get the upper hand with me.

He lifted his eyebrows, placing a toothpick inside of his mouth and chewing it. A cocky smirk ran across his face, one that I wanted to smack right off of him. He looked between me and Jake, leaning in to whisper to Kaylee, before they both walked towards the booth.

Jake finished ordering shots from the bartender, continuing to watch the TV overhead. I waited for him to look at me, and when he didn't, I gave him a reason to.

"I'm not trying to come off the wrong way. Jordan seems like a cool girl and I totally get that she's your sister. I have younger sisters too and they mean a lot to me. I just wanted to make sure that it's alright if I take Jordan out to dinner sometime... I would never do anything to disrespect either of you."

Jake pursed his lips slightly and scratched the back of his head, staring into the bar in front of him.

I knew he was aware I was barely coherent. Or untrustworthy. Or both. My past had to come and make an appearance someday, no matter how well I had avoided it before.

I had changed, but I hadn't changed enough.

Everyone fucking knew that.

Breaking the silence and tension you could cut with a knife, he turned his body to face me, one elbow leaning on the bar.

"Listen. You're a cool dude and all, but I don't want her to get hurt. You are a very different type of person than she is, and she doesn't need to be getting in more trouble than she has been.... I'm not saying you can't take her out, that's up to her." He sighed. "What I am saying is if you do anything to fuck her over, take advantage of her, or even say a rude fucking word to her, I will handle that myself. And I mean that. No hard feelings, but you gotta understand where I'm coming from here."

I paused for a moment, carefully trying to pull the right words from the back of my mind. Slowly nodding, I lifted my Jack and Coke to my lips, savoring the taste on my tongue before I spoke.

"I wouldn't do anything to disrespect either of you, I promise you that. You're my boy and I don't want to overstep. I just wanted to tell you where my head is at."

His jaw tensed. "I'm not just talking about disrespecting her. If you are still up to the same shit you used to be, don't bother taking her out. That's where I put my foot down. I won't let her go down that path."

Chest tightening, I nodded. It was difficult to change a reputation that I had tainted with years of mistakes and wrongdoings.

"I'm not doing that shit anymore. You have my word," I confirmed.

"Alright. But just remember what I said. And she will tell me if anything ever happens, so don't think that you can get around it. I'm not as clueless as some may think, and neither is she."

"I never would."

Jake shook my hand firmly.

This was really happening.

I had never been tied down, never even been on a goddamn date. Even though this technically wasn't a goddamn date.

For fucking years, I filled my nights and early hours of the morning with one-night stands, bottles of liquor, any drug I could get my hands on, and a lack of regard for the world around me.

Everything about seeing Jordan wearing my fucking shirt made me consider changing that.

We threw our shots back before I grabbed another drink, maneuvering through the crowd. My body sunk heavily into the cushion of a bench where I could see the dancefloor, Jordan and Camilla laughing and swaying to the music, Jordan's hips mesmerizing me from behind.

After a few shitty songs and another empty drink, I walked back to the bar to order a refill. I already wasn't sure how many I had drank, not that it would matter. I was already half asleep and out of touch with the surrounding room. A little more liquor wouldn't make it any worse.

Analyn turned around to face me from behind the bar, and I flashed her a lazy smile, trying to seem friendly enough to serve before all the assholes around me, who had surely been waiting longer.

Something that she would look deeper into, with good reason.

I never said that I was fucking perfect.

I was far from it.

"Hey babe, whatcha want?" She leaned towards me, resting her elbows on the bar to expose her boobs beneath her shirt. I dragged my eyes up to meet hers.

"Just a jack and coke," I said uninterestedly. Taking her home, and fucking her once again as a temporary distraction, ran through my mind, but I pushed it to the side. I needed to stop grabbing onto stupid ass ideas that floated around my head.

"Gotcha." She winked as the word left her lips, turning her back to me, and pouring a bottle of whiskey into an empty glass.

My eyes scanned the surrounding crowd, trying to focus in on the blurry room through the mental fog, before they landed on Jordan. Leaning her elbows on the bar next to me, as Analyn had been moments earlier, she was visibly trying to fight exhaustion, her dark eyelashes drooping in between long blinks.

"Oh, hey. Did you want something?" I asked with a half smile.

"Just a drink," she said, while looking forward to the glass bottles behind the bar.

"What kind?" I leaned my elbow on the wooden bar, turning my body to face her.

"Hmmm. Probably a vodka Red Bull. Basic, I know, but I need the caffeine."

"Yeah, very basic." I chuckled. "Analyn, make that a vodka Red Bull, too."

She looked at Jordan, and then at me, studying me for a few seconds, before turning to make the drink without saying a word. She placed the full plastic cup on the bar in front of Jordan.

"Do you have a tab open?" Analyn snapped.

"Put it on mine."

She darted her eyes to me before turning around to the computer behind the bar.

"You know, I have money." Jordan rolled her eyes with a smile, taking a small sip of her drink. Her plush lips on the rim of the cup, her drown worthy blue eyes laced with dark lashes, both teasing me by simply existing.

"Hey, my bad for picking up your $7 drink. I'm sure your yuppie money could suffice. I'm not doubting you, mija." I shrugged my shoulders and smiled, turning away from the bar and walking back to the dance floor, partaking in my internal game of tug-of-war once again.

What the fuck are you supposed to do when you can't get your mind to agree with your gut instinct? Just go against it and hope for the best?

For some, this may have been plausible, but for me, I would have been a fool to risk being wrong in that situation.

But I had proven to be a fool long ago.

The lights turned on over the dancefloor, signaling last call. Slowly, the crowd trickled from the building, all of them passing in a daze as I sat in the booth.

We stayed after closing, Trevor chatting amongst Camilla and Jordan, Jake desperately trying to stay awake, nearing failure. I snuck into the locker room and opened up the metal door that housed my shit, swallowing two last pills for the night. This was the most fucking sober I had ever been after being a patron at Hansen's all night. I threw the pill bottle back into the pile of Dickies pants at the bottom of my locker and shut the metal door.

As I turned the corner, Analyn ran into me from the opposite direction, placing her hand on the doorway to block my path.

"What are you doing after this? Wanna stay for a few drinks?" She asked tauntingly, knowing I would never protest whatever was planned for after our shifts.

"Can't, I have plans." I slipped past her, walking towards the main room of the bar.

"What, plans with that child you've been buying drinks for all night? I know that's why you kept her hidden all night at the bonfire, Adrian. You weren't afraid that I would hook up with her. You were afraid I would tell her the fucking truth about you. That you're a fucking scumbag, no matter how badly you don't want to admit it."

Her voice rang out across the hallway, though I shrugged it off. Rolling my eyes, I continued wading towards the bar, unable to give a fuck about anything that she said.

"My plans are none of your fucking business," I shouted over my shoulder.

My phone buzzed in my pocket as I walked back into the main area of the bar, signaling that our Uber had arrived. Trevor and Camilla climbed into the back row of the SUV. Jake, Jordan, and I sat in the middle row, with Jordan in the middle of us. Almost immediately, she nudged me with her elbow and pointed to Jake with a smile.

The wide and genuine smile, where cute ass dimples decorated her glowing cheeks.

Another glimpse.

I soaked in her joy until looking at Jake, who was already asleep, head hanging forward in a neck breaking position.

"Jake," Jordan said as she shook his shoulder.

"Hmm." The sound hardly left his body without lifting his head or opening his eyes.

"Getting him home is going to be fun." She rolled her eyes, smiling still, and looked at her phone.

"Where's Ryan?" I asked coldly.

"He left with Kaylee a while ago. I can call him to come over and get Jake inside."

"Why don't you guys just come back to our place? Ryan was hammered, and you're never going to get him in your house alone." I kept my eyes fixed out the window, tapping my thumb on my knee.

I leaned forward, told the Uber driver our address and directions in Spanish so Jordan couldn't understand or protest, and he zipped off in that direction.

"He's probably going to be pissed when he wakes up," Jordan said in a reluctant whisper.

"Why? It's not like he can make it inside without one of us carrying him. There's no way you could do it."

"I know." She looked at her feet. "I don't know. He just gets funny about stuff."

She spoke so quietly I could barely hear her over the music playing softly from the stereo. I didn't respond for a moment, and continued watching buildings whiz by outside.

"How'd you even know what I said?" I raised an eyebrow, looking in her direction.

"My family's from Mexico. She grew up speaking Spanish with us," Camilla chimed in around a yawn from the back seat.

I bit my bottom lip.

Noted.

I needed to watch what I fucking said in front of her.

"If he sobers up enough soon, I'll take you both home. Or just sleep on the couch and I'll drive you back first thing in the morning." My gaze stayed outside of the car.

"It's fine. We'll just stay. You can't take us home tonight anyway, we've all been drinking...."

I wanted to tell her I shouldn't probably ever drive because of my constant 'under the influence' head state. That I would have been fine – I had mastered the art of driving while not sober. That I had done things far worse than driving after a few beers.

But that wasn't something I wanted to admit to anyone besides myself, and I couldn't let her know I was borderline seeing double when I had driven her home the night before.

Trevor and I carried Jake up the concrete stairs to our apartment. I had Jake lay in my bed for the moment until we were all ready to go to sleep, and while I waited for my pills to knock me on my ass, so that I could actually drift off into a slumber.

Camilla asked Trevor to walk her home, thanked me for getting us a ride before hugging Jordan, and followed Trevor out of the apartment.

I got up and walked to the kitchen to grab a beer. I couldn't stop my hands from opening the cabinet and popping another pill into my mouth. Life had gotten fucking weird since I had come around my old friends again, and got my nose out of fucking trouble, and I couldn't stand how that this shit made me feel. To handle that, benzos and alcohol would suffice for the night.

"Want another drink?" I looked over at Jordan while she mindlessly watched my TV.

13. Jordan

Adrian passed me the same mixed drink he had before, pulling his shirt over his head and placing it in my lap once again. He made his way down the hallway, his shoulder blades moving beneath his bare skin with each step he took away from me. When he returned, pink sweatpants were now added to the pile of clothing on my thighs.

All I could think about was how much hotter he just got shirtless. My mind hadn't been coherent enough to realize it the night before, but now he was all I could see.

Colorful artwork covered his strong arms and abs etched into his caramel skin. He had changed into gray, baggy sweatpants, exposing another tattoo on the left side of his stomach, right above the waistline. It looked like the outline of a state or a country, filled in with a picture of a blue flag between rips in his skin. Blue stars ran down the middle of it.

I allowed my eyes to linger on his body, drinking him in before he inevitably caught me. On the inside of his right bicep, black ink caught my attention, which read, "*A veces el remedio es peor que la enfermedad.*"

'Sometimes the remedy is worse than the disease.'

Isn't that the damn truth?

"I'm not going to take your shirt," I said in a teasing tone.

"I don't sleep with a shirt on, anyway. Just take it. You didn't have a problem with that last night," Adrian stated plainly, his eyes trained in front of him.

I sat in silence, staring at the TV along with Adrian, before he took another gulp of his drink.

"Are you going to change?" He looked at me and smiled, lifting an eyebrow slightly. "The bathroom's down the hall. First door on the right." He lifted his chin towards the hall before looking back at the TV.

"I know, I know," I huffed before standing up and walking towards the bathroom. I would have been disappointed if I had come over and not ended up in his shirt again, covered in his delicious cedar scent. A stupid expectation that I needed to avoid obtaining.

I shuffled to the bathroom, locking the door behind me as I stripped out of my outfit and into the one he had given me. His bathroom housed photos of surfboards and the beach, with a Sublime poster hanging on the wall. I studied the fixtures that I had been too messed up to notice the night before until I finally exited the bathroom.

As soon as I returned to the living room, finishing my drink off with one last gulp, I plopped myself back down in the corner of the L-shaped couch, half laying down with my head laying against the back cushion. My body was begging for sleep, sinking into the cushions, while my mind kept racing.

How did I always get myself into these situations?

I should have been at home, watching Netflix or FaceTiming with my sister. Not making a fool out of myself with the same person for a second night in a row.

Adrian stood up, taking both of the glasses, and stepped out of my view as I continued to giggle at the dry humor of *The Office*. Jake had watched the show many times, though he hardly ever made it through an episode without being too stoned to fall asleep before it ended. I had never given it the time of day when he watched it at home.

Adrian immediately returned to the couch, holding another filled glass towards me. I hesitated for a second, given how late it was, but decided one more wouldn't hurt. I wouldn't be able to sleep much that night anyway, given that for the second night in a row I wasn't alone in my bed, and this time I wasn't on drugs that could help me forget about what I was doing.

His green eyes burned through me, staring confidently and expectedly as he pulled the corner of his lower lip between his teeth. This damn man always looked mischievous. Given the look on his face, he wasn't asking me to accept the drink, anyway. Either he knew how stressed I was about being in his house and wanted me to chill the hell out, or it was perfectly normal in his world to finish half a bottle of vodka after leaving a club.

"You alright?" He asked knowingly, as my eyes wandered every part of his shirtless physique and angel touched face.

I nodded, embarrassed, looking to the wall behind him.

14. Adrian

Jordan sat up in a criss-cross position on the other side of the couch as she took the glass from my hand. The front door swung open behind her, Trevor trudging back inside.

"You guys are still up?" He asked, sounding out of breath.

"Yeah. That took you a while." Taking a sip of my drink, I kept my eyes locked on the screen. I didn't want to see the cocky, judgemental look that he would surely give me for sitting on the couch with Jake's sister at 3 in the morning, drinking cranberry and apple juice with vodka. At that moment, I didn't care what he thought about my actions.

"Yeah, I'm exhausted. See you in the morning."

Jordan called out a goodnight as he trudged down the hallway and into his bedroom, shutting the door behind him.

"If you want help to move Jake out here so you can go to sleep too, I'll help you. He'll wake up if he has to."

She sounded as if she was imposing, when I knew damn well it was the exact opposite. All I wanted to do was be around her for no good fucking reason, even if just for the night, and I would do anything to make that happen now that I had the chance. I lay on my side with my head in the corner of the L-shaped couch, propping my head up on my elbow a few inches from where Jordan was sitting, and took another swig of my drink.

"Were Jake and your ex friends?" I asked, while keeping my eyes fixed on the TV.

"Alec?"

"Yup."

"Uh, kinda, I don't know. I didn't bring him around Jake much."

"Why?"

"I don't know."

"Don't want to talk about it?"

She sighed and continued looking down. "I don't know, no... it's just ancient history that always gets dug up. Kinda over it."

"Well, he seems like a fucking idiot, especially if he cheated on you. He needs to grow some balls and act like a man."

She scrunched her nose, looking away from me. "Can we talk about something less personal?"

I chuckled. "Everything's personal. How about this? My mom and younger siblings don't live in the United States and I haven't seen any of them in almost a year. Now you know something personal about me." I smiled at her and picked my drink up from the floor, finishing it before placing the glass on the coffee table.

"Where do they live?"

"A small town in Honduras, where we moved here from when I was a kid."

"Why did she move back there?"

I took a sip of my drink, not meeting her eyes. "Family shit. Things got complicated when my dad died. It was better that she went back home."

She stayed silent for a moment.

"I'm really sorry to hear that."

"Eh, it is what it is." I shrugged one shoulder and kept watching the TV. "I don't lose sleep over it. Life happens. But I get it if you don't want to talk about it. We all have our skeletons in the closet."

"Is that why you have that tattoo?" Her eyes lingered on my lower stomach.

I smiled at her. "Yeah. Gotta rep the motherland somehow, right? See, now you know more personal shit about me than most."

She smiled back. "Why didn't you go with them?"

"I just didn't want to. It wasn't fun when they first left, but I wanted to stay here."

She looked at me curiously, her blue eyes filled with childlike wonder. "How did you make it, though? I wouldn't last a day by myself right now, let alone at that age."

I let out an exasperated breath. "Honestly? And you can't think I'm some shithead if I tell you the truth. I did what I had to, and I was young and dumb."

She nodded innocently.

I didn't want to tell her, but I didn't want to lie to her either. I had kind of opened this can of worms anyway by asking her about her personal shit, and if I expected her to tell me anything, I had to fess up to some of mine.

So here it was.

The moment of truth.

The moment where I finally came face to face with my past, when I could no longer run from it and numb myself from the reality of my shadows.

"I stole shit, sold it online. Broke into cars and houses. Robbed dealers and sold their supply. You name it, whatever was needed. Made it work. Got involved with some shitty people to keep myself afloat. Sometimes people are pushed to do things they don't want to simply because they have to, and unfortunately that often becomes their defining moment – what they do in desperation instead of what they do when they have the resources and support they need. But it is what it is, and it's not who I am now. I know that." I swallowed with a dry throat. "Enough about my past. Anything you want to share about yours?" I smirked and lifted myself from the couch.

I expected judgment to be plastered across her face, but I found acceptance. My less than innocent past was something I hid from the women that I wanted to get into bed with. It didn't matter to share. But with her, it came naturally. Like I could finally vent and somewhat process all the less than acceptable things I had done, even if just momentarily.

She rolled her eyes with a smile, something that made a stupid ass grin come across my face. It was cute as hell when she did that. Like she wanted to have an attitude, but was too sweet to go through with it without smiling.

"I've shared more than enough with you for the next year." She laughed.

When I walked back into the living room with two fresh glasses, I sat myself next to Jordan, closer to her than I had before. My right leg pressed against her as I handed her a last drink.

"I'll need to go home in the morning so I can shower and get stuff to go surfing, if we're still doing that."

I placed my hand on her upper thigh and tilted my head back on the couch cushion, keeping my eyes fixated on the TV in front of me. "Just let me know what you need."

Her head fell softly on my shoulder. A rose scent, accompanied by her hair against my bare skin, brought my senses back to life. I savored the moment with her, watching TV and finishing my drink. A pause in time when I could just fucking breathe, for the first time in years.

15. Jordan

Sunlight peeked through the gaps of the living room blinds and danced across my closed eyelids. I squinted against the light, trying to gauge my surroundings. I had slept like a rock the night before, nothing waking me from the moment my head hit the pillow, until hours later.

Adrian was no longer sharing the couch cushions with me, as he had been when I fell asleep only a few hours before. My head spun, allowing in the ache that had been waiting to show itself the moment my sleep left. I sat up with my eyes half open to find him in the kitchen fumbling through cabinets, shirtless and in his relaxed, baggy sweatpants.

He was quite a sight to see, especially bare-chested and with sleep laced in his eyes.

"Do you ever sleep?" I said over the couch towards the kitchen as I stretched my arms up over my head.

He smiled at me underneath the cabinets, leaning against his hands on the counter. "I actually just got up. Are you hungry?"

"Um, I guess, kind of. I don't know yet."

He chuckled as I laid back down on the couch and opened up my phone.

I tried to gulp down the uneasiness I felt about ending up in his apartment two nights in a row. We had just become... *friends?* And even though we had spent the last two nights hanging out and talking for a while, I didn't know him well enough to be shit-faced, or on ecstasy at his house at 3 A.M., without feeling some shame.

I sat up to find Adrian sitting at the dining room table with a plate of food in front of him. He looked over at me with his signature half smile, then looked back to the seat next to him, empty with a plate of food on the table in front of it. Pointing towards the food with his fork, he raised his eyebrows at me before taking another bite.

Soft beige carpet was beneath my feet as I walked into the tiled kitchen/dining room area. I sat in the empty chair and looked at the breakfast he had made. Sunny side up eggs, toast, bacon and a glass of orange juice. He had cooked everything perfectly, the white of the egg fully cooked, with a delicious runny yolk. I swallowed a couple more bites, my mouth bursting with flavor, saltiness of the bacon dancing across my tongue.

"I haven't had bacon in years. This is delicious."

"You haven't? Why?" He asked as he watched his plate, cutting his egg for another bite.

"Jake and I don't cook a lot at home. We just munch on cereal and hope for the best, I guess."

"Your parents never cook?"

"I don't live with my dad, and my mom isn't much of a cook," I lied. My mom used to love to cook, but that ship had sailed years ago.

"You guys are missing out. I used to love to cook, but I've kinda lost that in the last few years, unless my mom's in town."

"Yeah, we usually opt for sushi takeout or something."

"You like fish?"

"Depends where from and how fresh it is. Usually only stuff that we catch or places that I trust."

"I didn't know that you fish?" His brows furrowed down his forehead as he chewed, watching me from across the table. I nodded silently, taking a sip of my orange juice.

"Fresh fish is hard to come by around here," he said in a matter-of-fact way. "Back home is the only place you can really get fresh fish unless you catch it yourself. Like *caught-that-day* kind of fresh."

"I wish we got that here. Jake bought a boat, but we've gotten skunked a lot this summer, so it's been a while since I've had fresh stuff."

I bit into my last piece of bacon, studying the art that hung on his walls. Photos that looked identical to the ones in his bathroom.

Living a plane ride away from my family, let alone in a whole different country, was unimaginable. I always imagined being independent, not having to deal with my mom's drunk antics and consistent desire to argue. But the thought of living on my own, in a different country than her or Jake or anyone else I was related to, would be terrifying.

Becoming an adult isn't that exciting once it actually happens.

"Where are Jake and Trevor?" I asked, the realization hitting me that both doors were open to silent and empty bedrooms.

"Trevor took Jake home before work."

My stomach turned as I scrunched my nose. Perfect.

Jake most likely had seen me asleep on the couch, wrapped up in Adrian's arms, and was pissed. The fact that he had left me here in the first place, and hadn't texted me yet, might as well have confirmed that.

"Jake mentioned going up to Big Bear with Trevor tonight before they left this morning," Adrian added.

"You saw them?"

"They left right after I got up. I told them I could take you home, so we didn't have to wake you." He grabbed my empty plate, his half full, and walked towards the sink. His muscular back moved with each step, one of the few areas on his body that was free of ink.

Maybe Jake didn't see us. If Adrian was up, maybe he was in the kitchen already. Hopefully Jake simply hadn't texted me because he thought I was still asleep, and he was too hungover to care either way.

"You're not going to finish that?" I asked curiously. Given he was the one who had prepared the meal, I had expected him to finish more than a few bites.

He shrugged his shoulders with his back turned to me, and I watched as the muscles beneath his brown skin tensed and relaxed. If muscular, bare backs weren't a turn on to me before, they sure as hell were now.

"I don't have much of an appetite in the mornings. Just figured you might be hungry," he said nonchalantly.

"So Jake's going to Big Bear?"

"Sounds like it. He wants to pick up on some of Macy's friends."

My eyes rolled as I spoke under my breath. "Of course he does."

16. Adrian

After dropping Jordan off at her house, I made my way back to my apartment to shower before going to surf with her.

Trevor was back on the couch, resuming his game where he had left off the day before.

"Where's Macy?" I asked, trying to seem like I actually gave a fuck.

"She's at home. Did you go to get food? I'm starving."

"No, I took Jake's sister home."

"You took her home?" He said, enunciating every word, and actually looking away from the TV screen towards me with both eyebrows raised.

"She didn't have anyone to come get her," I muttered.

"Pffft." Trevor shook his head and smiled slightly.

"What's that about?"

"Nothin', nothin'. Just funny."

"Whatever." I took my usual spot on the couch and shrugged it off. I didn't have the energy or mental capacity to care what he meant.

"Seriously though. What's up with you?" Trevor asked me while focusing on the TV screen.

"What do you mean? I told you she didn't have anyone to take her home."

"Just be careful with Jake. I know they're super tight," he taunted.

"Be careful with what?"

"Bro, you never talk to like anyone besides me because I *live* with you. Then you spend the last two nights with this chick you just met and actually get your faded ass off the couch to drive? And you're not even fucking her? Let alone leave Ryan's with her. Pshhh." He chuckled. "You're into her."

"It's not that deep. She was cool, but I know she's Jake's sister. I'm not gonna fuck around like that."

"If she wasn't Jake's sister, would you?" He teased.

I paused before replying. I knew I fucking would.

My desire to fuck her was becoming stronger, and masking it was my only option.

That's why I gave her my number.

That's why I brought her home.

That's why I couldn't stop myself from touching her.

Why I was hoping to see her again.

Why she took over all my senses every time that I was near her.

All that ran through my fucking mind was her for the past two days. But I was too far gone to let anyone else into my life, if she even wanted to be there. And even if she wanted to be there, there was no way Jake would allow me to corrupt his sister with my presence and lifestyle.

I waved off Trevor's interrogation. "I don't know dude, I barely know her. She's hot as fuck, but like I said, it ain't that deep."

"Alright. Just don't fuck things up with Jake, is all I'm saying."

I closed my eyes while lying on the couch, begging them to stay open. By the time they did, it was time to pick up Jordan. I made my way to her house, battling afternoon traffic to do so, and loaded her board into my car.

I felt like an ass when she didn't let me inside to carry her things, but I understood. She still lived at home, and that could have been awkward as hell. As much as she was intoxicating and beautiful and everything I never knew I wanted, that didn't mean I was looking to have an awkward-ass first meeting with her family already – or ever.

We pulled into a parking spot overlooking seventeenth street, my go-to place once again, and hopped out of the car to get our surfboards out from the trunk.

Jordan sat on the back bumper as she pulled her olive green and white tribal print sundress over her head, throwing it in the trunk of my car. She wore a light, baby blue bikini and beige, rainbow brand flip flops. When she let her hair down from the braid she was wearing, it fell to right above her waist in perfect waves, not as curly as she had worn it the night before, but still beautiful.

I tried not to drool at the sight of her nearly naked, as desire ran through my veins. This girl was breathtakingly beautiful. Sunlight had kissed nearly every part of her body, and I knew she was hot before I had seen her with no clothes on. Now, my cock was pulsing in my trunks, threatening to make me look like a fucking seventh grader who couldn't control himself.

She grabbed her board from my trunk and turned towards the beach, grabbing her towel from the back seat on the way.

"Are you forgetting something?"

"No?" She blocked the sun with her hand on her forehead, tilting her head slightly.

"No wetsuit?"

She laughed. "It's barely September. The water isn't cold enough to need a wetsuit yet."

With no regard for if I was following, she continued down the concrete steps and towards the sand. I grabbed my board and trailed behind her.

By the time I got to the shoreline, Jordan had already dropped her stuff on the sand and was paddling out into the waves. I sat for a moment, leaving my shit next to hers, and watching to see if she would catch anything decent. A few minutes passed as she sat on her board, facing away from the beach and staring into the open water.

I could easily watch her in her element, one with the ocean, all fucking day. Her head bobbing up and down with the changing direction of the water, long hair protecting her back from the strong sun.

Instantaneously, she turned her board towards the sand as she laid down and started paddling back in, allowing a wave to grab her and her board. She stood up on her board effortlessly and began carving up and down the rolling wave. She was made to be in the ocean, looking like she belonged there. Gliding across the water, she took control of her path.

Jordan was naturally good, really fucking good. Much better than I had expected. Everything about her was effortless – her surfing, her beauty, her humor, her captivating personality. Everything she wasn't showing me, which I was dying to see, parts of her I was slowly getting more and more glimpses of each time I was near her.

She jumped into the dark blue ocean and re-emerged seconds later, swimming a few feet forward to her board, before draping her arms across it and floating in the water. She bobbed up and down in the passing swells as she looked out on the horizon, where the Catalina Island silhouette contrasted against a pale blue sky, threatening to turn to gold when the sun moved just a sliver lower. Finally, her head turned to the beach as she waved to me. I hurdled myself towards the water and paddled out to meet her.

"Nice left you caught out there," I said as I approached her and continued paddling alongside her deeper into the water.

"It was fun."

"You're better than I expected." I sat up on my board and took a deep breath.

"What's that supposed to mean?"

"Why didn't you ever join surf team with Jake?" I looked out onto the horizon. It was a perfect, warm fall day. One of the last heat waves we would surely have all year.

"I don't know, didn't want surfing to become a chore, I guess. I like to do it for stress relief, not for class credit at 7 AM each day. Just for fun." She paused for a moment, her gaze fixed upon the horizon. "Why didn't you ever join?"

I took a deep breath.

"I did actually. My freshman and sophomore year. But that ended quickly when I started fucking off."

I turned my board back towards the beach and began paddling, catching the next wave worth my while that came in, not giving her time to question me. The perfect escape from a conversation regarding my past that I didn't want to have. She already knew more about me than I wanted her, or anyone, to know.

Jordan and I surfed for nearly two hours, laughing and talking in between waves. She laid on her board, studying the sky above her when she needed time to catch her breath, her dark lashes heavy with salt water.

Being with her was natural. It was fucking fun, and exciting, and relaxing all at the same time.

We finally called it a day when the sun started to dip and went to the outdoor showers to rinse off. The cold water pounded against my skin as I tried to process my thoughts and feelings. Something I hadn't done in so long.

My coping skills had become nonexistent due to always being numbed by benzos, opiates, and anything else I could get my fucking hands on. Being with Jordan forced me to kick-start them up again in order to understand how I felt about her, and what I could, and would, possibly do about it.

I didn't want to just *hope* everything fell into place – I wanted to make sure it did.

But falling into place with me was like hoping Jenga pieces magically fell into another tower.

After a few minutes, I walked over to the shower head she was soaking herself under and lightly pushed her to the side.

"Yours is warmer than mine."

She stepped towards me and pushed me back with her elbow, out from under the running water.

"Punk. That's why I chose this one."

Another glimpse.

I was getting a much bigger glimpse behind her walls than I ever had. She was like a vault, hiding away until you were worthy of a peek inside.

Jordan closed her eyes, tilting her head back into the downpour of water. I placed my hand on the side of her face, with my fingertips on the back of her neck, soaking her in. I could soak in her beauty like I was sunbathing on the sand. Slowly leaning forward, my lips inches from hers, I waited to feel her skin against mine, and *bam*.

The goddamn water shut off.

17. Jordan

After surfing and a bite to eat from a taco shop on PCH, Adrian convinced me to come over to his house for a bit. I didn't want to intrude, but I was also more than happy to spend the afternoon with him instead of at home alone.

Without Jake there, I didn't feel like dealing with my mom this late in the evening. Who knew what I would walk into?

We fell asleep quickly after getting to his apartment, wiped out by hours in the sun. When I woke, Adrian's chest moved with each one of his breaths, my head flowing with it.

I turned onto my back, placing my head on his thick bicep, and looked around the room. Various photos of the ocean covered the white walls. A large TV was mounted on the wall above a dresser at the foot of his bed, and a window with black curtains was on the wall to my right. A closet and the door to the hallway were on my left. His dark brown ceiling fan spun silently above the bed and I laid there, watching it.

I could sit and do nothing with him all week. Just being with him was more enjoyable than partying or drinking until my memory went black. Part of being with him felt freeing, in a weird way.

I finally had a sense of independence. Not just independent like I was getting older, but like I was my own person who could do things without the comfort of a friend or my brother.

Adrian rolled over on his side to face me and placed his hand on my leg. He picked up a piece of my hair and spun the end of it back and forth between his index finger and thumb.

"How long have you been up?" he asked.

"Not very long." I continued to watch the ceiling fan as it spun above us.

The sun had completely set, and the room was dark now, besides the light of his bedside alarm clock, and a little creeping in from the hallway underneath his door.

I sat up slowly and rolled onto my stomach. He propped himself up onto his elbow and began typing on his phone, tossing it on the bed in front of me.

"Order whatever you want."

Adrian lifted himself up, standing up and walking out of the room. I sat for a moment scrolling the menu to a Chinese restaurant and selected the meal I wanted to eat, apprehensive at the thought of staying for dinner.

I had been in his house for two nights in a row. Surely, he was ready for me to get the hell out and go home.

Adrian was in the bathroom as I walked past and went to sit on the couch. I rested my feet on the cool glass coffee table, placing his phone on the cushion next to me.

"Did you decide on anything?" he asked me as he walked into the kitchen. He reached into the cabinet to grab two wine glasses and began filling them up with a bubbly liquid.

"Yeah, I did."

"Good. Whatcha getting?" He dragged out his words in the cutest, chipper tone.

"Just orange chicken and rice."

He came back over to the living room and placed the glasses on the table before reaching for his phone. He typed quickly before locking his phone again, tossing it onto the couch a few feet away from him, and took a drink from his glass.

"Do you want some?" He looked at me, silently placing his glass back on the table.

"I've never really drank wine."

He smiled as he shook his head and handed me the other glass. I lifted it to my parted lips, bubbles containing crisp fruit flavors filling my mouth. Like candy and fireworks in liquid form. I had been missing out on heaven and trading it for vodka for years like an idiot. I took another sip, and then another.

"This is way better than I expected," I told him before sipping on my glass once again. He stood up and walked towards the wood entertainment center beneath the TV.

"It's my mom's favorite." He held a button on the sound system. "She found it when she went wine tasting with her friends a few years ago. She bought like thirty bottles or something fucking crazy like that. When they moved back, it was too much of a pain to fit with all of their stuff, so she gave it to me."

He sat down next to me as the sound of *I can't help myself* by Four Tops filled the room.

"You like this?" I questioned, pressure filling my chest. His deep brown skin contrasting against gray sweatpants, and brown curls shoveled together on the top of his head, shaved short on the sides and back, his perfect white smile and furrowed brows when he focused on something.

It had me entranced.

All of it.

He smirked at me, tilting his head to the side. "What the hell's that supposed to mean?"

"You sit in a bar full of rap every day."

He smiled, sending heat from my toes to my head. His gaze was intoxicating, green eyes like the strongest drink I had ever had. "You get used to it after a while, babe."

18. Adrian

We listened to some oldies and continued to talk while we waited for our food, finishing half a bottle of wine in the meantime.

Shit, the way this girl cracked me wide open with no hesitation and found her way under my skin, inside my veins, and swimming through my mind. I could spend all day with her, all week, all damn year.

If only I had a year to give to her.

I stood up and took Jordan's hand, pulling her with me to the center of the living room.

She smiled and turned her head slightly to the side, blue eyes glistening in the dim living room lights. "What are you doing?"

"Dancing."

"Here?"

"We danced at Hansen's to shitty music with total strangers surrounding us. I don't see how this could be worse..." I smiled and looked around at the empty apartment. *Feathered Indians* by The Tyler Childers spilled from the speakers as I placed my hands on her hips, and she placed hers on my shoulders. We swayed back and forth slowly, in unison to the beat of the song. She laughed about nothing and looked up at me, studying something about me.

"What?" I asked with a half smile.

"Just not how I expected to spend my Saturday night."

"Well, I hope you're at least enjoying yourself."

"If I wasn't, I wouldn't be here," she said quietly as she laid her head on my chest, and I wrapped my arms around her. How did this fucking angel waltz into my life without a clue, always smelling of salt water and roses in the perfect combination?

Why did the devil have to play tricks on me by dangling her in front of my face, surely only to snatch her away later? Right when I thought I could fucking have her?

"I like *this* you better," I told her quietly.

She chuckled. "This me? What do you mean by that?"

"The actual you. The one where you let me see more than just the surface."

I took my hand off Jordan's right hip and brought it to her chin, lifting her face towards mine. I studied her for a moment, letting myself drown momentarily in her blue eyes, intoxicating and refreshing all at once.

Her eyes traced mine before my lips crashed into hers, the biggest spark lighting off with the smallest touch. The first fucking kiss I had ever cared about, the only lips that ever left an imprint on every part of me.

We leaned further and further into each other, throwing caution to the wind. My lips parted, moving against hers fluidly as our tongues caressed one another.

I'd be damned – this girl was going to have me forgetting everything I thought I fucking knew. My fingertips braised her arm, leaving a trail of goosebumps on her soft limbs. The feeling of her on my skin felt like tattoos where we met.

How was I supposed to avoid getting completely hooked on her now?

I put my arm around her waist and picked her up as she wrapped her legs around me, latching on. Her plush body got me hard immediately, an erection growing between my legs, no chance of stopping it.

She was everything that I never knew I fucking needed.

We fell onto the couch; her legs still wrapped around me, kissing me without missing a beat. Our tongues danced in unison, heavy breaths flowing through our lungs.

I couldn't stop kissing her – she'd have to pry me off to get my lips to fucking leave hers – and then the goddamn doorbell rang.

Jordan jumped and turned to look at the door, startled by the sudden interruption.

"Leave it on the porch," I yelled from beneath her. She looked at me, smiling, before pulling my face back to hers. Her soft lips melted into mine, unable to tell where one stopped and the other one started. I ran my hands tenderly through her hair, letting her touch captivate my mind for a moment.

"We can't let it get too cold," I breathed, studying her lips with half-open eyes. Fire burned within me, watching her on top of me. Her in my shirt, on my skin, in my bed… it didn't matter where she was, she sparked a part of me I didn't ever think existed. My hands became feverish and my soul ached for every inch of her to be covered in my lips, to leave the feeling of my skin on her for as long as she lived.

We finally fetched the food from the front doorstep and sat and ate around the coffee table, Jordan sitting on the floor as she nibbled in tiny, mouse sized bites.

"It's more comfortable like this when eating from a low table. I always do it," she informed me when I asked why exactly she was sitting on the carpet with her knees to her chest as she ate.

We finished the bottle of wine during dinner.

We finished another as we watched TV.

I went to grab our third before I had even asked her to fucking stay with me again.

When I walked into the kitchen, I instinctively reached to the cabinet above the fridge where my pill bottles were, but stopped my hand right before it grabbed the handle.

I didn't feel numb.

I didn't feel the emotions I was trying to suppress and ignore.

Seeing her sitting on my living room floor like she had always belonged there filled every crack and crevice of me.

But those feelings in themselves were more than a good enough reason to throw a few more opiates in my mouth.

My life may have been crashing down around me, but I sure as hell felt good while it was happening.

I swallowed the pills dry and opened another bottle of wine, pushing off any second thoughts about being high as fuck when I was around her – without her knowing.

She only knew me when I saw high.

She wouldn't be able to tell the difference.

Plus, I had seen her higher than the moon at a party, so I knew she wasn't a saint with drugs, either.

She just wasn't as bad as me.

I poured two glasses full and brought them along with the bottle back into the living room, where I found Jordan laying on the couch, her thumbs quickly typing on her phone screen.

"Everything good?"

"Um, yeah, just talking to Jake."

"Did you tell him where you were?"

"Why would I?" She didn't look up from her phone.

"Sorry for assuming." I took a big gulp of the wine.

"I just don't want him to get upset... we have a complicated relationship."

"I don't see why he would be. He told me I could take you out."

"He did?" She looked up from her phone to me with surprised eyes, chewing on her cheek.

"Yeah, why?"

"When did he say that?"

"The last time we were at Hansen's."

"Wow." She bit her lower lip and returned to texting.

Jake had definitely told me it was alright to take her out. My memories may have been hazy, but that was one I knew for sure. I didn't know how he would feel about our date turning into a fucking twenty-four-hour one, but we hadn't discussed specifics.

"Why do you care so much about what he thinks?" I asked bluntly.

"Because he's my brother. I have to care. I wouldn't do anything to jeopardize our relationship."

"Well, then he has to accept what you do. Don't jeopardize your independence and happiness for a perfect relationship with him. He's obviously always going to love you."

"I know.... he's just the last one in my family I can rely on and am truly close with." She sighed, put her phone down on the couch, before sitting up and grabbing her wine glass.

"You don't talk to your dad? What about your mom?"

"My dad is remarried now, with twin one year olds. And my mom checked out a while ago. She's kinda hard to deal with. She's very up and down. Addiction is a powerful thing, so it's kinda just me and Jake."

She took a sip of her wine.

19. Jordan

After a few glasses of wine and a confidence boost from the new sense of drunk I was feeling, I ended up telling Adrian about more of my life than I had intended to.

He told me about his mom and how they were close, trying to grow accustomed to the American lifestyle as a family. Once his dad died, he left behind three young kids besides Adrian, younger than five, and a stay-at-home mom. His mom decided she had to move back to Honduras to be closer to his grandparents for financial support and to tie up some loose ends. Adrian stayed to see how well he could make it on his own.

"Why?" I asked him.

"I haven't lived in Honduras since I was thirteen. I had just graduated high school and couldn't imagine leaving all my friends, everything I had known for most of my life, behind, just to kinda start over."

"Did you like it over there?"

"Yeah, I love it. Just a different culture, it's like summer year-round and living in a small town means you know everyone. If you ever get the chance to go, do it."

"Were you close with your dad?" I practically whispered. Going deep wasn't something I was very used to.

"Kind of. He died when I was eighteen, so five years ago now. I don't have the fondest opinion of him. What he did was selfish and inconsiderate. I don't think I'll ever forgive him for it."

He finished the last glass of our bottle of wine after he spoke. If what happened had caused him pain, or agony, or any feelings at all, he never let it show. A trait I wished I had more of.

Something no one had told me about wine – the drunk sneaks up on you. It wasn't the same drunk that made me want to dance, like tequila brought on. It was a drunk that made me want to sink into the couch and talk and laugh all night long. One that, apparently, made me braver than usual, as well.

I leaned my head onto Adrian's shoulder and looked up at him to admire his features. His full, perfect lips, his long eyelashes, and relaxing green eyes. His thick hair that I wanted to run my fingers through.

"Can I help you?"

I held back a smile and looked away for a moment before returning my gaze back to him. He was still staring at me with a small grin, cocky that he was getting so much of me. Something that should have bothered me more than it did.

He was trouble, right?

Yes. He was trouble.

I had been warned, time and time again, by two of the people who meant the most to me.

Why couldn't I see that he was fucking trouble?

20. Adrian

Jordan's lips crashed into mine, and I slowly turned and laid on my back on the couch, pulling Jordan on top of me as we continued to melt into one another. Her personality, her looks, her laugh, her fucking lips when meshed perfectly with mine... all of it was something I couldn't get enough of.

We got more passionate by the second, turning from slow to needy. I ran my hands up and down her sides, feeling every inch of her body that I could without fear of her becoming uncomfortable. Of her turning me away and walking out my front door – like she should probably have done the first time she ever came here.

She lifted my shirt to place her hand on my bare stomach and my cock stirred, teased by her fucking proximity. I felt her fingers lift the waistband to my sweatpants and run lightly over my hip bone, and my instincts took over.

How was I ever supposed to stay away from her now?

I waited for her to come to her senses, to realize that she was too fucking good for me, but as her hands continued to trail my skin, my fingers intertwined with her blonde hair, I traded morals for desires. Her lips pushed me over the edge, her tongue caressing me as I fell into the spell of her skin.

She kissed my neck as I stood, picking her up and walking down the hall.

"Do you want to do this?" I whispered in her ear as we walked into my bedroom doorway. She was still kissing me lightly on my collarbone as I asked.

"I would have stopped you already if I didn't," she whispered, kissing my lips. Crashing into her, her hands ran through my hair as my tongue feverishly dove into her mouth.

How could one woman be so fucking exhilarating?

It surely wasn't fair to the rest of them.

I laid her down on my bed as she lifted my shirt over my head. Slowly, I slipped her sweatpants and panties down, running my fingertips along her soft thighs, kissing inch by inch.

"Tell me when to stop," I breathed as I threw her pants to the ground. Her thighs pressed together, her thumb between her teeth as she tried to control herself. Desire pulsed through me as I watched her on my bed, exposing me to what she hid behind her walls even more.

More than just a glimpse.
The best fucking sight I had ever seen.

I slid my fingers against her wetness, teasing her up and down, as moans quietly left her lips. I would have teased her until the fucking sun came up if I could have.

Control.

This was the only part of my life I had control over.

Over whatever happened to her in bed with me, which I was damn sure would be the best she had ever felt in her fucking life.

I kissed her center lightly, breathing into her skin before tasting her. Sweet, untouched flesh blessed my lips, and I was hooked fucking hooked at the first taste. I moved my tongue around her, sucking against her clit. My eyes stayed glued to hers as her back arched with each movement of my tongue, gripping the sheets by her waist. I continued to slide my tongue slowly, slipping my finger slightly inside of her.

The tightest damn entrance I had ever felt.

Her hands tugged at my hair as they grasped for some control, none of which I was willing to give her. She was fucking mine, even if just for the moment.

"Relax, baby, I'm not going to hurt you."

"Adrian…" she breathed as I held her thigh down, stopping her from pushing me away as she squirmed within my grip.

"I told you to stop me when you wanted to. Do you want me to stop?" I teased, my fingers continuing to massage her sensitive center.

"No," she gulped, pulling harder at my scalp.

"Good." My breath lingered on her skin as I moved my mouth back to her. Quickening my pace, I slipped a second finger inside, awaiting to see if she would protest. When she didn't, beyond a small flinch, I continued to sweep in and out of her tight pussy. Lost in her existence, I continued to search her for where she felt the best, the spots that made her melt. When her toes curled around my skin, I knew I had found them.

More than that, I had accomplished the only thing I cared to do. I could have spent fucking *hours* making her mine.

Within seconds, she was coming undone. She pulled a pillow over her head, trying to muffle the sound of her moans as she throbbed against my fingers, her legs shaking within my hold. Dripping down my palm, I slowed my pace until her moans quietly died out.

I climbed my way to her, removing the pillow from her face and taking in the sight of her euphoric state with a cocky smile. Her breaths were deep, eyes still shut, remaining in a spiral as my lips found hers.

I fucking did that.

"Do you have a condom?" She asked between pants, running her hands over the growing bulge in my boxers.

I scoffed. "I'm not going to fuck you, Jordan."

She frowned slightly, finally opening her heavy eyes to see the smile on my face. "Why not?"

"Are you a virgin?"

Her brows furrowed as she studied my eyes. "No."

My breath caught in my lungs. With how shy and damn tight she was, I had thought for sure she hadn't slept with anyone before. The thought of someone ever getting to touch her before me made me sick.

"I'm still not going to fuck you. I have to keep you coming back for more somehow." Kissing her forehead and rolling off of her, I pulled her to my chest. Blonde hair fanned across my arm, her head resting on my skin.

"Well, at least let me return the favor," she said after a few moments. I looked down at her comically. The quiet-ass girl was now half naked in my bed, offering to give me a blowjob.

"I won't stop you," I replied, pulling my bottom lip between my teeth.

Slowly, she kissed down my torso, nipping at my skin. I propped myself on my elbows as I watched her remove my length from my boxers, running her hands delicately along the size of me. Her soft lips kissed my shaft, followed by her tongue dragging across my skin.

Fuck.

My breathing hitched as she took me into her mouth, wrapping her plush, pouty lips around my tip, before taking me deeper into her mouth.

"Just like that, baby," I breathed.

She continued stroking me with her hand in perfect rhythm, sending fireworks off between my pelvic bones. Watching her claim me with her mouth was by far the sexiest shit I had ever seen.

"Damn, Jordan..." I groaned as my hips tilted towards her mouth, putting even more length inside of it. She welcomed me, focusing on finding the most sensitive spots to pleasure me with. Once she found them, running her tongue along my shaft, I grabbed the sheets and closed my eyes, focusing on holding out as long as I could. After minutes of a fire burning deep in my core, and slickness dripping down onto my waist, I grabbed a fistful of her hair, my hand following her movements, up and down.

"I'm gonna come," I warned, looking down at her.

Her blue eyes met mine as she kept the same movement, challenging me to do so. Instantly, my release arrived, and I bit my bottom lip to keep myself quiet.

"God help me," I whispered, pulling at the strands of hair in my fist. Once my head finally stopped spinning, I opened my eyes to find Jordan, with a satisfied smile, laying next to me.

"Get your ass over here," I teased as I pulled her next to me, her head back into its place on my chest. I kissed her hair, waiting for my heart to return to a normal fucking rate. We both lay in the dark room, listening to the sound of the fan as I spun Jordan's hair between my fingertips once again.

"You have no idea how badly I want to fuck you," I whispered into the darkness.

"Then why don't you?"

"I told you, I have to keep you coming back for more somehow." I ran my fingers lightly along her arm, taking in every inch of her skin in a mental snapshot.

She sighed obnoxiously. "You say that like I'm some whore who hooks up with every guy I've ever met and never talks to them again."

I chuckled at her annoyance. "Are you sure you're not a virgin?"

"Why do you keep asking me that?" She looked up at me with a suspicious expression, which I met with a shrug.

"You're just so damn tight, I would have bet everything I owned that you were."

Her cheeks flushed, bringing a cocky-ass smile to my face. Goddamn, this girl was the perfect fucking contrast of fire and ice.

"Well, I'm not, so quit asking me. I've only had sex with one guy, but that still makes me a non-virgin."

My thumb ran down the freckles that decorated her cheek, as I tried to wrestle the thought of her with anyone besides me out of my mind.

"Who?" I asked blankly, trying to disguise my distaste for whoever had been inside her before I even got the fucking chance to be.

"I don't think that's any of your business." Her eyes narrowed in my direction.

"Was it that tool trying to hit on you all night at Ryan's?" I asked before thinking.

It really wasn't my business, but I felt a weird need to know. I already had a bad feeling about him that night. If he had been the only guy to have sex with Jordan, and then fucking cheated on her, I would gladly ensure his death on my own.

Her gaze moved away from me to the ceiling as she began chewing on her cheek. "If you must know, yes. Alec's the only guy I've slept with, but I would rather not talk about him."

I took a deep breath to stop myself from going off about him. Anyone who was stupid enough to hurt her obviously just wanted to get in her pants and fucking ruin her for their own benefit.

"Stay away from him. I don't think he would be any good for you."

She sighed as she lay her head back on my chest. "Trust me, I'm trying."

I placed my hand on her hip under the blanket, looking down moments later to find her eyes already closed. She slept for probably an hour as I watched her, my eyes alternating between her perfect physique and the ceiling above me. Her chest rising and falling with each breath, dark lashes fanned across her freckle covered cheeks. Dirty blonde hair with streaks of brown that rested on my arm, her cheek pressed against my skin.

It was the best night of sleep I had ever gotten.

21. Jordan

I woke up when the sun was hardly above the horizon, initially confused about where I was. I blinked my eyes at the white wall, trying to differentiate one direction from another. When I sat up to reach for my glasses from my nightstand, a force of resistance held me still. Adrian was sleeping peacefully, his arms still around me.

I was at fucking Adrian's still.

Oh, crap.

What had I done?

No.

No fucking way.

I had been drunk the night before. Like, way more drunk than I realized. Drunk enough to try and fuck Adrian.

I was an idiot.

I had already hooked up with Adrian – I had been the one to initiate it – and without a doubt; he thought I was the biggest slut, with good reason.

My eyes traced around the room, soaking in every aspect.

I might as well enjoy my last few moments inside of his apartment for the rest of my life.

I had completely ruined any chance I ever had of seeing where things went between us by branding myself as easy. Ruined every chance of us at least being *friends*. Something that could never be changed.

I rolled over with my back to him, my head still resting on his arm.

How could I look him in the eyes when he woke?

He was in nothing more than his plaid boxers, me in nothing more than his shirt.

My heart ached, knowing I would never feel his skin against mine again.

What a fuckup.

What a dumbass, drunk decision.

One that I would surely regret the rest of my life, just as I had before.

An hour passed before Adrian woke up and interrupted me, as I sat with my thoughts. I pretended I was asleep, trying to avoid looking him in his eyes and feeling the new judgment he had against me. He slowly slipped his arm out from under my head and got up from the bed. After the bathroom door shut behind him, I grabbed my phone from the bedside table and checked the time.

It was still 7:30 A.M. I could easily pretend to be asleep until 9, and rush home like I had something to do that day before he had the chance to kick me out. A foolproof plan.

A few minutes later, Adrian reappeared into the bedroom. He silently lowered himself back into the bed and under the sheets, placing his skin against my back and arm around my waist. I looked down to see him scrolling through his Instagram feed, with his phone in his hand that was draped over me. He noticed my eyes were open and kissed me on the neck.

"Did you sleep alright?" He asked in a soft tone.

"Um, yeah, I slept good." I didn't turn to look at him as I spoke and closed my eyes once again.

"Do you have anything to do today?"

"No, not much. Do you?"

"I work at 2, but that's it. So we have all morning to be lazy until then." He kissed me on the neck again, dropping his phone and softly running his hand over my hip, back and forth on my side. I stayed still.

"Everything alright?"

"Yeah, I'm fine, sorry."

If he had thought I was just another easy girl, I liked to think he wouldn't be telling me to stay until he worked, and kissing me repetitively.

Or he was just taunting me. Trying to soften the blow of what an ass I had made of myself.

Only time would tell.

I rolled over in bed until I was facing him. He wrapped his arm around my back and pulled me right into his bare chest as I let my worries melt away for a bit longer.

Whatever was barreling towards me like a freight train could be dealt with later. I would cross that bridge when I got there.

22. Adrian

I was fucking dreading Jordan walking out my front door.

Dreading going back to work that afternoon.

I wanted to tell her that I had just had the best weekend of my life and that she should stay the night again every night for the rest of the year, and then next year.

But I couldn't tell her that.

Chemical-based pill residue covered my tongue from the one I had just dry swallowed after I went to the bathroom. I wanted to kiss her, to feel her tongue against mine and my hands in her hair, but fear took over that she would taste it. Knowing she was leaving today with no set date to come back held me back from doing so, and pushed me back into my self-destructive habits before she even woke up.

"Are you busy on Friday?" I asked her with my eyes closed, feeling her soft skin beneath my fingertips.

"It's only Sunday, so I guess I haven't thought that far ahead yet."

"That's true. So is that a no?"

"That's a no."

"Can I reserve you for dinner?"

"Are you asking me if I want to have dinner on Friday?"

"Yes, do you?"

"Yes, I do."

"Then it's a date."

We lay in bed for a few hours, talking and laughing amongst ourselves. I decided it was time to get up and out of bed, and headed to the shower. Jordan stayed in my bed as she watched YouTube videos on her phone.

When I came back from the bathroom, wet hair dripping onto my shoulders, she hadn't moved an inch and looked more tired than when I had left.

"You look comfortable," I laughed as I grabbed her foot teasingly through the dark blue blanket.

"Ughhhh, I am. I don't want to get up. Your bed is like a cloud." She rolled onto her back and stretched her arms to the wall above her head, letting out a sigh. "But I guess I have to."

I threw on boxers under the towel wrapped around my waist and threw a black T-shirt over my head.

"Not the shirt!" She giggled with a smirk as she taunted me from the bed.

I bit my bottom lip and smiled at her.

"I'm starving," I said as I stepped into my dark blue jeans and shook my hair with the towel.

"Um, I know, I'm hungry too." She sat up slowly with her legs hanging off the side of the bed and grabbed her sweatpants from the carpet below.

I made breakfast, and we both ate at the dining room table, Jordan as quiet as when we first met. I knew that she rarely initiated conversation, but this was even less talking than the days before.

As my shift approached, so did my dread of dropping her back off at home, marking the end of our wrinkle in time.

The best weekend I had ever experienced.

It had easily topped every weekend I had spent in a different universe, killing my brain cells with drugs, my lungs with clouds of smoke, and my liver with bottles of liquor. I finally had my feet on the ground and actually felt some connection with something outside of myself.

All weekend I hadn't spent a moment feeling sorry for myself, filled with never ending thoughts about the same things over and over.

Ones that I tried to numb.

Why was I still trying to be numb?

Now that I was driving towards her house, I could feel the wave of anxiety coming over me again.

I took a deep breath. I needed to focus on the day ahead of me, make it through work, and try not to spend my whole day, my entire week, looking forward to Friday.

I had to figure out what to say to Jake, if anything, about how this weekend had gone.

And most importantly, I had to find a fucking way to make sure I saw Jordan again sometime within the next few days. Or hours.

I looked over at her in the passenger seat of my car as I drove and placed my right hand on her thigh as she looked out the window.

She didn't look back at me.

My eyes stayed focused back on the road ahead of me and my hand rested on her the rest of the way to her house.

I pulled into the alley and parked in front of her garage door. She gathered her things from the floor of my car below her feet silently. Tapping my thumbs on the steering wheel, I stretched in my seat.

I tried to stop myself from saying; *You know what? Don't go, I'll call out of work, and we'll lie in my bed all day.*

Every bone and muscle and instinct was begging me to stop her, to drive away before she got out and take her back into my arms.

But I knew I couldn't do that. Jake and Trevor would be home soon. I had shit to handle, and things wouldn't be the same as they had been over the weekend.

Our wrinkle in time had ended. Things would resume as normal, with people to please, and things to do, and lives to live.

"I had a good time. Thank you for everything," she smiled back at me.

"See you Friday," I replied as she climbed out of the car and shut the door behind her. I waited until she was inside of her house to drive off to work.

23. Jordan

The hot water ran down my back as I sat on the floor of the shower, my routine to ease my hangover and reflect on my weekends.

Nothing cured a feeling of death from too much drinking, smoking, and MDMA like a room full of steam and nearly burning my skin off with scorching hot water while sitting on the cool tile floor.

This time my feeling of death wasn't from drugs, and alcohol, and no sleep, and self-hate.

Well, maybe a little self-hate.

I had a slight headache from the bottles of wine wc drank the night before, but nothing like the hangovers I would have regularly from hard liquor and no sleep.

I had fucked up with Adrian.

Like, *fucked up.*

And it wouldn't leave my damn mind.

How he would tell Trevor and all his friends that he nearly slept with me, and they would now assume I was easy.

It would eventually get back to Jake and I would have to live with how disgusted he was with me for what I had done, and for the impression I made on Adrian and everyone he told.

Even worse than my reputation, that was sure to take a major hit, so did any chance I had of being friends with Adrian.

I couldn't stop replaying the weekend over and over in my head. His smile and eyes made the world melt away. His arms around me as we slept gave me a feeling of home that I so longed for. Thoughts of being back in his presence, to being held by him, his fingers lightly tracing my spine, danced in my head as I pushed them to the side.

Now I would never have that again. He would surely take me out just so he could hook up with me again, and eventually have sex with me.

Hooking up with him repeatedly would only make me even more attached to him than I had already quickly become.

How was I supposed to act like I didn't fall for him even more every time I saw him, every time he touched me, or even talked with me?

Every thought of him made my head spin and my heart skip a few beats. I waited two and half years after meeting Alec until I did anything more than kiss him, and he still never saw me as more than a piece of ass. After not waiting more than a few days before hooking up with Adrian, he would think of me as even worse than Alec did.

I turned off the water and continued to sit on the shower floor, debating whether I should go out with Adrian on Friday, if he even followed up on it.

My skin raised in goosebumps from the swirling cold air, unable to penetrate my mental wall.

In the back of my mind, I *knew* he was just wanting to take me out with other intentions.

But I still had a bit of hope that giving him the benefit of the doubt wouldn't bite me in the ass. Maybe he was different from every other guy I had ever known in my life, besides Jake and Ryan. Though the odds of that, though, were practically nonexistent.

I sighed, massaging my temples.

Jake.

The last person I wanted to see.

I wrapped my towel around my hair and slipped on sweats before leaving the bathroom. Turning the corner into my bedroom, I found him sitting on my bed.

Shit.

"How was Big Bear?" I asked before he could speak, turning to my closet so I didn't have to look at him.

"Good. How was your weekend with Adrian?" His tone was ice cold as all the blood left my face. He never was one to shy away from how he truly felt.

"Um, it was good. After you left on Saturday we just went surfing and hung out at his house…"

"And you spent the night." He finished my sentence for me.

I sighed and turned around to face him. He kept his eyes on me, unblinking, as he waited for an answer.

"Yes, I spent the night there. Now get off my case." I crossed my arms, leaning back against the wall.

He ran his fingers through his hair. "Goddamn it, Jo, I fucking told you not to hang around him. He's dirty, too far gone for you."

"It was one time."

"For now. Who knows where this will go? And when it all bites you in the ass, I'm going to have nothing to say besides I fucking *told you* so!"

"Stop telling me what to do! I don't tell you what to do, Jake. I already know about Adrian's past. And we aren't even seeing each other. We didn't even sleep together!"

His eyes got wide, redness slowly creeping across his face. "You better not be fucking sleeping with him, Jordan! This is more than just his past. I don't trust him, and you shouldn't be so quick to, either!" He stood with his finger pointed at me, ready to release his rage on me.

I softened my tone, trying to calm the situation. "I don't trust him, Jake. We spent one weekend together. If things progress farther, I'll tell you, but I highly doubt they will."

He sat back on my bed and interlaced his fingers, his elbows on his knees.

"Seeing him again isn't a good idea, just so you know. I just don't want you to get hurt. This isn't me trying to control you. I'm trying to protect you, so try to understand where I'm fucking coming from."

I let out an exasperated breath. Jake never stepped into my life like this, so I had to give him some validation.

"I do understand, Jake. I promise I won't be stupid. Why are you so nervous about me being around him anyway?"

He shook his head, eyes focused on the floor. "It's a long story, Jo. Just… trust me on this."

24. Adrian

I walked through the grungy feeling bar and dropped my stuff into my locker, keeping my phone on me this time, which was unusual.

I walked over to where Ryan and Marco were standing at the bar, as Ryan served beers to our few customers scattered throughout the room, watching the NFL game.

"Hola amigo, cómo estás hoy? Porque ya estás aquí?"

Hey man, how are you today? How come you're already here?

Marco was from El Salvador, somewhere in his mid-thirties, with three kids and one on the way. He reminded me of home and my family. I could talk to Marco for an unbiased, upfront opinion about everything, and he would smack me in the fucking face with truth when I needed it.

Besides Trevor, he was the only one who knew about my fucking drug habits. He knew how badly I wanted to stop, how many times I had tried and failed, how they had a death grip on me I couldn't seem to escape.

He knew about Analyn and any other one-night stand I had ever had, all the details. Knew about my dad's death, my mom, the money problems that overcame my family, that I was here riding it out as long as I could without returning home. He had a sense of home in a place that had become just as foreign.

"Estoy muy bien. Dormí sobre 8 horas o más anoche, que es raro. ¿Y usted? ¿Cómo está?"
I'm really good. I slept about hours last night, maybe more, which is rare. And you? How are you?

"Estoy bien, más o menos. Preocupado con mis niños y esposa. No te he visto este fin de semana. ¿Dónde estabas?"
I'm good, more or less. Busy with kids and my wife. I haven't seen you this weekend. Where were you?

"Estuve con una chica durante todo el fin de semana. No trabajo ayer o viernes. Solo pasaba tiempo con ella, y mis amigos por un poquito."
I was with a girl all weekend. I didn't work yesterday or Friday. I was only hanging out with her, and my friend, for a little.

He looked at me as he smiled. We continued to talk until my shift officially began and his break ended. He asked me if I was going to fuck her again, and when I told him I hadn't yet, his cocky fucking smile grew even more. He nodded and told me, "Camarón que se duerme se lo lleva la corriente"
The sleeping shrimp is carried by the water current.

The Spanish equivalent somewhat of, "the early bird gets the worm."

Those who acted first got what they wanted, and those who waited, didn't.

I sat quietly and considered what he had said.

184

Was it too soon to move things along with Jordan?

Or was I just afraid of what I would have to overcome to be with her?

Afraid of being sober, having to face the things I was running from, telling her the shitty-ass truth about my life. Afraid of not living up to her expectations, of who she thought I was.

I pulled out my phone and texted Jordan.

Me: I don't think I can wait until Friday to see you again. Do you want to come over for a little tonight?

I waited five minutes before getting a reply.

Jordan: Jake's home and I have homework tonight...

Me: I can handle Jake and you can do homework at my house. Deal?

20 minutes passed this time before another response. My heart sank with every passing minute, doubt and disappointment overtaking me. Finally, my phone vibrated in my front pocket.

Jordan: Deal :)

25. Jordan

I hid in my room all day until Adrian came to pick me up.

I could hear my mom slurring her words while on the phone in her room with one of her friends, or maybe my sister, as I walked out down the stairs and towards the front door.

Jake was asleep on the couch when I passed the living room and left the house silently. I didn't know why I was hiding from him.

He didn't control me, yet I acted as though his opinions of me were holier than hell.

Bitterness formed in my chest, stinging my tongue as I clenched my jaw.

Not at him, but at myself.

For never standing up for myself.

For pleasing everyone around me no matter how miserable I was.

Putting everyone first.

Relying on others to make me happy.

Defining myself by those in my life.

Yet I would still continue to do those things, whether or not I wanted to.

I sat at Adrian's dining room table, flipping through pages of my Spanish book for definitions as I wrote in my notebook. Adrian was in the living room, switching between shows and trying to convince me to sit with him every few minutes.

"You could do your homework over here. I won't bother you."

I smiled and continued writing. "I could, but then I wouldn't focus."

He walked towards me and leaned into his palm on the tabletop, the other hand grabbing my shoulder as he read what I was working on.

"Look at you, my bilingual mija, why didn't you tell me you were working on Spanish?" He smiled at me and lightly shook my shoulder back and forth. Hearing him refer to me as his sent a flush into my cheeks, with stupid reason. My face turned away so he couldn't see my overly excited facial expression and redness as I bit my bottom lip. It was reassuring to feel wanted.

Maybe I was worth it to work for.

Sike.

"I didn't think it mattered. It's my homework, not yours."

"But I could still help you. Seems like you're doing fine without me, though." He walked away from me and into the kitchen. With all my strength, I tried not to stare at him.

"Did you learn all that from school? Pretty impressive."

"Kinda, Camilla's from Mexico and half of her giant family doesn't speak English, so that helped me learn."

"Good to know that you can understand me when I speak. Necesito recordar que no puedo hablar sobre ti cuando estamos con mi madre."

I need to remember that I can't talk about you when we're with my mom.

He faced the cabinet as he finished speaking.

I paused. "What?"

What did he mean when we were with his mom?

Thinking about being with him, actually *with* him as more than just a hookup or fling, like a meet the family type of with him, brought on a whole new type of feeling.

Falling for him had already been out of the question, but before, I had planned on just keeping that to myself and mourning in silence when he broke my fucking heart.

"I'm sorry. I guess I overestimated your level of Español." His words snapped me out of my thought tornado.

"I understood what you said, just not what you meant."

"What about it?" He leaned his back against the counter, facing me with a sideways smile and empty glass in hand.

"Never mind." I looked down at my book.

"You said it, now I have to give you clarification. What do you not understand?"

"Um, nothing like I said… it's nothing. I'm just being presumptuous."

"You didn't answer my question, Jordan." My name rolled off of his tongue, his accent decorating each syllable, which made it sound sweeter than it ever had before.

"Just about when we're with your mom, but I'm sure I misheard you…"

"You didn't."

"Oh."

He walked back over to my side and rested against the dining room table beside my open textbook.

"What's wrong?" Adrian looked puzzled, though far from worried.

"Nothing, just me looking too deep into things."

He pushed a strand of hair behind my ears and kissed the top of my head.

"I wanted to get to know you better, and that hasn't changed. I also think I've gotten to know you pretty well this weekend and I don't want to stop, so unless you don't want the same, then just let me know and I'll back off," he replied casually and finished his glass of water.

"I didn't say I didn't want that, but your mom doesn't live here. Just took me off guard, looking that far into the future."

He chuckled at me while I sat confused, secretly giddy at the thought of having him in my life for more than a weekend.

Stupid.

I scolded myself for allowing any excitement to run through my veins. Why would I have set myself up for failure like that?

"She doesn't, but she'll come to visit, and if I'm dating someone, she'll expect to meet them the next time she's here, at the very minimum."

Butterflies flew from my stomach to my throat.

"Entiendo."

I understand.

26. Jordan

The hot September days were officially in full swing, and the month was close to being over.

My days working at the yacht club felt longer than usual. If it weren't for the ocean breeze, the job would be nearly unbearable in the heat.

Since my mom's house didn't have an air conditioner, as most coastal houses in California didn't, hiding in the walk-in freezer during slow times was my best bet at getting some much-needed relief from the heat.

California natives weren't built for anything besides mild temperatures. Anything above 85 degrees was miserably hot, and anything below 65 meant layering up in sweaters before going to the grocery store.

Resilience wasn't exactly our specialty.

Dropping onto my couch after working the morning shift, I let my body sink into the cushions. I had pulled my hair into a high bun on the drive home, loose strands sticking to my sweat-ridden forehead.

I pulled my phone from the back pocket of my jean shorts and my thumb slid across the screen, scrolling through my Instagram feed.

Adrian's latest post popped up, a photo of Trevor and Ryan lounging in hammocks that were tied to palm trees along the boardwalk. Trevor held a joint to his lips, and both of them were looking out into the yellow and orange sky as the sun set.

Analyn had left the first comment: "Such a sick day."

My stomach knotted at the sight of her name.

Something was off about her and I. I didn't know what it was, but she made me feel uneasy.

When the front door slammed shut, I kept scrolling to Jake's new post. A photo of his surfboard by the beach, with muted colors and no caption.

"Hi, baby."

"Hey, mom."

She sunk into the cushion next to me, pulling her dirty blonde hair over her shoulder and twisting it around her finger.

My mom was where I had gotten my small figure, my blue eyes, and my dimples. Her humor and care for others had also been passed down to me – though so did her short temper. We liked to bottle things up and then explode all at once, when we couldn't take it anymore.

"I missed you. How was work?"

I locked my phone and dropped it on my chest. "It was fine, just hot. Where did you go?"

"Oh, I just had to run some errands." She exhaled. "I got this *really* good cheese from Trader Joe's, if you want some."

"Sure."

She pulled herself from the couch and I did the same, following her to the kitchen, where she pulled a purple log-shaped cheese from the refrigerator.

Did I mention our house was hot? Because wow, it was suffocating, even with the ocean breeze entering through the windows.

"Goat cheese with blueberries," she enunciated. "I think I like this stuff even better than brie."

"I didn't think you would ever like a cheese better than brie." I laughed, taking the cheese covered cracker she offered to me. With one crunch, sweet berries and soft cheese tangled on my tongue, a slight saltiness from the cracker following.

"Wow, this is good," I breathed, inhaling another bite.

"Right! Where's Jake? He's going to *love* this stuff."

"I don't think he's home." My thumb slid along the corner of my mouth, picking up excess cheese along the way.

"Where is he?"

"Nooo idea."

"Well, he's missing out. Where have you been all freaking month? I feel like an empty nester, and I'm not ready for that." She laughed, turning to the refrigerator.

I breathed a sigh of relief when her hand reached past the beer and towards a can of sparkling water.

"I, uh, went out with Jake and everyone over the weekend and got caught up with them. You know how that goes."

She shot me a suggestive smirk. "You did not go out with Jake every night for the last *two weeks*, given he was home half of that time."

A smile crept across my lips as I focused on cutting another slice of the giant cheese log. "No, not every night. You caught me there."

"Who is it?"

"Who's who?"

"Oh, shut up. I can read you like a book. You don't have to tell me if you don't want to, but I am still going to be nosey like you would expect me to be. That's my job." She tapped my hand, leaning her hip against the counter.

"One of Jake's friends."

"Oooof." She sighed, crossing her arms. "I bet Jake loves that."

"*Totally* loves it." I laughed, mimicking her posture.

"Well, if he hasn't killed you over it yet, I guess that's a good sign. I don't know when he got so goddamn cynical."

"Don't make me telling you nip me in the bud." I pointed my finger at her, a smile growing across my lips. "I know how you can get."

"What's that supposed to mean?" She laughed, brushing a loose strand of hair behind her ear. "Jake is the one that you need to worry about, not me."

Not you when you're sober, I thought to myself, before biting my tongue.

This was the mom that I loved with my whole heart. The one who I could tell anything to, who was like a best friend to me.

Can family members be your soulmates?

If they could, then this version of my mom was definitely mine.

Mourning someone who is still alive is so contradictory.

You mourn the version of them you love when the other side of them shows face.

But when the good side is around, you learn to enjoy it. To try not to think about how long it will last before they flip on you once again.

"Anyway, I'll be gone this week. Your aunt just got surgery and I have to go take care of her."

I took a deep breath.

Here comes a week of them arguing and my aunt getting upset because all she did was drink the entire time she was there.

"You be good." She began walking away from me and towards the stairs.

"*You* be good." I chuckled, a sense of seriousness clipping my tone. She shot me a pointed look over her shoulder, guilt coating her small smile. Like a kid who had gotten caught eating cake before they were supposed to.

I stayed in the kitchen, wrapping up the cheese and refilling my water bottle. My mom had impeccable taste, she was quite the foody. That love for the simple finer things, such as fancy cheese and craft soda, hadn't missed Jake or me.

My phone began buzzing on the couch as I walked over, plopping down on the cushions. Adrian's name lit up the screen, and I held it to my ear with a smile.

"Get dressed mija, I'm picking you up in ten minutes."

"What do you mean? I just got home from work, and I look like hell." I chuckled, switching the phone on speaker phone.

"It is impossible for you to look like hell. Believe me, I've seen you in the mornings with a hangover, and it's still a sight that I would fight to see."

"Lying to me won't get me to agree to you picking me up."

His laugh floated through the speaker.. "I'm not lying, and I'm picking you up whether you like it or not. We're going to dinner, so I hope that you're hungry after working all day."

"Dinner! Adrian, I need to shower and change. Ten minutes isn't enough."

"Then I'll come in and wait. I'm already on my way."

I paused, my eyes tracing the room. The large TV was mounted above our fireplace, silently playing reruns of Modern Family. "Just wait in your car. I'll be quick. See you in a few."

I ended the call before he could protest. My mom may have been sober momentarily, but that didn't mean it would last more than a half an hour. I was lucky to have her sober past noon, and I wasn't about to push that luck.

After a quick shower and slipping on a lace sundress, I put on minimal makeup and blow dried my hair as quickly as possible. By the time I stepped out the front door, Adrian's car was waiting right in front of my house. He hopped out of the sleek black SUV and came around to the passenger side to open my door, my eyes trailing down his body. He had on loose black jeans with a black button-up shirt, his Mayan tribal tattoos peeking out from below the sleeves. A gold watch glistened in the sun, black Ray-Bans hiding his eyes.

"You sure clean up nice." I smiled, sliding into the seat.

"You look beautiful, baby."

"Thank you."

He lifted his sunglasses onto his head, leaning against the door as he stared at me for a moment with the corner of his mouth lifted. "You ready?"

"Yeah, I'm starving. Where are we going?"

"Javier's."

He shut the door, walking around the front of the car before sliding into the driver's seat.

"What do you mean Javier's? That place is so expensive."

My family had money, and we never even went to Javier's. My mom's family was old money, my dad new money. She loved to splurge, but my dad had always been strict on saving for a rainy day. Which meant we *never* went to pricey restaurants unless we were with my mom's family. That was more their taste.

"I don't care how much it costs. I want to take you somewhere nice, so that's where we're going."

His hand found my leg, bringing a sense of comfort over me. A sense of comfort that I was getting used to far too quickly.

Eating somewhere so expensive made me feel guilty. He had no family to fall back on financially, and I knew that working at the bar didn't come with a luxurious salary. Ryan had always complained about how little they paid.

Not that he, of all people, needed the money. I think he just worked there because he was bored, being by himself at his house all the time.

Since I had met Adrian, he was never unwilling to splurge. He bought me large spreads of food daily, filled my car with gas, bought me a new wetsuit, and spent ungodly amounts on bar tabs when we went out. He had a brand-new car and an apartment that was steps from the beach. All of that, his bouncer pay couldn't cover on its own.

He had to have another source of income that I didn't know about. But it was too soon, and too psycho, to be questioning his personal finances, when all he wanted to do was take me to a nice dinner.

"How was work today? Busy?"

"Yes and no, it was just so hot I couldn't think straight."

He chuckled, his eyes staying on the road in front of him as we drove down PCH. "I'm sure you were happy to get off then and hang out inside of the AC."

"Oh no, we don't have AC. Just a few old box fans to make it work."

"You're telling me you don't have AC in that nice of a house?"

"Yeah, it's an old house. Didn't come with one. My dad didn't want to spend the money to install one, and my mom hasn't bothered to look into it since he moved out."

"Babe, you're probably burning alive in there."

I shrugged, twisting my ring on my finger. "I'm used to it, I guess. It's not a big deal."

"It's a good thing I was going to ask you to spend the night. You can cool off at my place."

My eyes landed on him, studying the way his tattooed hands gripped the steering wheel. The way his strong jaw shaped his face, how his hair transitioned from buzzed to curls on top of his head.

Whoever created Adrian was sure to give him an extra dose of beauty – both inside and out.

Good genes.

"Are you sure? I've been there a lot, and I feel like Trevor is probably tired of it."

"Trevor doesn't care. Macy practically lived with us for like a year. After dealing with her for so long, he has no room to complain about the only girl I've ever had around there."

"Who's Macy?"

"His girlfriend."

"I didn't even know he had a girlfriend."

"You're lucky. She's a fucking bitch. I doubt they'll be together much longer."

"I just feel bad stepping on his toes."

He chuckled, shaking his head with a smile. "You're not stepping on anyone's toes, baby. Would you rather stay at your house then? I don't care where we sleep, mija, it could be under a goddamn bridge, as long as I get to be with you."

I bit my bottom lip, trying to suppress my smile. How did his stupid words get this reaction out of me so easily?

I shook my head slowly, watching the ocean slowly shift as we drove down PCH. My mom hadn't clarified when she would have been leaving, so my house wasn't an option.

Not that she would have cared if I had a guy spend the night anyway – avoiding Adrian coming over was much more for my sake. The last thing I needed was to run him off with a drunk mom.

"No, we'll stay at your house. I just need to grab some stuff from my house on the way there."

Adrian pulled into the parking lot of Javier's, opening my door for me before escorting me to the entrance. His hand was on the small of my back as we walked to our table, overlooking the ocean and oncoming sunset.

Javier's was stunning – inside and out. Crystal chandeliers hung from the ceiling, with beautiful dark leather booths spread throughout the large room, and brown wood covering the ceiling. White curtains hung against cream walls, sporting beautiful Spanish style arched windows.

"This is amazing," I gasped, sliding into the booth.

"Have you ever been here before?"

"God, no." I shook my head. "My family never went out to eat much."

A young server came to our table, placing menus and waters down. He looked at her with a half smile.

"Can we do two of the house margaritas to start out with?"

I shot Adrian a wide-eyed look, avoiding the server's gaze.

"Sure, anything else to start with?"

"Just chips and salsa, thanks." Adrian sat back in his booth, his charming smile lay comfortably on his face as she retreated from our table. "What was that look?"

"I can't order drinks yet."

"Well then, it's a good thing she didn't ask for I.D." He winked, taking a sip of his water.

"How did you know that?"

"Know what?"

"That she wouldn't ask for I.D."

He shrugged casually, adjusting the watch on his wrist. "Just had a good feeling."

The server returned with our drinks, her eyes fixed on Adrian, as she placed them on the table. His eyes stayed on me. "Thanks, Isabel."

"Are you ready to order?"

"Yeah, let me do the enchiladas de camarones and…" his green gaze fell on me, eyebrows raised, as he looked up from the menu.

"I'll do the same, thanks."

She nodded, taking both of our menus. "Your food will be right up." Slowly she walked away, her long black hair swaying with every step that she took.

"You know her?" I questioned, taking a small sip of my drink. Tequila overtook my tongue. She made this one *strong*.

"Oh, Isabel? Yeah, she's an old family friend."

I nodded silently, dipping a chip into the salsa that she had just brought out.

"So, I was thinking, you should probably start leaving some more clothes at my house so that you don't have to keep running back and forth. I cleaned out a drawer for you, and we can stop by the store to buy extra face wash and whatever else you need."

My breath hitched in my throat as I stared at the table. "Are you sure?"

"Of course I'm sure," he affirmed. "It'll make things easier on both of us, especially when you have work or what not."

"Okay."

Isabel approached with our food, placing the steaming hot plates in front of us. "Let me know if you need anything." She smiled at Adrian, her eyes casting a quick glance in my direction.

Digging into the mouthwatering, and I mean life-changing good food, our dinner passed in a breeze.

We spent two hours laughing and talking, drinking margaritas and enjoying tres leches cake when we finished our meals. By the time we left, my stomach was heavy and full of food, my mind loose from the tequila.

Adrian drove to my house, pulling into the alley and blocking my garage. "Do you want me to come up and help you grab some of your stuff?"

I shook my head, unbuckling my seatbelt. "No, that's okay. I'll be fast."

"Are you sure you don't want to stay here tonight? I feel bad that I've been stealing you so much. I'm sure your mom would like to have you home." Adrian ran his hand along his chin, resting his elbow on the center console.

"I'm sure. She's going out of town this week, anyway. She won't even notice I'm gone." I opened the door before he could protest and follow me in, hopping into the alley and punching in the garage code.

Strolling through the house, I tiptoed up the stairs and stuffed a bunch of clothes into my backpack. Bursting at the seams with bathing suits, shorts, tank tops and underwear, my backpack swung over my shoulders. I probably packed far too much, and I didn't want to look like I was trying to move in, so I took a handful of stuff out of the bag and zipped it back up. I began trudging back down the stairs, my eyes heavy with sleep.

"Where are you going?" My mom slurred, her hands planted on her hips. I let out a deep breath, trying to plan for an easy escape.

This was the last thing that I needed.

"I'm spending the night at Camilla's."

"Well, you need to move your car. I'm trying to leave and it's in the way."

I scoffed, rolling my eyes. "You're not driving like this."

"Like what?" She seethed, her bloodshot eyes narrowing in my direction.

"Drunk. You're going to kill someone, or yourself."

"I'm not fucking drunk, Jordan. I have made it 47 years just fine on my own without your guidance."

I inhaled, smelling the vodka oozing off of her body. "I'm not letting you drive like this."

She shook her head slowly, her arms crossing over her chest. "Wow. The disrespect in this house is unreal. If you think you're just going to fucking walk in here and tell me what to do and put me down after all I do for you, you're sadly mistaken. I'm so fucking sick of this shit."

"I'm not being fucking disrespectful. I'm telling you it's not a good idea to drive for two hours at night when you have been drinking."

"Does it look like I give a fuck what you are telling me?" She boomed, her breathing labored. "You are such an entitled bitch and I'm fucking tired of it. I have had enough! Go off to wherever the fuck you are going and let me be, fucking spoiled brat!"

"I'm telling you that it's not a good idea to drive. Quit this shit."

"I heard what you're telling me, Jordan!" Her voice grew louder, surely loud enough for half of the City of Long Beach to hear. "Alright, I got it. You fucking know everything. I got it. Just get the fuck out of here already!"

"Okay," I breathed, making my way towards the garage. Tears gathered in the corners of my eyes as I grabbed her keys off of the hook, stuffing them into my backpack. Reaching under her car, I snatched the hide-a-key that was magnetically stuck to the frame, and put it in my backpack, too.

I jumped into Adrian's car, sniffing as I blinked the tears away.

"Everything okay?"

"Yeah, sorry it took so long. I couldn't find the jacket I wanted." My eyes stayed fixed out the window, avoiding his.

"It's fine, baby. I'm not in a rush. I just thought I heard someone yelling. Are you sure you're okay?"

"I'm fine. Must have been the neighbors or something."

27. Adrian

"Do you care if Camilla comes over?"

Jordan's head lay in my lap on the patio couch. I ran my fingers through her hair, tucking a strand behind her ear.

"Of course not, mija."

"Thanks," she breathed, typing on her phone. Trevor sat on the couch across from us, watching a video on his phone. We had plans to get margaritas in a few hours, and were passing time until then.

That's all we did together, really. Pass time.

And it sure as hell was time well spent.

"She'll be here in five minutes," Jordan chirped, sitting up. She made her way to the sliding door, opening it as Trevor's face twisted in something I couldn't read.

"I'm going to the bathroom, and then I'll let her in." Jordan shut the sliding door behind her.

"You good dude?"

Trevor sighed, leaning his elbows on his knees. "Uh, yeah. All good."

"It doesn't bother you too much that Jordan's here a lot, right?"

He scoffed, a smile growing across his face as he shook his head. "No, she's cool, man. It's nice to see you in love for the first time."

I leaned my head against the cushion, running my fingers through my curls. "I'm not in love. She's not even my girlfriend."

"So you're telling me that if someone came up to you at Hansen's and said 'Yo, I'm trynna fuck her, is that your chick?', you would say no?"

My throat tightened as I tugged at strands of hair, pulling at my roots. "Fuck no."

Trevor laughed, interlacing his fingers together. "So you're in love with her. Call her what you want, but I think we can all see it."

"Then what the fuck was that sour face for?"

He shook his head, focusing on the sliding glass door. "Just going through some shit."

"Long time no see!" Camilla squealed, her smile lighting up her face as she walked through the open door. Kaylee trailed behind her, Jordan sneaking past them to sit on my lap. Her plush hips melted into mine as I wrapped my arm around her stomach, pulling her closer to me.

"Sorry, I didn't know Kaylee was with her," she whispered in my ear. Her blue eyes darted around my face as she bit her lip.

"Mija, it's fine. Stop stressing."

"My two lovebirds, what have you guys been up to?" Camilla said in a sing-song voice, flipping her long black hair over her shoulder. Kaylee's bleach blonde hair reflected the afternoon sun as she sat on the end of the couch.

"Cam," Jordan warned, narrowing her eyes in her direction.

"What?" Camilla shrugged. "At least one of us is getting some action."

I watched behind her as Trevor's eyes trailed up Camilla's body, taking his bottom lip between his teeth.

When she turned to face him, he quickly glanced away, not making eye contact with her as she spoke. I held back a smile, watching the two of them interact.

Fucking liar.

28. Jordan

Adrian and I lay on his couch, watching old horror movies for hours after spending the day surfing. Our skin was still covered in salt water, kissed a few shades darker by hours in the sun.

"Where's Trevor?"

"Visiting Macy's family, I think." Adrian held his lips to my hair, pulling my shoulders into his chest. "We got the place to ourselves tonight."

"Why doesn't he ever bring her around here?"

"Their relationship is fucked up, and he knows I can't stand her after the shit she's done to him. Easier to just keep her separate from everyone."

I nodded, my eyes trained on the flat screen across the room.

"Come on," he commanded, sitting up and leading me off the couch, a beer in his free hand.

"I thought we were going to finish the movie before bed," I groaned as he dragged me down the hall.

"The movie can wait, but a shower cannot. We both smell like ocean and sweat, though that is a sexy scent on you."

I giggled, resisting his pull, only for his fingers to grasp me tighter. "Well, you can shower first then, and I'll finish the movie."

"*We* are taking a shower, babe."

My eyebrows scrunched together as I watched him. "Like together?"

"Yes, like together, why is that such a big deal?" He spun around to face me, lifting me by the back of my thighs. I wrapped my legs around his sturdy frame, my hands finding his shoulders, as my legs clung to him.

"I've never, um, done that before."

"Done what? Showered?" He flashed a cocky smile, low eyes trained on me.

"Um, with a guy, no. I haven't."

A sexy half smile grew across his face, the corner of his bottom lip between his teeth. "Well, that makes this way more fun." Adrian flicked the light on and sat me on the bathroom counter, his hands running up and down my bare thighs.

"And if I'm being honest, if you had said you had showered with anyone before me, I would have had to hunt them down and kill them. This is *my* first to give you, and I'm going to savor every bit of it."

He pressed a kiss to the tip of my nose, resting his hands on my thighs. Heat rose across my cheeks as I studied him. His glassy green eyes, and mop of brown curls on top of his head. Carved to a perfection that I was lucky enough to ever put my fingers on, to trace the ink that covered his flesh as his presence engulfed me.

"Okay," I whispered, my eyes locked onto his.

"Okay." He chuckled, pulling my shirt over my head. Adrian spun around and flicked the shower nozzle on, leaving the door open as he turned to face me. "Relax, amorcita, it's not that big of a deal. I've already seen you as naked as a newborn baby, anyway." He winked, and I whacked him lightly on his shoulder. Unclipping my bra, I let it fall to the floor and slipped from the counter. I walked over to the shower, dropping my sweats and underwear softly onto the ground in front of me.

"God, you're fucking perfect," Adrian breathed, his green eyes trailing every inch of my bare skin. He pulled me into his chest, grabbing my hair softly and planting a tender kiss on my lips. I hooked my arms under his, holding onto his muscular shoulders as he kissed my head.

Could you find a feeling of home in a person? *One that had been ripped away so long ago.*

Feelings of your favorite breakfast, and birthday presents, and a glass of chocolate milk after you had been crying, eyes heavy with tears.

Could those things take a human form, to find you in any way that they could?

Because if so, Adrian was every drive to school, and congratulations on a good grade, and day at the park, wrapped into one.

I backed away from him, pulling my hair over my shoulders. It fell on my upper back, stiff with salt water and sand that needed to be washed out.

"My hair is disgusting." I laughed, stepping into the shower. Dipping my head under the hot water, I closed my eyes and let it run through the strands that had been stuck together, blanketing my body.

When I opened them, Adrian was standing right outside of the open shower door, beer bottle in hand. He leaned casually against the wall, his eyes unapologetically trailing over my flesh and face. I crossed my arms over my chest, turning away from him.

"What was that about?" He laughed.

"You're making me feel too exposed."

"I'm not trying to make you feel like anything. That's just you letting yourself feel exposed. You're too used to being closed off, and this is what happens."

I narrowed my eyes at him over my shoulder, hot water trickling down my chest as I held the shower head close to my body. "Still."

"Come here." He motioned to the ground with his beer, before taking a long drawl, green eyes pinned to mine.

"What do you mean come here? I'm not getting out yet. I haven't washed my hair."

"Exactly my point. Come sit."

"I told you I need to wash my hair."

"Would you stop being so goddamn stubborn?" He laughed, leaning into the shower and taking the nozzle from my hands. "*Siéntate.*"

With a sigh, I planted my butt on the hard bathtub floor, Adrian sitting on the edge behind me. He lifted the shower head above me, rinsing my hair carefully. Warm water blanketed my back as I tilted my head up, letting my eyes slide shut.

"See, now was that so hard?"

"Shut up." I laughed, watching the ceiling above me. Adrian flicked open a bottle, and I turned to see the same shampoo that I use at home. "Where did you get that?"

"The girl that I had over last night."

I nodded slowly, pressure forming on my chest.

Stupid fucking question.

Stupid, stupid fucking me.

Adrian chuckled, massaging my scalp with shampoo. "Wow, not even a reaction. I thought I would at least get something out of you."

"What do you mean?" I questioned, trying to keep my tone even.

"If you had told me some other guy left shit at your house, I would have lost my fucking mind, but you didn't even flinch."

"It's none of my business."

"I'm kidding, Jordan. I texted Jake and asked what type of shampoo you used when I went to the store, since we forgot to get it last time."

I let out a sigh of relief, keeping my eyes on the white tile in front of me. "Thank you."

"You got jealous." He laughed, rinsing my hair of the purple suds. "You can try to hide it all you want, but I'm getting good at this."

A smile crept across my face as I looked at him above me, taking another drink of his beer. "I was not."

"Okay." He shrugged, "Whatever you say. You can have this one, if it makes you happy."

I rolled my eyes, turning my head back around as he ran conditioner through my ends. I let myself relax into his touch before he rinsed my hair once again.

"Hold this."

He placed the shower head into my hands, and I stood up and put it back into its place on the wall. After pulling his sweatpants off, Adrian stepped into the shower, closing the glass door behind him. He leaned under the flow of water, running his hands through his hair, his muscular frame stretching with each movement. Water trickled over his skin and the ink that was intertwined with it, dampening his dark lashes.

"See, this isn't so horrible, is it?" He smirked at me, green eyes heavy.

"I guess not," I mumbled, watching as droplets slid down his body. Wrapping his arms around me, Adrian pulled me into him, letting me melt into his skin. We stood like that for a few minutes, or an hour, or a lifetime, before his phone rang.

"Fuck," he grunted, stepping outside of the shower. I turned the water off, reaching for the towel that hung on the rack.

Once I grabbed it, my feet stepped onto the plush bathroom rug and I toweled off, wringing my hair out over the tub. Adrian stood scrolling through his phone, a towel wrapped around his waist as he typed quickly. "Sorry. Just a bunch of bullshit."

"It's okay," I replied quietly. Realizing that I had forgotten my fresh clothes in his room, I made my way past him and out of the bathroom. I dug through the dresser drawer that housed my items, looking for something comfortable to wear to bed.

It wasn't a big deal.

Anyone could have been calling him.

But his phone was *always* ringing. At odd hours of the night, when we went on dates, always. And he never answered it in front of me.

But it could have been his mom, or his brother, or someone that he didn't want to talk to in front of me – in a harmless way. I was just letting my doubts get the best of me.

I mean, he did just buy me shampoo and conditioner to keep at his house without me even asking. I had to give him some credit where credit was due.

I let out a deep breath, digging deeper into the drawer as Adrian walked in. His arms wrapped around my waist from behind, hiking my towel up slowly as his hand traced up my thighs. My core clenched together, sensitive to his touch, as he placed kisses down my neck. His sturdy frame pressed against mine, and I relaxed back into him, letting myself enjoy the feeling of his skin against mine.

"I can't find my sweats," I whispered breathlessly, his fingers continuing to tease my skin. Sucking lightly on my neck, his hand got a firm grip on my ass, digging his fingers into my flesh.

"Good, then we'll sleep naked." Adrian pulled my arm that was holding my towel, letting it pool by my feet. Turning me around, his lips crashed into mine, hands caressing my back softly. Oxygen dissipated from my lungs as I melted into his touch, letting him own every part of me without needing to say it.

He fucking knew.

He had known that he owned me since the day he brought me home with him.

His hands slipped underneath my ass, gripping my thighs and lifting them to wrap around him. Making his way to the bed, Adrian lowered me to my back, resting his body between my open legs. His tongue licked my bottom lip, causing them to part as he slipped inside. Moving carefully, he explored the inside of my mouth, jaw working mine, getting to know me from the inside out, whether I liked it or not.

My hands found the back of his head, making their way from the fuzzy, short hair to the curls that sat nestled on top. My fingers ran through his caramel brown locks, grabbing at them as he took my bottom lip between his teeth, sinking into it. I yelped at the pain, a dirty form of pleasure pulsing thickly through my veins. He pulled my lip farther towards him with his teeth, sucking on it and biting it as I tried to catch my fucking breath, a hopeless victim to the power he had over me.

Adrian groaned into my mouth, his tongue gently caressing mine as his hands gripped the inside of my thigh. We went from slow and careful to needy and powerless and back again at a moment's notice, going full circle time and time again, as I ran my fingers lightly down his back.

His mouth moved from my lips to my collarbone, sucking at my skin and lighting a fire inside of me.

How could I become a victim to his flames so quickly?

My brain became fuzzy as his tongue traced my skin, leading down to take my nipple into his mouth. I clenched my thighs around his waist, lost in the way his tongue moved along my nipple, sucking and nibbling at it. My eyes rolled to the back of my head, biting on the knuckles of my fist, as I let the sensation of his mouth take over. His hand squeezed my breast, his mouth awakening every fiber of my being as he worked me carefully, skillfully, like he had been studying how to build me up and make me come undone for his entire life.

"Adrian," I breathed, my eyes still lightly shut as my brain only focused on everywhere that his skin met mine. His warm mouth released my nipple, tight and hard from the bare emptiness it now felt. His lips continued to kiss down my torso, on my hipbone, and across my pelvis.

"What, baby?"

"You know what," I panted, curling my toes against his sheets.

"Enlighten me," he taunted, his warm breath dancing across my clit. I waited for his mouth to meet my flesh, for his tongue to send sparks up my spine and stars inside of my eyelids. When that didn't happen, I let out a needy groan, letting my shoulders go limp in defeat.

"Good girl. Just relax and let me do my job."

His tongue licked the inside of my thighs, teasing me with only inches between him and my clit, tracing from my mid-thigh all the way to my waist. While sucking my upper thigh, his thumb slowly circled my clit, massaging it in the most heart-stopping, breath-stealing, fucked up way possible.

Arching my back, my hand dove into his hair, desperate for a grip on reality. For some form of control.

He released my thigh from the grasp of his mouth, where a purple mark now surely laid, but I didn't care. When his tongue replaced his thumb on my clit, sucking lightly, sensations rushing through my entire body, an audible gasp left my lips, my fingers tightening around his hair.

All that my reaction did was motivate him, and his tongue slid slowly down to my entrance, diving inside and out through my folds. My core tingled, tightened, responded in every way possible to his careful touch, methodical with every move. When his warm mouth wrapped around my clit, diving two fingers inside of me, I swore my heart stopped, unable to take the euphoria that he was putting me through.

Working me, his hands gripped my thighs roughly, forcing them apart to make more room for his face between my legs. Fireworks lit off inside of me as I found my release, letting him guide me all the way through it.

After all, he was apparently the one who knew me best.

Knew what I wanted, what I so desperately needed.

Adrian slowly climbed over me, achievement shining in his hooded green eyes, as my chest rose and fell violently with pants. Reaching over me, his hand dug into his nightstand drawer, fishing out the foil wrapper that housed a condom.

Upright on his knees, between my spread legs, he ripped the condom wrapper with his teeth, stroking his length as his eyes locked on mine.

"Are you sure you want to do this?" Adrian asked, his robust physique placed perfectly between my legs.

"Are you sure *you* want to do this?" I breathed, watching as his hand worked himself slowly, twisting slightly when he reached the tip of his cock. "You're the one that's rejected me before. A lot."

A cocky smile grew across his face as he rolled the condom on. "That one stung, didn't it?"

"Yes," I gulped, trying to control my heart before it beat out of my chest.

"That'll only make this time that much sweeter."

His cock slowly sunk into my entrance, slipping in and out of me carefully, more length making its way each time he entered. His eyes squeezed shut with a deep breath, gripping my thighs strongly, his thumbs sure to leave bruises on the inside of my legs.

He worked deeper into me, his length filling me completely, as I arched my back at the invasion, fisting his sheets. Slowly, my muscles relaxed for him, melting around his cock. He thrusted in and out of me carefully, holding back the feverish desire that glistened in his green eyes.

"Fuck me," I begged, arching my back, pressing my hips into him.

"I could watch you take my cock all day."

He began plunging into me, going to the deepest parts of my core, as his thumb dipped inside of his mouth before he brought it to my clit. Circling it tenderly, he lit me on fire, from where his thumb met my skin, to where his cock dove inside of me, to the inside of my thighs, begging for more, like I had been starved of water my entire life.

"You were fucking made for me," he panted, continuing his assault, our bodies slapping together as he pushed me closer to the edge of ecstasy. He knew how to get me going, how to make me come repeatedly, and he would do so until I couldn't take it, and then maybe once more. My boobs bounced as he dove in and out, digging my fingernails into his forearm, leaving half-moons indented in his skin.

When my core pulsed around him, I let paradise run through my veins, growing with each advance he took inside of me. My moans caused my throat to become dry, out of control and unsure if I could handle the electric bliss he was making me feel. Unwilling to let me off easy, he continued at a steady pace until I clenched for one last time, stars dancing inside of my eyelids, the room spinning around me like I was on the fucking teacups at Disneyland.

"Fuck, Jordan," he groaned. With one final bury inside of me, he exploded into the condom. His grip on my thighs pressing so hard I swear he could feel my femur. Sweat rolled down his chest, over the black lines of the tattoo that decorated the left half of it, as he pulled the corner of his bottom lip between his teeth with a smile.

I pressed the back of my head into the mattress, running my hand down my face. "I'm seeing fucking stars." He dragged his cock out of me, leaving me empty and dripping onto the sheet below me. Pulling my knees together, I kept my eyes shut, somewhere between breathing and dying, as I prayed for my heart to slow down.

Adrian ran a towel between my legs as I pulled the pillow that our sex had pushed against the headboard beneath my skull, sinking into the cloud that it offered my heavy mind. Once he cleaned me off, Adrian flicked the lights off and sunk into the mattress next to me, pressing a kiss to my temple.

"I'm going to have bruises," I mumbled, fighting against the sleep that he had forced over me like a fucking spell.

"Good." Another temple kiss. "That's the goal, baby."

29. Adrian

"I'll be there in ten," I told Jake over the phone, driving towards his house. Dragging him to the yacht club while Jordan worked probably wasn't my best idea, but it was all I had.

If I didn't want him to fucking hate me, I had to be the one to call a truce. Jordan and I were in a gray area, we both knew that. But that didn't mean that I hadn't fucking rubbed Jake the wrong way in the past few months – a lot.

I knew he had a pass to the yacht club, since Jordan had mentioned their dad was a member. Reluctantly Jake agreed, and shortly after, we sat with Trevor, Anthony, Ryan, and a small crowd of others I was sure I had never met before, overlooking the harbor.

Jake drank Hennessy and sprite disguised in a Hydro Flask as we watched the tide. I could feel the tension between us, but tried to act like nothing had ever happened. I already had told him my intentions with Jordan and that they were pure. Now all I could do was show him – and show myself.

The entire night, my eyes were pinned on Jordan as she moved through the crowd. Her eyes were unfocused as she blankly scanned the yacht club, looking for the next polo-wearing asshole to serve.

"Are you just watching Jordan?" Trevor grinned at me tauntingly and took a swig of Jake's drink.

I snapped out of my trance.

"I'm trying not to fall asleep."

"That's the most bullshit lie I've ever heard. Unless you had one too many zannies before you left the house." Ryan taunted, chewing on a toothpick.

I shot Ryan an irritated look after his stupid-ass remark, hoping that Jake hadn't caught onto what he was saying.

"As long as you're keeping your fucking eyes off of her, I don't give a shit what you have to say about me." I grumbled.

That was the last thing anyone needed, to blow this out of the water and fulfill Jake's low-life expectation of me fucking over his sister.

I leaned back and grabbed the Hydro Flask for myself, gulping down some much-needed alcoholic relief from the bomb Ryan had just dropped.

"Does Jordan know?" Jake broke the silence as he asked sternly, staring forward at the dark harbor.

"Know what?"

"About the drugs. Does she know?"

"I don't know what you mean."

"I do. And I know you do. Are you still using them and if you are, does she know?"

"Uh, no, she doesn't know," I replied quietly as I ran my fingers through my hair.

"Then you need to tell her, or I'm going to. She won't get hurt like that, dude. I told you that already, and I will take matters into my own fucking hands if I need to."

"How did you even know?"

Jake scoffed, shaking his head. "How did I even know? I've known you for years. Why do you think I've never brought her over before?" He took a deep breath, drawing a long drink from his Hydro Flask. "I'm not stupid. We all know when you're sober and when you're not. I wouldn't be surprised if she has caught on by now, too."

A wave of shame rode over me. I knew my memory was faulty, especially the more I took, but I hadn't realized it was to where I had forgotten so many major things in my life, even conversations that completely slipped from memory. I felt like an idiot for thinking Jake, or anyone, was clueless about my habits.

"Are you going to quit?" He looked over at me with stern blue eyes, staring through me.

I let out a deep breath. "I'm fucking trying. Trust me, bro."

"Then tell her that. But if you aren't honest and she finds out, you'll see a different fucking side of her, I guarantee it."

The words lingered in my ears. I didn't want to tell her and see the disappointment spread across her face. I wanted to quit before it ever got to that point.

As I sat with my thoughts, conversations ringing out around me, I saw Jordan look up at me from a table she was serving. She hadn't made eye contact with me the entire night, and I could tell by the look on her face she was just now realizing any of us were even here as her eyes lit up, her heart-melting smile flashing in my direction.

I smiled back, trying to hide the look of guilt and shame that was spreading across my face.

30. Jordan

"I think Brian's sister is going to come to Mexico," Jamie said, the sound of her chewing a sandwich going through the speakers of my phone. She always held the phone ridiculously close to her face when we talked.

"Oh, lovely," I grumbled, squinting my eyes in the sun as I laid on the beach. "That'll go well."

"I know. I tried to talk him out of inviting her, but he's so clueless sometimes, he doesn't get it."

"Well, I know who I will be staying away from." I grabbed a carrot from my tupperware, breaking off a piece with a crunch into my mouth.

"Your hat is cute. I didn't know you were a bucket hat girl now. So trendy."

"Thanks. Hand me down from Cam."

"I always have the cutest shit, huh Jamie?" Camilla yelled from her towel, not bothering to open her eyes as she laid on her back, sun rays soaking into her brown skin.

"Yes you do, babe." My sister laughed, shifting positions on the couch. For only being half siblings, we looked a lot alike. Even with our ten-year age difference.

"God, I wish it was warm here. You're making me jealous."

"Shouldn't have moved to butt-fuck Michigan then, loser. You sure don't get any October heat waves there, do you?"

"I know," she groaned, rolling her blue eyes. "We'll be back, eventually."

"Before you make me an aunt, I hope."

"Before I make you an aunt," she confirmed. "I'm gonna call Brian and get him to bring me some dinner. I love you," Jamie dragged the last word out.

"I love you too. Call you later."

My phone dinged as her face was swooped into a black screen, ending my call.

Stupid Jamie.

Moving across the goddamn country before I had even gotten out of high school.

"When is she coming to visit?" Kaylee called out, her sunglasses covering her face as she laid on her stomach next to me.

"I don't know. Besides Mexico for Thanksgiving, we probably won't see her until Christmas."

"Brian sure has her on a tight leash."

"Or she has him on one." Camilla laughed.

"Yeah, I think he's the one on the tight leash." I moved my elbows from my towel, letting my head lay flat. "I should have brought my board."

"It's only like two-foot waves today. Not worth getting in a wetsuit for that."

"I know." I sighed, resting my body on the sand. "Just haven't been out in a while."

"Because you've been too busy riding Adrian's dick," Kaylee laughed.

"Shut up."

"What are you guys doing tonight?"

"I don't know. I haven't heard from him."

"Why don't you text him and ask? I think margaritas are calling our name." Kaylee announced.

I was the youngest out of our group, so with Kaylee and Camilla's new ability to buy drinks when we went out to eat, we were spending a *lot* of time and money on overpriced alcohol.

"Let's just walk over to LB Cantina after this and grab some drinks."

"Are you going to invite him? Or is this a girl's night?"

I paused, chewing on my cheek. "I haven't heard from him in a while."

"How long is a while?"

"Like a week."

"A *week?*" Kaylee exclaimed, sitting up and sliding her sunglasses down her nose. Her brown eyes looked at me in shock. "What the hell do you mean you haven't heard from him in a week?"

I shrugged, trying to minimize the situation. I hadn't heard from him since last week, which was odd for us. Some nights I wouldn't spend the night when he got off late, but we never went more than two nights without sleeping together – let alone hearing from one another at all.

The last time I had heard from him was when he got off of work last Wednesday. When I texted him early the next morning, I got no reply. By the time Tuesday had come around, my messages had gone from blue to green. That was when I stopped trying.

If he was going to ghost me, I wouldn't embarrass myself by forcing him to give me an explanation. It stung, *really damn bad*, but I had no control over him and what he wanted – even if I really wished it were me.

"I don't really want to talk about it. It's not that big of a deal."

"Yes, it *is* a big deal, Jo. Why the hell didn't you say anything?" Kaylee asked.

"I don't want to turn it into something that it isn't. If he still wants to talk to me, he will, and if not, he won't. Nothing I can do about it."

"What a dick," she exclaimed, shaking her head. "Well then, fuck LB Cantina. We're going to Hansen's and getting *hammered.*"

"I don't know if that's a good idea."

"Oh trust me, it is. Fuck him. He's not just going to blow you off and never have to see you again."

I sighed, rolling onto my back. Wind picked up lightly around me, bringing goosebumps onto my legs and arms. "I'm freezing. Are you ready to go?"

"Yes," Camilla mumbled, rubbing sleep from eyes as she sat up. "You guys always want to stay here until the sun goes down."

"Not very much for a few months now," I laughed. "Those days are almost over."

We packed up all of our things, driving to my house and rinsing off in the shower. After quickly toweling off, we all sat scattered throughout my room, doing our makeup and hair before heading off to 2nd street. On our way, my phone buzzed with a new message.

Ryan: Heard you're coming to Hansen's tonight.
Me: I guess that's the plan.
Ryan: Text me when you're here, youngin'. I'll meet you at the front door.

Our Uber sat in a line of traffic, slowly inching towards Hansen's, red tail lights in front of us lighting up the inside of the car.

"Fuck it, I'm walking." Camilla opened her door, climbing out of the backseat. I scooted across the bench, placing my feet on the street, and following her.

"Thank you!" Kaylee exclaimed as she shut the car door, all of us shuffling down 2nd street. We squeezed in between people on the crowded sidewalk, running across the streets in between red lights. Heels clicking against the sidewalk, we made our way to Hansen's, a short line already forming at the front door.

"What's up, ladies?" Ryan greeted us from inside, waving us past the bouncer. Wrapping his arms around me, he held me to his chest. "If it isn't my little Jo Jo. I've missed you."

"I missed you too."

Releasing me from his embrace, he looked down at me with furrowed brows. "Where's Dre?"

I shrugged, my eyes tracing the crowded room around us. "I couldn't tell you. Haven't heard from him in a few days."

He nodded slowly, grabbing the back of his neck. "Pulled a disappearing act?"

"I guess. I don't know."

"He does that sometimes." Ryan sighed. "Come on, let's get you a drink."

Waltzing over to the bar, Camilla grabbed my hand as we weaved through the drunk patrons. Ryan slipped behind the wooden counter, grabbing a bottle of Don Julio 1942 and pouring it into four shot glasses.

"Make it five."

I turned around to see Anthony walking towards us, a beaming smile across his face. "You really thought you would get away with drinking some forty-two without me?"

"Anthony!" Camilla said in a sing-song voice, passing him a full shot glass. "Of course we didn't, we were just getting ready for ya." She pulled out her phone, pointing the camera towards our hands as we clinked our glasses together to cheers one another.

Scanning her camera over all of us, Ryan reached over the bar and squeezed my cheeks together, placing a kiss on my temple as Camilla recorded us.

My eyes found Kaylee, who watched the whole thing. Camilla dropped her phone down, typing quickly and tagging all of us in the video.

"I'm sorry. I don't know why he did that."

Kaylee took a sip of her fresh margarita, waving me off. "He wants Adrian to see. It's fine. I couldn't care less."

I tilted my head, pulling her in for a hug. "I don't deserve you."

"Yes, you do," she laughed, squeezing her arms around me. "Now come on, let's give him hell."

Wet sand squished between my toes as we walked down the beach, towards my house, after Hansen's closed. Kaylee had declared that we were all having a sleepover at my house, and we trekked down the peninsula, the moon reflecting off of the still bay next to us.

"Turn around," Ryan called out to us as we walked, snapping a photo of us on the dark beach, heels in hand, eyes heavy with liquor. I hadn't let myself get that drunk, but I was still tipsy enough for there to be tingling in my gut and giggles to leave my lips. For the first time in ten days, I wasn't letting

Adrian's unexplained absence consume every part of me.

My phone buzzed in my pocket, and I opened it to a notification of Ryan tagging me in his story. He had written "my favorite angels" on the photo of us walking, and I tapped repost before tucking my phone back into my jeans.

"Jake is going to kill us," I sang, laughing next to Camilla.

"Oh, fuck him. I'll blast Tupac in his bedroom to piss him off even more."

"We might as well." I giggled, taking a deep breath. We hopped over the seawall and onto the sidewalk, trudging up my front porch steps. Jake sat at the dining room table, eating a bowl of mac n cheese, his eyes burning from the joint he had surely just smoked.

"How did I know?" he grumbled, taking another bite.

"Jakey wakey," Camilla laughed, sitting on Jake's lap and wrapping her arms around his shoulders. "Did you miss us?'

"Not especially."

"What's up, dude?" Ryan slapped Jake on his back and walked to our refrigerator. I took a seat next to him, Kaylee and Anthony across from us.

"You missed one of the hottest chicks that I've ever seen in my life," Anthony hollered, pulling his vape from his pocket and holding it to his lips. "Like, Megan-Fox-type-of-hot."

Jake lifted his eyebrows, focusing on the bite of mac n cheese he slowly moved towards his mouth.

"No way she was that hot."

"Swear," Ryan said over his shoulder. Kaylee's eyes narrowed in his direction.

"I am going to shower," Camilla announced, pulling herself up from Jake's lap. "And then I am going to sleep. Goodnight everyone, see ya in the morning."

"Goodnight," we all called out. It had to be close to three in the morning.

"We should go to Laguna tomorrow, leave early and beat the crowds," Kaylee said, relaxing into her chair.

"I'm game," Jake agreed.

"Same," I muttered, picking at my split ends. "I haven't been to Laguna in a while."

"Or we could go to Trestles," Ryan said with a full mouth, leaning his elbows on the dining room table. "Bring our boards, catch a few waves."

I nodded, focusing on picking the white ends from each strand of hair. "We can take my car. I don't mind driving if you guys want to drink."

"Then it's set. To Trestles we go," Kaylee chimed, stealing Anthony's vape and taking a hit.

My phone began buzzing in my back pocket, Adrian's name flashing across when I held it in my hand. I let out a deep breath, holding it to my ear. "Hello?"

"Come outside."

"Why?"

"Just come outside, Jordan."

I rolled my eyes, lifting myself from my chair. Leave it to Adrian to walk out of my life for ten days and then show up at my house at 3 in the morning.

"Looks like he finally went on Instagram," Ryan said to Kaylee, shooting her a cocky smile. I flipped him off as I made my way to the garage door, shutting it behind me. Adrian's black SUV sat in the alley behind my house and I walked up to the passenger window, the black tint rolling down in front of me.

Adrian sat inside, one hand on the steering wheel, the other resting on his center counsel.

"Hi."

"What the fuck was that?" He sneered, his green eyes burning into me. His eyelids hung low, dark circles on the top of his cheeks. Whatever had been keeping him so busy for the last ten days had also sucked the life out of him.

"What was what?"

He scoffed, nostrils flaring. "What the fuck was all over Instagram, that's what."

"What are you talking about?"

It was a stupid question. I knew what he was talking about. What I didn't know was why he was bothering to ask when he had just disappeared for a week and a half.

"You and Ryan?"

I shook my head, holding my hand to my forehead. "I am so sick of you asking about me and Ryan, especially after you just vanished for a week, and are now showing up at my house in the middle of the night."

His jaw clenched, veins throbbing under the skin on his neck. "I'm coming in."

"No," I snapped. "That's not a good idea."

"Why?"

"It's just not."

Over my dead body was I letting him into the same house as my mom at this hour.

He sighed, pinching the bridge of his nose. "Listen, I'm really sorry for not getting a hold of you. I had some shit going on."

"It's fine. It's none of my business, anyway."

"What do you mean, it's none of your business?"

I shrugged, looking away from him. "It's just not."

"I had some family shit I had to deal with, Jordan. I'm sorry, I really am. Just let me come in."

I yawned, pulling my hair into a bun on top of my head. "It's late. I'm just going to go to bed. Talk to you later."

"Will you at least come to my house?"

"I can't. We're going to Trestles in the morning."

"I'll have you back by then."

I chewed on my cheek, studying the asphalt below my feet.

He sure was nonchalant about this whole disappearing thing.

I was fucking pissed at him. Livid, honestly.

But remember that thing I said about bottling up my emotions until I exploded?

Case in point.

Taking a deep breath, I sorted my thoughts. I wasn't his girlfriend. We were hanging out, hooking up, whatever, but I wasn't his girlfriend. He had no obligation to tell me where he was, or even contact me every day. No matter how frustrating and irritating it was, I had no right to be mad at him.

"Okay," I breathed, swinging the car door open and climbing into the passenger's seat. His hands grabbed my face, crashing his lips into mine. Finding the back of my neck, he pulled me farther into him, tenderly slipping his tongue into my mouth. I stiffened before welcoming him, letting his tongue caress mine, as he melted me beneath his touch.

Ten days without him had been misery, no matter how much I denied it.

Pulling away, he rubbed his knuckle down my cheek, green eyes darting between each of mine. "I'm really sorry, Jordan. I promise that won't ever happen again."

"Okay," I whispered breathlessly, my mind tangled with doubt.

What the hell was going on?

I think I had stopped knowing long ago.

He shifted his car into drive as his hand found my thigh, squeezing it lightly our entire drive to his house.

31. Jordan

The sun beamed down on Adrian and me as we lay on the boat. With October already halfway over, our warm days floating on the ocean were ending soon.

"Throw me a beer!" Jake shouted from the raft that was tied to the stern of the boat, bobbing in the passing waves. Camilla and Anthony lay on either side of him, Kaylee, Ryan, and Trevor resting on a separate raft right next to them.

My eyes stayed shut, covered by my sunglasses. "Come get it, I'm not moving."

Adrian slapped me on the ass, surely leaving red marks spread across my cheek. "I got it, babe."

Bringing my lip between my teeth, I rolled to my back and watched him stroll over to the cooler.

"Anyone else?" He yelled, reaching his hand through the ice and grabbing a beer.

"Yup!" Ryan yelled, not lifting the baseball cap that was covering his face. "Just send out six, make it easy."

Adrian tossed the beer through the air, landing on the raft by Jake's feet. He did the same with five more, his muscles flexing and stretching beneath his skin, tattoos rippling over the tissue that they were hiding.

I squeezed my thighs together, trying to suppress the throbbing I was feeling for him.

I hadn't been a sexual person before I met Adrian.

I had always felt insecure about having sexual desires, never knowing that sex was meant to satisfy me, just as much as it was meant to satisfy the person who I was having it with.

Adrian had taught me how to let someone put me first, to put myself first. And he would never get that sexually timid side back.

Walking over to me, he slipped his sunglasses down his nose, green eyes trailing up my body. His tongue slipped out, wetting his lips, before a sideways smile grew across his face. Slipping his knee between my thighs, he lowered his body over mine, elbows on each side of my head.

Pressing my lips to his, I lost myself in him all over again.

How was my head supposed to handle all the spinning that he caused it?

It couldn't have been healthy, I was sure.

His hands trailed down my side, feeling each inch of bare skin. His fingers dipped beneath the fabric of my bikini, teasing over my clit. Pulling my lips from his, I pushed his sunglasses back up his nose.

"Stop, punk."

"Why?"

I rolled my eyes, despite him not being able to see them behind my sunglasses. "Because our friends are getting a full view of us, including my brother, and I don't want them to see my cooch."

"They can't even see us," he said with a smirk, pressing his thumb to my clit. A deep breath escaped my lips, parted as I watched him. "If you tell me to stop, I will."

He leaned in to kiss me, my mouth opening for him as our tongues danced with one another slowly.

Usually, our kisses were needy, desperate for more.

This time he was smooth, calculated, but demanding nonetheless.

His thick finger slipped into my entrance, and I stifled a moan by biting into his shoulder. Adrian chuckled, massaging his thumb over my clit as his finger slipped in and out of me. His kisses tasted of beer, his tongue careful as it moved around mine.

"Adrian," I groaned through a whisper, clenching around his finger as it teased me slowly.

"What, baby? I thought you were worried they would see us, hmm?" He taunted me, pressing his bare chest against me as he gained speed between my legs. My nipples perked to his touch, my head rolling back as I neared release.

Pleasure rolled over me like a tidal wave, and I gripped his biceps as I tried to control myself. His mouth found my neck, nipping and sucking up it until he found my ear, taking it into his mouth and sinking his teeth in.

"Fuck," I breathed, electricity rolling through me.

"Quit holding back," he whispered into my ear, running his tongue from my collarbone to my jaw bone. "You can let go. I'll make sure that you're not loud enough to hear."

Bringing his thumb to his lips, he snuck it inside of his mouth before his hand slipped back into my bottoms, another finger diving inside of me. Finding all of my sensitive spots with ease, he slowly nudged me towards the edge, fireworks exploding deep inside of my core. I rode the assault all the way through, welcoming the ecstasy that his movements brought on.

"Tell me what I'm going to do," Adrian whispered, his fingers not missing a beat. He was slow and controlled, ensuring that I melted completely in his hands as he watched me squirm.

Fire and ice.

Though this time, I wasn't sure who was which.

"Adrian," I groaned, biting my tongue to keep from moaning.

"Jordan," he drew my name out, slowing his thumb over my clit as his fingers pressed deeper inside of me. "What am I going to do to you?"

"You already know," I whined, biting into the pad of my thumb to grasp some control over myself.

"Say it."

"Adrian…"

"Say it," he demanded, his thumb gliding over the most sensitive area of my clit, his fingers continuing to thrust inside of me.

"You're going to make me come," I breathed, my head tilting back as his mouth continued to assault my neck. He slid his fingers steadily in and out of me, finding the perfect rhythm to push me over the edge. My thighs clenched together as my ears drowned out any noise. Clenching around his fingers, I found my release, letting euphoria contain me from the inside out.

Adrian continued to work me, not letting up until he knew I was finished. My teeth dug into the tattoo on his bicep, fighting off the scream that was building in my chest. Finally, with one last restriction, my head stopped spinning as he slowed his pace, kissing the top of my head.

"And I'm the only one who's going to do that, ever." He placed a kiss on my lips, sucking my bottom lip into his mouth and taking it between his teeth. "Don't you forget it."

His lips pressed against my forehead as he shifted off of me, picking up his beer and taking a long chug. I lay panting, shifting onto my elbows and sitting upright on the cushions. Lifting to my feet, I took a swig of my beer and dropped it into the cupholder, making my way to the edge of the boat.

"What are you doing, mija?" Adrian said with a mischievous smile, taking another drawl of his beer. He shook his wet hair, making the perfect wave on top of his head.

I stepped off of the edge, cold water rushing around me as I submerged beneath the surface of the ocean. Once my downward motion had stopped, I floated in the stillness, letting the water overtake me. The current bobbed me slightly, moving up and down with a passing wave.

I kicked my feet and looked towards the surface, making my way towards the sun. Tilting my head back as I emerged, my hair stuck to my shoulders in a slick carpet. Adrian stood on the edge of the boat, beer in hand, as he looked down at me.

"Rinsing off," I replied, answering his question.

"Ahhh. And what exactly are you rinsing off?"

"Sweat."

"I see." He took a long swig of his beer, tossing the empty can into the hull before jumping into the water. His head slowly rose from the water, his fingers running through his hair and pushing it backwards from his forehead. His arms glided through the water as he made his way towards me, wrapping his hands around my back. I kicked my feet steadily, keeping us at eye level as he studied me.

"What am I going to do with you, amorcita?"

"Hopefully more of what you did to me on the boat," I teased, my hands intertwining behind his neck.

"Definitely more of that." He placed a deep kiss on my lips. "I swore I never would, but you're making me turn soft. I'm not very sure that I like it."

"I hope so."

"Do you?"

"Yes," I mumbled, my lips only inches from his.

"Why is that?"

"I think you could use it."

After another deep kiss, I wiggled from his grip, swimming over to the back of the boat and pulling myself up the ladder. Adrian stopped by the rafts, hitting a joint that Jake, Camilla, and Anthony were sharing.

I dropped onto the cushions, covering my face with a towel as I let the sun dry me.

How quickly things had changed.

I had begun the summer not knowing who Adrian was, and I was ending October by letting him bring me to my knees on the boat.

I had spent almost every day with him, falling asleep in his embrace and waking up to the sun sneaking in his bedroom window. We hadn't talked about the future, or even the present. I wanted to think that when he went out without me, his hands stayed reserved for once we were together again – as mine were with him.

His phone began buzzing against the cushion next to my head, and I ignored it, remaining still under the sun rays that I so desperately needed. It would buzz for a minute, stop, and then begin again. Whoever was calling clearly needed to talk to him – urgently.

I heard him make his way up the ladder; the boat shifting with each step that he took. His hand grabbed my foot, shaking it lightly, as the cushion next to me dipped with his weight. "How you holding up over here?"

"Never been better."

"Your phone is ringing, Jordan."

I rolled onto my stomach, using the bunched-up towel as a pillow. "That's your phone."

"Who is it?"

"I don't know."

"Will you check, please?"

I lifted my head, reaching towards the device. It felt weird, checking his phone – like I was going somewhere that I wasn't supposed to.

I wasn't his girlfriend.

Who knew what was in his phone?

I lifted it, tilting my head forward to let my sunglasses slide down my nose. Squinting, I saw Analyn's name lighting up the dim screen.

"It's Analyn."

He sighed, holding his hand out to me as I placed the phone in his open palm. He pressed his screen, throwing the phone towards our feet and resting his head on his arm.

"Aren't you going to get it?"

"Nope. Probably wants me to go into work, and I'm not doing that."

I nodded silently, looking out into the water.

Something about her had never sat right with me. Whether it was from the thought of her fingers tracing the tattoo on Adrian's forearm at the bonfire, the way she acted towards me when we met, or how cold she was whenever we went to Hansen's, I wasn't sure. Maybe all of it.

"What's wrong?" He asked, lifting his head to look at me.

"Nothing."

"What's going on in that head of yours?"

I let out a deep breath. "I just feel weird about Analyn."

"Why?"

"I can tell that she doesn't like me."

He chuckled, shaking his head lightly. "It's not that she doesn't like you, babe. She just has a… personal vendetta against me, and she's using you as collateral. You don't need to worry about her. She's all bark and no bite. I won't let her get to you."

I twisted my ring on my finger, keeping my eyes focused on the ships out in the distance. "It's not that big of a deal. I'm not your girlfriend, so your relationship with her is honestly none of my business."

"You're not my girlfriend, but there's nothing between me and Analyn, if that's what you're asking." His hand found my ass, squeezing tightly. "And just because you're not my girlfriend doesn't mean I'm willing to share. Ever. So since no one else gets any of me, I expect that no one else gets any of you. And I'm firm on that from here on out." He paused.

"You're the only thing that I do not share."

32. Jordan

Hansen's had become like a second home since I started dating Adrian – besides his house, which I had slowly moved half of my stuff into. He had insisted on me staying with him almost every night, and I wasn't one to turn him down.

We walked through the dim bar, squeezing in between crowds of people standing too close together. Once we arrived at a booth, I slid in before Adrian, who placed his hand on my bare thigh.

Adrian wore a dark blue t-shirt and black jeans, his curls flipping out from under a black beanie. I studied the way his tattoos moved over his skin as he talked, placing his hand on his chin.

I had fallen for him – hard – no matter how hard I had tried to avoid doing so. Despite trying to hide it as much as I could, he knew. We both knew.

What the hell was I going to do now?

Camilla grabbed my hand, pulling me away from the booth. "Let's get a drink!" She shouted over the music, leaning into my ear.

"Okay."

Kaylee followed behind her as we made our way to the bar. Lights flashing in every direction, I leaned my elbows against the wooden counter. Ryan was working tonight, instead of Analyn, and I breathed a sigh of relief. Sometimes I swore she didn't put a drop of alcohol in my drinks when she made them.

"If it isn't my favorite babes." He smiled, leaning against the bar top. Throwing a rag to hang on his shoulder, he shot us a wink. "What can I get you, guys?"

"Three shots of forty-two" Camilla answered without asking for any of our approval.

"It's that kind of night?" Ryan laughed, moving around the bar. "Don't get too wasted before I get off. I want some of that bag, Cam."

"We'll save you some," she taunted, grabbing the lime he placed in front of her.

"Cheers," Camilla said, holding her glass in the air. "To fifteen years of friendship and many more to come."

We clinked our glasses together, simultaneously licking salt off of the rim and throwing the burning tequila down our throat. My teeth dug into the lime, letting the sour juice wash away the fire of the tequila.

I shook my head, squeezing my eyes closed. "That was rough." I laughed, wiping my lips with a napkin from the bar.

"I've got a surprise," Camilla announced, a white smile beaming across her face.

"You're pregnant."

"No, stupid." Camilla swatted Kaylee on her arm. "I just took a shot of tequila. I'm not fucking pregnant. I got some fish scale from Anthony."

"Oh fuck yeah," Kaylee breathed, grabbing the drink Ryan had made for us from the bar. "It's been too long. We never get the party-Jo anymore."

I rolled my eyes, leaning my head on Camilla's shoulder. "You act like I never see you anymore."

"Because we don't! We went from seeing you every day to seeing you like once or twice a week."

"I know, I know. I'm sorry."

"Don't be sorry." Kaylee waved me off. "I'm happy for you guys, even if he's so in love with you it makes me want to puke."

"Kaylee! He is not in love with me. I'm not even his girlfriend."

"You may not be his girlfriend, but even a blind man could see that he's in love with you."

"Kind of like you and Ryan," Camilla teased, signaling to him for another round of shots. "No," Kaylee clipped, watching him as he maneuvered towards the tequila on the other side of the bar. "Not like me and Ryan. Not even close."

Once Ryan dropped the glasses in front of us, we made our way back to the table, a shot and mixed drink in each of our hands. I found my spot in Adrian's lap, letting his hand travel to the top of my thigh, teasing me with proximity. I pulled my hair over my shoulder, letting him place kisses up and down my neck.

"Alright, lovebirds, that's enough. We're getting drunk," Camilla laughed, and we all downed another shot as my cheeks became warm. I was always the first out of everyone to get drunk, no matter how hard I tried to hide it.

Ryan walked up to the table, resting his elbows in front of me as he snatched the drink from my hand, helping himself to half of it.

"You off?" Jake leaned back in the booth, hitting his vape and holding it inside of his lungs so that no one would notice the smoke he blew out.

"Nah, not for another hour or so."

I waited for Kaylee to lean into him, but her eyes never found his. Something was clearly going on between them that neither of them had told me about.

"Tryna go back to your place after this, Dre?" Ryan leaned forward on the table.

"Yeah, that's fine."

"I'll be back then."

Camilla was in the corner, on the cushion next to Adrian and me. She tapped me on the shoulder, cocaine on the tip of a key hidden beneath the table. "Your turn."

Looking over my shoulder for a worker, I leaned towards her lap and let her bring the key to my nostril. Snorting up the white powder, chemical infused mucus immediately ran down my throat. I sniffed through my nostril, wiping my nose to get any excess cocaine off my face. The room slowed around me as I blinked my eyes to stop the tears that pricked at the corners.

Adrian's hand grabbed the back of my neck, forcing my ear next to his mouth.

"I don't want you doing that shit anymore."

I turned in his lap, my brows furrowing down my face as I tuned into his mood. "What? Why?"

"You don't know what's in it. I don't trust the people who make that shit, and people have been dropping like flies from fentanyl."

"So? I just took some, and I'm fine."

His head leaned back against the booth, humor gone from his emerald eyes. "I don't care. I don't want to have to worry about you. Tonight or any other night."

I chewed on my cheek, studying his expression. "You don't want me to do it like ever? What about molly?"

"No. None of it. I would never forgive myself if something happened to you."

I took a deep breath, trying to calm my adrenaline ridden heart. "Okay. I guess."

"Just listen to me on this one thing, please."

My eyes drifted along the tabletop as I reached for my drink, taking a sip. "Okay."

33. Adrian

"Hey, mom," I said into my phone, hopping out of my car after surfing. I had been given the day shift, which meant I was off in time to go catch a few waves and visit Jordan at work.

"Hola mijo, ¿cómo estás? ¿Qué estás haciendo?"

Hi honey, how are you? What are you doing?

I laughed, holding the phone between my shoulder and cheek as I unlocked my front door. She was always nosy, even from thousands of miles away.

"Nada, acabo de llegar a casa del trabajo."

Nothing, I just got home from work.

"Ah. ¿Y qué vas a hacer esta noche?"

Ah, and what are you going to do tonight?

I dropped my keys on the counter, slipping my shoes off. Trevor and Macy sat on the couch, and I avoided looking in their direction.

Why the hell hadn't he ended it with her yet?

I was far from an angel, but the things she had done to Trevor topped even the scummiest person I knew. At least the feeling was mutual, and she would avoid me like I avoided her.

"Voy a ver una chica mientras está en el trabajo," I told my mom.

I'm going to go see a girl while she's at work.

"Ooooh," she replied. "Ella es tu novia, ¿verdad?"

Oooh, she's your girlfriend, right?

A stupid-ass smile took over my face.

"Mas o menos."

More or less.

I could feel her smile through her words. My mom had been worried about me far before she moved back to Honduras, and she had been hounding me to find a girlfriend for years now. She thought that would be the answer to all the things that I was running from – hell, so did I – but while I had cleaned up my act tremendously since I met Jordan, I still had a way to go.

"Bueno. Quiero conocerla."

Good. I want to meet her.

"En navidad, posiblemente," I muttered.

On Christmas, maybe.

My mom chuckled. "Bueno. Te quiero mucho. Adiós, Adrian."

Good. I love you so much. Bye, Adrian.

"Te quiero. Adiós, mama."

I love you. Bye, mom.

I looked over at Trevor, who had a cocky smile plastered across his face. "Waiting until Christmas to introduce them, huh?"

I furrowed my brows. "How the hell do you even know what I'm talking about?"

"Jordan's the only reason I've ever seen you smile like that. Pretty easy tell."

I rolled my eyes, walking to the cabinet and grabbing a glass to fill with water.

"Why not Thanksgiving?" Trevor yelled from the living room.

"She won't be here. She's going to Mexico with her family," I answered before gulping down some cool water. I walked over to the couch, leaning onto the back of it. "Hi, Macy."

"Hey. You got a girlfriend?" She asked.

"Kinda."

"Are you going with her to Mexico?" Trevor inquired.

I shrugged my shoulders. "Cross that bridge when we get there."

"That bridge is coming up pretty quick. Thanksgiving is in a month," Trevor reminded me.

"I know. We'll see."

"You finally got your passport, right?"

I nodded. It had been quite the uphill battle to get my citizenship, but I had finally gotten all the legal paperwork handled in the last few years, earning me a passport and the ability to see my family. I had been planning to go visit my mom, but when Jordan timidly asked me about going to Mexico, I reconsidered. How could I ever say no to my blue-eyed angel?

"You should go, dude. Mexico is sick."

"Where in Mexico?" Macy chimed in.

"I can't remember," I answered without looking at her. This was the longest conversation we had held in years, and I didn't exactly love the fact that it was about Jordan – not that Macy could ever corrupt her. I didn't think that anyone could, but I still wanted to keep her ass as far away from her as she could get.

I pulled out my phone, looking at the calendar. I had just over four weeks until Jordan left for Mexico, and the thought of her going without me – and spending that much time apart – was something I wanted to avoid. But we needed to have a serious conversation before taking that step. Not just about us, but about me and my demons I was fighting. A conversation that I would avoid for as long as possible, hoping it would magically disappear and we could have continued in this love-stuck honeymoon phase forever. Impractical, I know, but I never said that I had been realistic.

Was I really going to do this?

34. Adrian

"And so I just don't talk to his family much anymore." I inhaled the joint, holding the burning smoke inside my lungs as Jordan's foot rested in my hand.

Our new nightly routine. Days ended with her in my bed and began with her bare skin against mine, between silk sheets. Unpacking all the things we didn't yet know about one another – though that list was quickly growing shorter. Only on days when she felt like fucking talking, that is.

"How did he die?" she whispered, her head by my feet in my bed. I watched her eyes as they studied the ceiling fan above her, blonde hair fanned on the mattress.

"It's a long story, not something I really want to get into right now. Kinda depressing." I took another deep breath of smoke, my eyes becoming heavier. "What about your dad? You close with him?"

"No."

"Were you ever?"

"When I was younger."

I scoffed, shaking my head with a smile as I passed the joint down to her. The frustration this girl caused me made me fucking wild. Sometimes simple answers were like begging for winning lottery numbers.

"Do you ever give more than just a glimpse into your life?"

Her eyebrows furrowed as she inhaled the smoke, holding the joint to her lips. "Yes."

"Alright, no more smoking my weed if you're going to be like this. I only share when you share." I leaned forward to snatch the joint back from her.

She held it out of reach before taking another inhale, focusing only on the ceiling above her.

"Fine, my dad and I were very close until he and my mom split. After that he just kinda went into his own life and I just kept living mine. I see him when I visit my brother and sister, or my older sister comes into town, but it's mostly surface level stuff now, and holidays." Another puff of the joint. "Are you happy?"

"I am, actually." I taunted, massaging her foot as it rested in my hand. "Why do you always have to be like this?"

"Like what?"

"Guarded."

She inhaled the smoke again, passing the joint down to me without moving her eyes from the ceiling. "I'm not."

"Oh, but you are, mija."

Her words came out quieter this time. "I don't try to be."

"You just don't trust me yet, do you?"

"It's not that I don't trust you, it's that I was told not to. I'm not supposed to trust you."

I shook my head. "You can trust me on your own schedule. But I wouldn't let whatever Jake, or fucking Ryan for that matter, tells you have such an influence on your life. Beyond just how you feel about me. You're missing out on life by focusing so hard on not letting anyone in."

"I am letting you in."

"Hardly, but I'll take what I can get, I guess. You would be much happier if you changed your ways a little. Took some risks."

"Hm. And how do you suggest I do that?"

"Throw caution to the wind, for starters. Quit being so inside your own fucking head, focusing on everything you can't control. The only thing that matters is what you're doing right now."

"That's a bit harder than it sounds."

I blew air into my cheeks, leaning my head against the headboard. "Not really. Who cares about what's going to happen tomorrow or what happened yesterday? It's all just a drop in the bucket. Being yourself and making the most out of what life offers you is much more fulfilling than worrying about the what-ifs that will never come true."

She shifted onto her elbow, looking at me with narrow eyes. "I am being myself."

"Maybe inwardly, but not outwardly. I've spent almost every day with you for the last, fuck who knows how long, and sometimes I feel like I don't even know who you are. Some days I feel like I know you better than anyone, and other days I feel like I hardly know you at all. It's pretty goddamn frustrating, you know that?"

"So I'm being analyzed for not giving as in-depth answers as you would have liked. Three months, by the way. I'll be more open, I guess, if that's what you want."

"What I want is for you to say fuck it, to grab life by the balls and make it your bitch. To not care what anyone thinks or says about you. You're going to get hurt and disappointed, so quit trying to hide from it and start disappointing some people yourself. Get even before it even begins."

Her eyebrow lifted as she studied me, a small smile finding its way across her lips. "You're sick in the head. Do you know that?"

"Yeah." I shrugged, inhaling one last puff of smoke. "Aren't we all?"

Pushing my hands into the mattress, I sat up and dropped the joint into the ashtray on my nightstand.

"Where are you going?" Jordan questioned as I made my way to the bedroom door, shutting it.

Not like it would do much good.

Trevor had already heard us fucking many times, closed door and all. Which, of course, he loved to give me shit for regularly.

I lowered myself onto my back next to where she now sat, using my elbows to prop me up. My eyes trailed up her body, wearing black sweat shorts and a baby blue hoodie, which made her blue eyes pop even more than usual. Dark lashes lined them, with pouty lips to match her heart-shaped face. If angels had found a human form, it would be Jordan. No one had seen genuine beauty until they had seen her.

Jordan's finger began lightly tracing the Aztec calendar tattoo on my chest, following each little line.

"Why did you get this one?"

I let out a deep breath, her fingers nearly bringing goosebumps to my skin. "My heritage. As a tribute to the beginning and end."

"Beginning and end?" Her brows furrowed down her face, eyes focused on the ink now infused with my skin.

"Yeah. Everything begins, everything ends. Life. Love. All of that stuff. Figured it was fitting."

"I guess. I prefer not to think about that stuff."

"Why?"

"I don't do well with change, with beginnings or endings."

"That's okay. I kind of gathered that from the beginning of us, but it's not a bad thing."

She paused for a moment, keeping her eyes on the same place on my chest, before her finger continued gliding across my flesh moments later. "I don't know if I would use the word us, but sure."

I laughed, throwing my head back to hang between my shoulders. "That's exactly what I mean."

"What?" A small smile crossed her lips, her eyes following the finger that continued to trace my skin.

Grabbing hold of her wrist, I pulled her on top of me, letting her legs fall on either side of my lap.

"You can keep resisting all that you want, but as long as you're sitting like this, ready to ride me like a fucking carnival ride, you're mine. You're all fucking mine." My hand found the back of her neck, pulling her lips to mine. "And I've known that you would be since the days that I laid eyes on you."

"You're lying," she gulped, her blue eyes staring into mine from an inch away. Her breath fanned across my lips, deep pants taunting me with each molecule of air.

"No, I'm not."

"Then why did you let me leave at the bonfire?"

"Because I needed to see if you would come back. Once you did, it was over. You've always been mine."

"I know," she breathed, my hand gripping the back of her neck tighter.

"Should I remind you?"

My lips were on hers before I could get an answer, pulling her bottom lip into my mouth and sinking my teeth into it. She yelped lightly, letting her body sink into me. Hips grinding against mine, her tongue darted into my mouth, sweetly caressing mine.

When I was fire, she was ice.

Where I was greedy, she was patient.

And where I was merciless, she was pure bliss.

My cock pulsed against my jeans, begging to be freed. To dig into her and assault her pussy until she was praying to the fucking heavens above. A frenzied wind took over my mind, as it always fucking did when I was near her.

Like a caged animal that had finally been released.

Flames took me captive, victim to her presence.

Bringing my hands to her shorts, I ravenously pulled them off, not giving a fuck if I ripped every piece of fabric she wore just to get her skin against mine. Squeezing her bare ass in my hands, I was sure there would be bruises where my thumbs pressed against her flesh.

Good.

Let there be marks.

If my lips left scars everywhere that they met her skin, I would cover her from head to toe, just to let everyone know she was fucking mine.

Slow moans left her mouth, meeting mine in a hasty fever. There sure was something satisfying about turning her from a saint into a fucking sinner. I wanted to wrap it up and keep it in a jar, only for me to see.

I let my hands grab around her thighs, pulling her to sit on my face. "Adrian!" She exclaimed, half in defiance and half through a desperate moan. My tongue dove through all her folds, studying every inch like a piece of art. Needy hands wrestled through my hair, pulling at strands and threatening to rip them from my scalp.

Her sweet pussy melted onto my face, wetting my chin as I found all the spots that made her tick. Stroking her clit with my tongue, my hands gripped her ass, pulling her into me as her back arched.

I guided her hips in a grinding motion, tracing her over and over until I heard soft moans leave her lips. My hands studied her figure, feverishly grabbing ahold of her hips, then slowly trailing up her sides. Writhing above me, I knew she was close – so fucking close – but we were both aware that this wouldn't be the end.

The fires she lit inside me were stubborn to extinguish. They wanted more, craved more, and I would lose myself inside of her until the sparks took over her entire fucking soul.

"Come here," I groaned, pulling her down to my cock. Unbuttoning the button on my jeans, I hurried out of the fabric, my cock springing free against her wet pussy. Grinding her over me, I let her warmth tease me, driving me to dangerous places.

Desperation can be severe when heaven's legs are spread across you.

"Fuck, let me grab a condom," I breathed, bringing her to my lips, swirling my tongue around hers. My desire for her wasn't just a hunger, it was a fucking demand that couldn't go unsatisfied.

"I'm on birth control," she said between pants, keeping her eyes locked onto mine.

"You're on *what*?"

Her head tilted, stilling her hips from grinding into me. "The pill?"

"Why the fuck are you on that?"

"I've been on it since I was sixteen," she whispered, oblivious to what her words had just done to me. That I would fuck all of my anger out on her, and then some.

Images of her with Alec spun through my head, my need for her becoming animalistic. To wipe the fucking idea of any guy ever with her right out of both her head and mine.

Her blue eyes poured into me patiently, innocently, waiting for me to respond.

"Don't fucking tell me that."

"I'm sorry," she whispered. "I just figured you would want to know. In case you didn't want to use a condom…"

I pulled her face towards mine, clasping my teeth on her bottom lip as I pulled it into my mouth, sucking possessively at her soft skin. Lifting her hips, I lowered her onto my cock, my entire length plunging inside of her.

A husky groan left my mouth as her hips moved rhythmically, her pussy slowly melting around me. My hand slapped her ass, vibrant moans ringing through the air.

"Dear god," she whispered, riding me faster with each breath. I kept my eyes fixed on hers as they rolled back, lost in ecstasy – one no drug could ever give her.

Our bodies slapped together, the air thick with sex as she moved over me in a harmony that only we knew. I yanked her hips closer to mine, filling her completely. Sweat rolled down her forehead, dripping onto my bare chest as she leaned forward, meeting my lips with hers. I kissed from her collarbone towards her neck, sucking lightly each time that her skin was against me. Trailing up her neck, I savored the taste of her salty skin, the feeling of her clenching against me with each push closer to the edge of an orgasm. When I reached her earlobe, I took it between my teeth, sucking the life out of her flesh.

My arms grabbed around her waist, lifting her and dropping her onto her stomach. Bent over the edge of my bed, I thrust my cock inside of her, grabbing a fistful of her thick blonde hair.

"Fuck, baby," I groaned, my head falling backwards as her ass slapped against my skin. She convulsed against me, digging her teeth into my sheets to stifle her screams.

Shaking from the inside out, I continued to bury myself inside of her, pulling her hair until her back arched off the mattress. Electricity burning in my chest, I watched as her eyes slid shut, mouth agape on the purest high that life could fucking offer. With the sight of her coming undone, I erupted inside of her, my fingers digging into her lush hips with each thrust. Ravaging with each pulse, I slowed my pace.

This girl was going to be the fucking death of me.

But for her, I would have jumped into the deepest oceans to fuel her release.

Jordan rolled onto her back, wiping sweat from her forehead as drops rolled down my skin. Her boobs, neck, and ear lobe were decorated with purple, floating with each deep breath she took. I studied the marks on her skin, a feeling of satisfaction rushing over me.

"Hopefully those marks remind you that you're only taking birth control for me, that you've only ever been taking birth control for me."

"What?" She shot up, rushing over to the mirror that rested on my dresser. "Adrian, I have work!" she laughed.

I shrugged, cleaning my cock with a towel from my hamper before tossing it to her. "Call out."

"All *week*? I can't call out until these go away. I have bills to pay."

"Relax, babe. I'll pay for your shit, and I'll call out all week too, so we can fuck until you're black and blue."

35. Jordan

"Hey," I breathed, falling to my back on the patio couch and studying the blue sky. The sound of small water ripples lightly floated through the air. Camilla sat beside my mom, flipping through magazines. I pulled my hair above my head, desperate for some airflow on my neck.

"Mom, I think it's about time we think about getting AC. This is like torture and it's October. I can't do another July like this."

"I know, I know." She laughed, licking her finger and flipping the page in her magazine. "How was work?"

"Oh, fine."

"Work," Camilla said, a smile across her face as she made air quotations with her fingers. "That's where she was."

I rolled my eyes, my mom not looking up from her magazine as she spoke back. "Yeah. We'll go with that."

"Oh, shut up." I rolled onto my stomach, propping myself up with my elbows. My mom's eyes flicked to me slowly before returning to her magazine.

"Honey, I love you and I don't mean to like, *call you out*, but you should really cover those hickeys with some makeup. Put a spoon in the freezer or something." My mom laughed, casually flipping through her magazine.

My mom and Cam were close, obviously. She had known Cam since we were kids, and Cam clung onto her like she did me. Cam had never had a good family relationship, and it was much easier for her to look over my mom's flaws than it was for me. Though we all equally loved our afternoons spent gossiping and lying on the patio furniture with my mom.

"Just be careful, Jordan. I worry about you." My mom spoke without judgment. Like a friend simply sharing their opinion. "I'm glad Jake hasn't lost his mind on you yet. You should probably put on a turtleneck or something so he doesn't when he gets here."

"Mom!" I laughed, covering my neck with my hands. "They're not that bad!"

"Oh, please, Jordan. It looks like you went eight rounds with Mike Tyson and lost *horribly*."

"Fuck-"

"I don't want to hear it." Jake walked out with his hands up to stop me. His eyes were bloodshot as hell, carrying a bag of Taco Bell in hand. He plopped down on the couch next to me, digging through the bag of food.

"Who wants Cinnabon Delights before I eat them all?" His words were slow, laced with smoke. Jake was a stoner – like a huge stoner – but this time I knew he was high as *hell*.

"How many did you get?"

"Fourteen."

"Jake!" my mom exclaimed, tears forming in the corners of her eyes with laughter. "There's going to be a shortage because of you."

He nodded, throwing one into his mouth.

"Sit up when you eat, loser," my mom scolded teasingly, folding the magazine open in her hand

"I'm not listening to this Fleetwood Mac bullshit," Jake said between bites, pulling his phone from his pocket and connecting to the outside speaker.

"Oh god, you always play awful music."

"I'll play something you like," Jake taunted, scrolling through his screen. *Vienna* by Billy Joel began flowing from the speakers moments later.

"Thank you," my mom confirmed, turning her attention back to her magazine.

"You know, I'm doing pretty good for fourteen. I've only got six left."

"I wanted some!" I laughed, hitting him on the shoulder.

"Oh." He laughed, stuffing another ball of bread and frosting into his mouth. "You should have said that."

"And if we didn't, you were just going to eat all fourteen to yourself?" Camilla questioned, her eyes locked on her magazine.

"Fuck yeah."

36. Adrian

"Wow, the infamous room. I never thought I would get to see it."

"Oh, hush." Jordan waved to me over her shoulder, flicking on her bedroom light.

The room was perfectly *her*. Light beige walls with white macrame hanging on one portion, green plants scattered throughout the space. A plush white comforter covered her bed, soft white pillows taking up a quarter of the mattress.

Jordan's house was fucking *nice*. Her kitchen held a large granite island, with two guest bedrooms downstairs and Jake's room next to hers upstairs, her mom's across the hall. Everything was perfectly manicured, with expensive-ass art by Wyland covering the walls.

Photos of her with Jake, Ryan, Camilla, and Kaylee sat on her dresser and built-in shelves, as well as her nightstand. A few photos of her family, including her sister that I had never met but seen on her social media.

"Wow, I didn't make the cut?" I asked, pulling a selfie of her and Ryan from the shelves. She turned from her closet to face me, studying which photo I was holding.

"We don't have any photos together."

I nodded, replacing the photo on her shelf. "You've got me there."

Falling onto her bed, I kicked my shoes off and lay on my back. Sitting next to me, she typed quickly on her phone, chewing on her bottom lip. Her eyes were narrowed as she focused on the messages.

"Sorry. My mom is just a pain in the ass."

"Let me guess. Out of town?"

"Yeah."

"So that's why you actually let me step foot in her house."

Her blue eyes looked up from her phone, a slight blush coming across her freckled cheeks. "You caught that."

"I'm not stupid, babe."

"I know you're not."

I pulled my baseball cap off my head, placing it on the bed next to me.

"That big of a deal if I meet her, huh? We've been together for a few months. It's going to have to happen sometime, unless you're planning to cut things off before then."

I gulped at the thought, pushing the thought of life without her out of my mind. Either that day would never come, which I prayed to fucking God that it didn't, or I would have to deal with the downward spiral caused by her absence once I got there.

No point in dreading bad dreams.

"It's not that."

"Then what is it? Why are you so elusive with your mom? You *live* with her baby, and as much as I would love to move all your stuff in and lock the both of us behind the same door forever, we both know it doesn't work like that."

She sighed, putting her phone flat on the bed before pressing her fingers to her temple. "It's just complicated with her."

"I can see that, but I'm here to help. Quit shutting me out so much, mija."

"She just has a bad drinking problem, and it gets draining. I don't like talking about it."

I nodded, my throat constricted.

I should have known that addiction ran in her family. She could drink, and she did, *a lot.* That was half the reason I finally put my foot down with the fucking drugs when we were at Hansen's.

"Why didn't you tell me that?"

"I just don't like thinking about it."

I pulled her down to my chest, her hair tickling against my chin. "You have to decide on what you want to do. Either you let your walls down with me completely, or you don't. But going back and forth like this must be as exhausting for you as it is for me."

"I know," she breathed. "I'm trying."

"And you're doing better." I kissed her hair, pulling her delicate frame further into me. "Come here." I fished my phone out of my jeans, holding it out to take a selfie of us.

"Oh God, don't take a picture of me right now."

"Why?" I laughed, snapping a photo of us. Jordan's hand covered her face, her hair spread on the mattress behind her. "Smile, baby. We don't have a single picture together."

She sighed, sitting up. "Fine. Sit up then."

I sat next to her as she leaned into me, letting a slight smile creep across her lips. "Jesus, at least look like you want to be with me."

"Shut up." She laughed, looking at me with smile driven dimples. I snapped a few blurry photos of us, saving one as my background.

"So what movie will it be tonight?"

"You pick. I'm tired"

I sat up, walking to get her TV remote off of the dresser. Opening the window on my way back to her bed, I noticed a black sedan sitting in the alley behind her house. I watched it for a moment before it pulled away slowly, the outline of someone familiar in the front seat. Too bad that I was too fucking out of it to recognize who it was.

"I have to go to the bathroom." Jordan slid out of her bed, making her way to the bathroom door and shutting it behind her.

My hand slipped into my pocket. "I'm a fucking piece of shit," I whispered to myself. Pulling out two benzos, I swallowed them dry, the taste of chemicals burning the back of my tongue.

37. Jordan

"Jo." Adrian shook my shoulder softly, his fingers lightly tracing up and down my arm. I savored his soft touch, resting deeply on the pillow. "Wake up, baby."

"Hmm," I mumbled, rubbing my eyes with the heel of my palm. My limbs were heavy with sleep as I rolled onto my back, the room still dark. "What time is it?"

"Around four. Someone keeps trying to call you."

Running my hands down my face, I sat up and slid my hand over the side table next to Adrian's bed. I squinted at the light from my phone, a random number flashing across the top of it. Laying back, the plush comforter pulled up to my chin, I held my phone to my ear.

"Hello?" I mumbled, my voice laced with sleep.

"I've been calling you for a damn hour, Jordan! What the fuck!"

I let out a deep breath, rolling my eyes. "Forgive me for not answering at four in the morning."

"I don't give a shit what time it is. I need you to come get me."

"From where?"

"The police station." My mom dragged out her words, annoyed at me for even asking.

"DUI or drunk in public," I breathed. Only *my* mom would get arrested and then get mad at me for it.

"Does it matter?" She snapped, her words slurring. "Just come fucking get me. I'm sick of waiting around this place."

"Call Jake. I'm not home and I don't have my car."

"Well, where the hell are you?"

"I'm at Camilla's."

She scoffed, and I could picture her face over the phone. Bloodshot eyes looking through you, rather than at you.

"Have her come get me."

"I'm not waking her up, mom. Call Jake."

"You don't think I tried that?" Her words dragged out in drunken annoyance, like I was the stupid one in this conversation. "His phone is off."

An exhale left my lips, trying to control my anger. There was no point in arguing with her. "I don't know mom, call an Uber."

"Jordan, my phone is dead and these fucking assholes won't let me use a charger. I can't call a stupid Uber." She breathed heavily into the phone, hiccuping every few seconds.

"Fine, I'll come get you. Wait out front." I hung up the phone before she could answer, resting it on my chest. My eyes closed heavily, still half asleep.

Taking care of her had gotten old years ago. She was the eternal victim of her own life, and somehow, I was to blame. This would never change, and I was tired of it. The only way to keep myself sane was by keeping my distance and not expecting anything more than disappointment from her.

And even then, in the back of my mind, I clung onto a tiny glimmer of hope that she would change one day. That hope grew whenever I spent time with her sober, laughing until we cried and gossiping for hours. When she was like this, that hope got smashed back into the ground.

"Everything okay?" Adrian asked, pulling me into his bare chest. I breathed in his cedar scent, letting his firm hold melt the world away for a moment.

"Can you take me home? I have to go get my mom."

"I'll just go with you. I'm not letting her steal you that easily."

"No, I don't think that's the best idea."

He softly brushed a few loose strands of hair out of my face, tucking them behind my ear and pulling me tighter into his chest. "Still that big of a deal if I meet her?"

"No, she's just complicated."

"Why are you always so vague about this?"

I let out a deep breath. "It's not that. She's just super fucked up right now."

"So? I don't care about that. And she won't even remember meeting me, so it works out good. If that's what you're worried about."

I chuckled, trying to make light of the situation like he did so well. "I don't know about that. About any of this, honestly."

"Come on, baby." His fingers lightly traced my spine beneath my shirt, his body relaxed against mine. "I'm coming with you. Let me help you with something, for once."

"I don't know…"

"Please."

"I really don't feel comfortable with this, Dre."

"I know, and it's fine. It'll be fine. I don't want you going by yourself right now."

"Okay," I breathed, sitting up and swinging my legs over the side of his bed. The pads of his fingers continued to trail lightly up and down my spine as I slipped my sweats on, pulling my hair into a ponytail. "Let's get this over with, I guess."

Adrian rolled out of bed, moving across the room and throwing a black hoodie over his head. The muscles beneath his light brown skin moved with each swift gesture. Slipping his loose black jeans on, he made his way to his closet and kicked his black Vans sneakers on.

"So, do I pretend I'm Camilla or what?" He teased.

The drive over to the police station was short, the black sky decorated with distant stars. While living by the ocean was beautiful, the city lights took away the gift of a clear night and the specks of light that decorated it.

Adrian's car pulled into the parking lot of the police station, slowing to a stop in front of the entrance. I rested my head against the seat, staring through tired eyes at the dimly lit glass door. Moments later, my mom came wobbling down the steps and towards the car. She held her high heels in her hand, her blonde hair a frizzy mess, falling over her shoulders.

The back door swung open, the smell of vodka overtaking the car. I kept my eyes away from Adrian, flames burning in my chest and throat.

This was the most humiliating part of my life that I never wanted him to see. Yet here I was, allowing him in spaces he should never be. I should have fought harder, demanded that he took me home and let me get her alone.

"Took you long enough," my mom slurred, squirming into the car and buckling in the backseat.

I turned around in the passenger chair, looking at her with dead eyes. "Nice to see you, too."

She rolled her eyes obnoxiously, swaying in her seat. Her gaze moved slowly from me to Adrian, who was driving in the direction of my house.

"And who is this?"

"Adrian. Jake's friend."

She scoffed, studying Adrian with lazy eyes. "My own son won't come pick me up, but his friend will. Pathetic."

I shifted in my seat, flames growing up my spine to the back of my skull.

How could I have been related to someone who made me this fucking livid on a regular basis?

"I'm not going to treat you like a two-year-old." I waved her off, turning back in my seat to stare out the windshield. There was no traffic, meaning that the drive from the station to my house was going quicker than usual.

Thank God.

"Well, thank you for coming to get me. I'm sorry that my daughter is such a bitch."

Adrian smiled at her in the rear-view mirror. "No worries at all. It's nice to meet you, Mrs. Langford."

"Call me Shannon, please."

I rolled my eyes at her sweet tone, like she hadn't just been acting like a complete bitch moments before.

"It's nice to meet you, Shannon." Adrian's sweet smile caught my eye, shooting me a wink when I looked over at him. My heart caught in my throat, electricity spreading through my chest.

How did he make one of the many most irritating moments of my life feel calm and secure?

Adrian's car pulled to a stop in front of my house, my mom grabbing her Louis Vuitton tote from the backseat. "Are you coming in?" The liquid words fell from her lips with an attitude, struggling to come out coherently.

"No."

Adrian looked at me sympathetically, placing his hand on my thigh with a squeeze. "Are you sure? I don't mind coming in."

"I'm completely positive. Trust me."

He nodded his head, looking out the window.

"Are you going to come in at least, Jordan?"

"Nope."

"I thought he was dropping you off."

"No, we were dropping you off. I'm going to go surf."

"Suit yourself," she said with a knowing smirk as she got out of the car. Shutting the door with one last hiccup, she made her way up the porch and inside of the dark house.

"Jake's friend?" Adrian teased, lightly pushing my shoulder. "That's how you introduce me?"

"What do you mean? That's what you are."

He tsked, shaking his head with a smile. Playful green eyes met mine. "Okay, Jake's sister."

I rolled my eyes, looking at him through my lashes. "Can we just go to the beach, please?'

"You were serious about that?" His eyebrows shot up as I nodded. "I still have all our shit in my car. Wanna run in and change?"

"No." I sighed, waving off his offer. "I'll change in your trunk. I just want to get on a damn board."

38. Adrian

I walked into Hansen's for my shift after spending the day surfing with Jordan. We watched the sunrise transform the sky before slipping into wet suits to catch the early morning swell. My hair was still damp as I punched in my timecard, dropping my phone into my locker.

Jordan opted to stay at my house all day, finishing homework and waiting for me to get home. When I knew she was lying on my bed without me, the days took ten times longer. Minutes dragged on, testing my patience with each damn second.

"What are you doing tonight?" Ryan shouted at me over the music as I walked through the bar. To say that our friendship had been strung thin the past few months would have been an understatement. I was still pissed at him for the way he acted towards Jordan when we first met, but I understood. I could only look past my disgust for him when we were working in the same building.

"Just going home. What about you?"

"A few of us are going over to Analyn's. You should come."

I shook my head, tapping my fingers on the wooden bar. "Nah, I don't think I'll make it. Have a drink for me, though."

Ryan rolled his eyes and wiped a glass cup clean. "We haven't seen you in ages. I'm sure Jo won't mind if you stop by for one drink."

I hesitated to answer. I knew he was right, that he was one of my best friends and we hadn't hung out since I started dating Jordan. But I also knew that Jordan was at my house, lying in sheets that would smell like her by the time I got home. Odds are she would have been asleep for hours by the time I clocked out.

"Yeah, sure. I'll come by for one drink."

39. Jordan

I woke up at 7 A.M. for class to an empty bed.

Immediately, it dawned on me.

Adrian had never come home last night.

I knew he had been working the closing shift and wouldn't be off until 2 A.M., but he still always came home.

Except for when he disappeared for over a week.

I walked out of his bedroom to check the living room in case he had fallen asleep on the couch, trying not to wake me by watching TV in the bedroom, as he had before. When the couch was empty, my heart sank. I couldn't help but panic as I thought of the worst possible scenarios.

Where the hell was he?

"Hey, Jo," Trevor said from the kitchen as he filled a small cooler with his lunch. I had such tunnel vision, I hadn't even realized he was there.

"Hey," I replied, trying not to sound distressed.

"Adrian still asleep?"

I walked to the dining room table and took a seat, twisting the ring on my finger.

"Um, I'm not sure, actually. He, uh, he never came home last night, I guess."

Trevor seemed unaffected. "He didn't? Well, sometimes if he's had too much to drink or is too crossed, he'll stay at the bar. Maybe he's there and just forgot to call."

"Yeah, I hope so."

He looked at me sympathetically. "I'm sorry, girl. I'm sure he's fine, though. Don't worry too much."

A deep breath left my body. He was right. Adrian had to be fine. But why did he leave me alone at his house without even bothering to tell me where he was? I would have just stayed home if he had been busy. What had he been up to that was so important he couldn't come back to me?

"I know. Hey, can you do me a favor and take me home? I need to get ready for school."

He closed the lid to his cooler. "Yep. Be ready in 10."

Questions swirled through my mind, though I tried to push them to the side and not become consumed by Adrian's absence. We had only been together for a few months, and we hadn't labeled anything, so I had no right to panic like I was.

I also knew I would never leave him sleeping alone in my room all night, waiting for me. But that was probably only because I was much more into him than he was with me.

My classes passed quickly as thoughts consumed me. I didn't hear a word my professors said while I watched my phone on my desk, waiting for it to light up with his name.

After hours of anticipation with no cure, I finally called him as I walked across campus.

"Hello?" He answered with a groggy voice.

"Hey…"

"Hey, babe. What's up?"

How the hell could he sound so carefree when I had been worried sick about him all morning?

"Um, I just wanted to make sure you were okay, since you never came home last night."

After a few moments of silence, he finally spoke.

"Yeah, I'm really sorry about that. I had a few too many drinks and slept at the bar with Ryan. I should have texted you, my bad."

My bad? No, you shouldn't have left me alone at your house to drink with your friends.

I didn't want to seem bat-shit crazy, so I bit my stupid tongue.

"It's fine. I was just worried something happened."

"Nothing happened. I'm fine, mi amor. Want me to pick you up today?"

"I'll let you know. I have to go. Talk to you later."

I hung up before I could get a response, walking into my next class. Shuffling between desks to the back row, I rested in the seat and flipped open my laptop.

If I had left him at my house, he would have been much more upset than I was showing him I was. But since his story matched Trevor's assumption, I didn't want to make it a bigger deal than it was. This was something that we could surely talk about later.

And besides, him calling me amor still made my heart pound faster than I wanted to, despite my current frustration.

40. Adrian

I stumbled into the hallway towards the bathroom as Analyn rounded the corner. My head pounded as everything I had ever eaten threatened to travel back up my throat.

"Morning cupcake, you sleep good?" She leaned against the doorway with a satisfied grin on her face. I wanted to smack it off of her, though she wasn't the one to blame for my actions. I was.

"No, I slept like shit," I lied. I was practically in a coma all night, thanks to the mass amounts of opiates that had entered my body. Faint memories of stumbling through the apartment, my head spinning after puking in her toilet, lingered in my mind.

When I would nod off, which was often, I was in a pure lucid dream state. It was hard to tell the difference between being asleep and awake when everything felt so good, regardless. Usually I knew my limits, but apparently last night was an exception to this.

Plus, the fucking heroin I had shot into my veins didn't help.

As hard as I had tried to forget last night, it was impossible. Regret ate at me with the thought of Jordan alone in my bed, her soft skin waiting for me to be pressed up against it. Usually I was exceptional at forgetting the past and not worrying about the future, but currently I was doing the complete opposite of that.

She made my careless, live-for-yourself view on life much harder than it had been before she found her way into my life, under my skin and flowing through my veins, a twin to the heroin.

I don't know what had taken over, pushing me to do the fucking lowest thing possible – the unimaginable and unspeakable.

I had never craved to try it. All I had craved was to stop everything, but something inside of me had other ideas. I was destined to drown, and my body wouldn't forget it, even if my mind had tried so very hard to.

Instead of soaking in every moment I had with Jordan, I was here in a state somewhere between dead and alive, a needle sticking in my arm as I floated in an orgasmic, out-of-body experience.

Opiate molecules were by far the greatest gift life had to offer, especially in the pleasure powder form called heroin. The equivalent of kissing God.

The comedown was the complete opposite. Buckets of sweat poured from my pores as I fought the urge to vomit. I needed another hit, or at least a handful of pills, to take the fucking edge off. All I craved was another euphoric rush to take away the horrible flu I had been hit with now that it was gone.

I couldn't bring myself to look at my phone, half because the screen was only a blurry form of excess light, and half because I would do anything to avoid remembering what I had indulged in the night before – including facing Jordan.

I pounded on the closed bathroom door until Ryan opened it, wearing nothing but boxers and a smug grin.

"Look who's alive," he mocked me as I tried to regain my balance. I was coming down hard, my head pounding with each breath I struggled to take, and I was ready to fucking kill someone for any reason if they crossed my path. "Shut the fuck up and take me to my car," I sneered at him before pushing past him into the bathroom.

"Why? Jo gonna be pissed at you for leaving her all night?"

I pushed him up against the wall, his eyes challenging my sudden movement. "Call her that again and I'll snap your fucking neck."

"What? I know my little Jo Jo, she'll forgive you for what you've done. That is, if you tell her. Which you're too chickenshit to do."

"Quit acting like this wasn't your goal. We all know you would do anything to get into her pants, even if it meant knocking off your best friend."

He scoffed, staring back at me with eyes free of any ounce of fear.

He thought I wouldn't fucking touch him.
Oh, but I fucking would have.

"My goal was to hangout with you, and try to get rid of some of the beef between us. The heroin?

295

That was all you, bud. How could I talk you into doing something I would never consider doing myself?"

I clenched my jaw, staring at him with narrow eyes. Ryan didn't falter, almost looking amused with my anger.

As much as he was my friend, he was also Jordan's, and I had to remember that. He was always going to have her back as much as he had mine, even when I was the one wronging her.

I dropped my arm from his chest, shoving him into the hallway and locking the bathroom door. My elbows leaned on the sink as I ran my hands through my hair.

Heroin.

I had done fucking heroin.

I was trying to get sober from all opiates, and instead I had turned to the strongest one – the one I had promised myself I would never do.

The one that had killed my best friend before he lived to see nineteen.

One that would kill me if I gave into those damn cravings that now had a death grip on me.

The only somewhat good thing that had come of this twisted, fucked up night, was Analyn fucking Ryan. At least now she had someone new to keep her busy, and to keep her the fuck away from me.

All I wanted was to see Jordan, to fall into bed with her and never let her go, to beg her to take this pain away. To use her to fill the void that heroin had now left in every state of my being. One that I never knew existed twenty-four hours before.

I took a deep breath, splashing cold water on my face. My eyes reflected back, bloodshot to no end.

Tonight was the night.

I could, and would, come clean to her. I would get on my knees and fucking beg her to support me in getting clean, and hope to God that she didn't abandon me at the mere mention of my fucking addiction.

Though that night never came.

Once Ryan dropped me off at my car and I struggled to keep my eyes open as I drove home, I slept for almost thirty hours – in between trips to the bathroom with vomiting spells. Trevor knew something was up – that I had fucking taken something harder than usual – as he stuck his head into my room or the bathroom every few hours. I flipped him off when I could muster the energy and gave him no answers.

Heroin was somewhere between Wednesday night and early Thursday morning, before darkness had subsided. By the time Friday night rolled around, I could finally get myself up off the bathroom floor. Making my way into the kitchen, I walked past Trevor and grabbed a water bottle from the fridge.

"Have you been shooting up again?" He asked me blatantly, like he knew my actions before they even took place.

"No, I haven't been shooting up morphine again, it's been a while since I even took that shit."

He scoffed at me. "I didn't ask if you've been shooting up morphine, I asked if you've been shooting up in general. What did you use last night?"

I rolled my eyes. "Not jack shit Trevor, so shut your fucking mouth."

"So you want to tell me you aren't being an asshole from shooting up something yesterday?"

I sighed, my patience wearing thin as I rubbed my temples. "That's exactly what I'm telling you."

His voice raised as he slammed his fist on the countertop. "Then show me your goddamn arm. Show me you don't have track marks where you stuck that needle in your arm last night, with whatever fucked up shit had you puking all day."

My mouth stayed shut, my eyes unable to meet his. When my silence gave him his answer, he shook his head and grabbed the back of his neck.

"What the fuck did you use, Dre?"

"It's not that big of a deal. It was a one-time-thing and I'll never do it again," I mumbled.

I didn't even have to say it. He knew what I was talking about. He had been there, alongside me and my friends, when Clay spiraled down the drain with his heroin addiction, eventually to his death. The symptoms of my fucking heroin hangover were no secret to someone who had seen them before.

His booming voice interrupted my mental pity party, for both myself and my late best friend.

"You did fucking heroin! Are you stupid? Actually, don't answer that, because you clearly are. More importantly, do you want to die? Because you sure are trying to with that shit!" Anger seeped into his expression further. I ran my fingers through my curls, tugging at my scalp.

"I told you, it was a one-time thing. No matter how badly I want to do it right now, which is really fucking bad, I'm not going to. I'll just pop an oxy or something to make it through the cravings, so chill the fuck out."

As much as I knew he just cared about me and was concerned, it didn't matter. I just wanted to be left alone to my vices, which allowed me to reset reality as much as I needed to.

He spoke through gritted teeth, "If you're just going to keep supplementing one form of poison to replace another, then at least end it with Jordan. She was sleeping here by herself, worried half to death that you got in an accident, while you were doing fucking smack. She deserves better than that."

My shoulders slumped as I looked to the ground, a deep breath leaving my tight chest. She deserved better than a junkie who was going from one fix to the next, while she had been waiting innocently to love me for who I was – and nothing more. Yet the selfish part of me told myself I would get clean before I would ever consider letting her go, the only form of hope in my dark, fucked up life.

I pulled out my phone to text her for the first time in over 24 hours.

Me: I'm sorry about this. Can I please pick you up?

For three hours, I sat on my couch lifelessly. My hope for Jordan coming over had diminished until my phone finally buzzed.

Jordan: Sure. I'm off work at 11, but I have plans to go out with Camilla, if you want to come.

I knew the only reason she agreed to see me was to get into the bar, which I deserved. She hardly spoke to me all night, shooting me emotionless glances whenever I tried to get near her. It was obvious she wanted nothing to do with me, no matter how hard I tried to weasel my way back towards her.

Finally, when I caught the right moment, despite my piercing headache and lack of reality, I grabbed her waist and pulled her towards me. Her silky hips leaned into me, overtaking my senses.

But still not more than the heroin had.
Fuck.

How was I going to get clean when all I could think about was opiates, and the fucking death grip they had on me and my life?

I wanted to; I fucking wanted to so bad, but all I could think about was the euphoria another hit would give me, even while dancing with the love of my life, being her only focus, as I had wanted to be for so damn long.

Camilla and I smoked on the balcony while Jordan showered after our night at Hansen's. I could see the hesitation on her face as Camilla told her she would call an Uber to my apartment.

The only reason she had agreed to come was because everyone else was already planning on it, and because she couldn't leave Camilla alone when she was as high as a kite.

Trevor was asleep in a drunken slumber in his room, Jake in the same state on the couch. I could tell by Camilla's dime sized pupils, eyes as wide as a deer in headlights, that she was on the same shit as the time I saw her and Jordan at Ryan's party, which was now so long ago.

"Do you like her?" She asked, chewing her gum and packing the biggest bowl of weed I had ever seen.

I stumbled on my words, confused about the root of her question. "What do you mean? Of course I do. That's why I spend every day with her."

"That's good. She's really into you. I can tell." She lit the bowl, packed to the rim with green weed, and inhaled until her lungs were about to pop. Her eyes closed as she blew the smoke into the cold air.

"What are you on, anyway?"

"A good one, that's what."

Her stupid response made me laugh. "No shit, Sherlock. A good one from what?"

I grabbed the bong from her hands and lit the bowl for myself.

"One hell of a euro I got from Anthony. That boy has the best ecstasy hook up in the country. Even though he almost got me killed for it before."

I exhaled smoke and tried to suppress a cough. "Is that the same place you got it from the night I saw you at Ryan's?"

"I'm sure it was. I don't really remember one party compared to another anymore. But that's what we always take when we go to house parties, makes them more bearable."

As she answered my fears, I swallowed with a dry throat. I didn't know how to feel about Jordan taking party drugs every weekend, especially when I saw her. There was no right for me to judge, given my own drug-fueled demons, and the fact that we were far from together at the time I saw her. Still, the image of her high out of her mind ate at me internally, causing my stomach to twist.

"Yeah, I know what you mean. My memory's pretty shot." I lit the bowl and inhaled smoke once more before leaning back into my chair.

"What do you mean your memory is shot? You're like the most sober Sally out of all of us."

"Not really, but I'll take that as a compliment." I shrugged and inhaled more smoke.

"What am I missing?"

"Nothing major, but just things aren't always as you see them." I tapped my temple with my index finger, trying to play on her ecstasy driven state to my advantage.

It was hard to believe that she couldn't see how drug use had affected every part of me, but I guess she had never known me sober, so she had nothing to compare it to. I knew by the look on her face she wasn't going to let me get away with not exposing myself.

Ecstasy did that, made you want to talk about all the deep shit you can't face when you're sober. Everything festering in your mind was easy to put out on the table and process, even if just momentarily. I had only taken it once and hated it, this being part of the reason why. My need to get high was to further bury the things I was avoiding, not to examine them underneath a fucking magnifying glass.

"You have to tell me now."

I sighed. "Just the short version, because Jordan's going to be back soon..." I looked over my shoulder into the empty living room. "I've been on pills for a few... years, now. I've got a handle on it, but I need to quit completely. It's really not a big deal. I'm not like addicted or anything, but I'm quitting right now."

I justified saying that I was quitting because, to me, it was the truth. When I was with Jordan, I was hardly using them. I never took them when she was at my house, which meant I had gone from 8 or more pills a day down to 4. I had chosen to discount the heroin run-in.

"Does she know?" Camilla asked me innocently.

"It doesn't really matter. I've seen her fucked up on ecstasy before and I've never said anything about it."

"Yeah, that's true, but two wrongs still don't make a right. Is it a daily thing? Because if so, you can't compare her actions to yours. She used to take it every weekend or so, but she has a handle on it. I know she doesn't like taking it as much as I do, and she takes it more often than she would if she wasn't friends with me. Plus, she hasn't taken it since you came into her life, which shows me she can stop whenever she wants." She bit her bottom lip. "But you never answered me. Does she know?"

Camilla continued chewing her gum and patiently staring at me. I couldn't compare the two, but I still tried to.

Jordan would smoke with me at night, before we watched a movie, or after we surfed. She only drank when I did, and rarely on weeknights. I knew she definitely hadn't taken any drugs since we had met. I also knew I hadn't gone a day without all three.

"No, she doesn't know."

Camilla studied me with hyper focused eyes as I lit another bowl. As I passed the bong back to her, she grabbed my wrist and extended my arm towards her.

"Adrian, are these track marks?" She asked me, studying the inside of my elbow, seeing that bruising had formed around the spot where a needle had entered my vein. I thought my tattoos had covered the evidence, but apparently, I was wrong.

"Um no, they're not."

She shook her head at me, studying my arm. "*Yes,* they are. I know what they look like. My brother was a heroin addict for years. What the hell are you doing? You said it was just pills."

"Catch me up, what are we talking about?" Jordan appeared suddenly, my head snapping toward her voice as I yanked my wrist from Camilla's grip. Jordan leaned against the opening of the sliding glass door to the balcony, braiding her wet hair as it dripped onto my shirt that she was wearing.

My heart fucking sank.

I glanced at Camila, who kept her eyes locked on Jordan, before looking up at her myself as I rolled my eyes. Now I was at risk of being caught because of Cam, and she didn't even have the nerve to help me.

"Nothing important. Do you want to go lie down?"

She studied me as her fingers continued weaving pieces of her long hair in between one another.

"In a second. I'm not quite ready for bed yet." She sat on the couch next to Camilla, who had a concerned look plastered across her face.

"Alright, well, I'm pretty tired, so let me know when you're ready." I tried to sound nonchalant as my heart was beating out of my chest.

"I'm sure you are," she said coldly. I had really dug a deep fucking hole to get myself out of.

My phone lit up on the table in front of me and began ringing loudly with an incoming call. I quickly silenced it and put it face down on the couch next to me.

"Who is it?" Jordan asked.

"Ryan," I answered quietly, keeping my eyes fixed on the floor as I tapped my foot.

"Answer it," Jordan said sternly.

I looked at her with her stone-cold eyes, ones I had never seen before. I knew trying to avoid this would just make everything worse. Yet I still didn't want to face the music.

I slid my thumb across the screen and held it to my ear, and before I could even say a word, Jordan continued. "On speaker."

I threw my head back and looked at the night sky, reading her suspicion like a book, before putting the phone on speaker.

"What's up?" I asked Ryan emotionlessly. Music played in the background of wherever he was, conversation ringing out around him.

"Yo bro, you left your wallet at Analyn's. I forgot to tell you to hit her up when you want to get it!"

I immediately looked at Jordan, who was already walking inside with a disgusted facial expression, not shooting as much as a glance in my direction.

41. Jordan

This was the end.

He had had his fun with me, and now it was onto the next one.

I was always just a stepping stone and never anyone's end goal. I should have seen it coming.

He couldn't have ended it with me before hooking up with someone else?

"Listen…." the word tore me wide open. I didn't say anything. "I've been needing to tell you this, and it just never felt like the right time."

My chest got heavier and heavier with each breath as I continued to throw my clothes into my backpack.

He took a deep breath. Silence pierced the air between us as I waited for him to continue.

"Jake told me I need to be honest with you and that you'd understand, and I hope you do. If I mess this up, I will never forgive myself. The last thing I want is to lose you, so I hope that me telling you this doesn't cause that."

Adrian's eyes remained locked on the side of my face.

"Can you just say it and stop dancing around whatever you're trying to tell me? You fucked

Analyn last night and you think I'll forgive you for that? You're delusional, Adrian."

Harshness edged around my words. A side of me he hadn't seen yet. A tone and attitude reserved only for my mom and others who had disappointed me.

"What? I never fucked Analyn!"

My eyes shot to him, calling him on his bullshit. He grabbed the back of his neck.

"Okay, okay, I did fuck Analyn, but that was way before you. I haven't even talked to her since I met you, before last night. Ask Ryan, he was there."

"Oh, so you didn't fuck her, but spending the night and lying to me about it makes it better?" I scoffed at his stupidity, and at my own. I never should have trusted him. Jake and Ryan had warned me, and like the clueless bitch that I was, I ignored them.

"Fuck, I know, and I'm sorry. I just knew it was fucked up what I did, and I didn't want you to think I was doing something shady." I could feel him step closer to me, though I didn't turn around. Mindlessly, I continued to pack my things, on some form of autopilot.

A deep exhale left his lips. "I've been taking prescription pills. I'm trying to get off of them and I'm taking them a lot less than before…"

"So? If they're prescribed to you, who cares?"

"They're not."

"Not what?" I said between gritted teeth.

"Not prescribed to me. Some were when I was in high school, for rare occurrences, but I get them from a dealer now."

"Like what kind? What pills?"

"It depends on the day, benzos, pain killers, opiates…"

"The *day*?" I drew my words out. "You mean you've been on something everyday we've hung out? And you're just now telling me? *After* you asked me to stop doing any drugs, even occasionally?"

He stayed silent, staring at me as I processed what was going on – what had been going on since I met him, and even before that. Anger fired inside of me. Resentment and rage festered in the deepest part of my chest.

I paused.

"So this is what you and Camilla were talking about."

He sighed again. "Yes."

"So you mean to tell me you told my best friend and my brother before you even told me? What the fuck, Adrian?" My voice rang louder with each word.

"I didn't tell Jake. He already knew."

"Oh, so you just told my best friend before me. That makes it better. I can tell what I mean to you now!" I threw my clothes into my backpack with more force.

"I knew Jake was wrong when he said you wouldn't do this."

I snapped my head around and locked my eyes on him. Now lying on his bed on his back, his fingers ran through his hair as he stared at the ceiling.

"Jake said I wouldn't do what?" The sternness of my words sliced the air between us.

"That you wouldn't leave me when you found out I was using."

His words became a weight almost too heavy to bear. My anger melted away into sadness.

It hurt. *So fucking bad.*

My insides ached and my brain felt swollen inside my skull. The one person I thought I could let in and change my fear of anyone new had, in fact, confirmed my worries.

"I wouldn't leave you because you're using. I would leave you because you lied to me. Everyone is in on this secret besides me. You have been acting completely selfish. I look like a fool, Adrian. And not only have you hid your addiction from me, you lied straight to my face about where you were and what you were doing. How can I ever trust you?"

I chewed on my cheek as I stared at him in disbelief. "Let me see your arm."

He shot up from the bed and looked at me with furrowed eyebrows.

"Let you see *what*?" He asked, trying to make me feel insane.

"Camilla was looking at your arm. Let me see it."

"She was looking at my tattoo. You're acting crazy."

"If I'm acting crazy, then let me see your arms," I said, holding my hand out to him.

42. Adrian

Her words were punches, thrown at me one after the other. I never knew her beautiful, big blue eyes could be so piercing and cold. They had finally swallowed me up whole, the inevitable drowning in them making its promised appearance. Shame had eaten me alive as I tried to walk myself back from the edge of this cliff.

I held my arm out in front of me and she studied it for a moment, before looking at me with a horrified expression. I heard her breath leave her body, and I knew.

"You've been doing heroin?"

"What? No! I haven't been doing heroin!" I lied. I knew it was only making it worse, but I couldn't even admit to myself what I had done, let alone her. Raising my voice was my only defense.

"Shut the fuck up with your lying, Adrian. Those are track marks and I know it! I know what veins look like from fucking heroin, what those scabs and bruises are from. I'm not fucking stupid! I have been best friends with Camilla for 15 years. Her brother almost died from that shit!"

"I haven't been doing it, Jordan." I tried to speak calmly before we woke up the entire fucking building from our screaming. "I did it once, but I'll never do it again. It was a huge mistake."

"You did it on Wednesday."

She didn't ask. She stated it knowingly.

She already fucking knew.

"Yes, and I'm sorry. That was the first and only time I've done it, and I was fucked up beyond belief. That's the only reason I did it. I didn't know what was going on before I decided to do it, and that morning I regretted every second of the night."

She laughed mockingly.

Fuck, I hadn't known she could be so cold.

"So you mean to tell me, you were so fucked up on prescription pills and drunk, that you decided to go to the girl's house you used to fuck, do heroin, then spend the night there, all while I was waiting for you here?" She looked at me, amused. "You're fucking delusional, and I look like a fucking fool."

"You don't look like a fool, I do." I kept my eyes fixed on the floor.

"I *do* look like a fool! How can I trust you to be honest when you have been honest with everyone else besides me? If we're together, I should be the first one you tell. That's how these things work. Better yet, don't do something you need to lie about in the damn first place!" She crossed her arms over her chest, staring through me.

"I didn't know we were together, Jordan. Every time we go to your house, you make sure your mom isn't home. The only people that know about us are your friends."

Her eyes turned even colder. My response was stupid, trying to put the blame off of myself, but I was searching for any way out.

"You didn't know? Don't give me that bullshit, Adrian. I don't take you around my family because I don't want you to see that part of my life! My mom is a disaster! I can't stand the sight of her. Why would I want to be a part of that? You've seen it with your own eyes."

My heart sank with each word.

"I was afraid to tell you because I knew about your mom and how much she hurts you. I was afraid you couldn't handle another addict in your life."

Her eyes looked away from me, up to the ceiling as tears formed at the bottom, trickling down her cheek. She bit her bottom lip and kept her gaze fixed.

"You're right, I can't. More than that, I also can't handle dishonesty. If this was ever going to work, it would only be when you're clean. At least now I know who you really are and I can stop getting my hopes up. You're just like the rest of them, and it's my fault for thinking you weren't and letting you into my life. It was a stupid, childish decision."

She turned back to the dresser and picked up her backpack full of clothes.

"What are you doing?"

"I'm going home?" She didn't miss a beat on tearing my heart out as she spoke. Coldness edged around each word that left her mouth.

"Why? I'll get clean for you. No more drugs, drinking, nothing. You can watch me throw everything away. I'll do anything to make this work. I'll check into rehab tonight. I'll take a damn drug test everyday if I have to. Please give me a chance."

She shook her head, slipping her shoes on.

"You can only get clean for yourself. Doing it for me will never last. You have to want this for you, not for me. I see how it worked out when you already had that chance. You were selfish with your addiction, with your lying and deceiving, so maybe now you can try to be honest with sobriety."

"I will do it for me. Just please give me another chance to show you and fix this." I was begging, pleading for her to not walk out of my life forever.

"I'll believe it when I see it. This has already gone on long enough. You don't deserve another chance to rip my heart out in multiple ways."

"I'm sorry, Jordan. I love you." It felt so natural to say, but I knew the timing was the worst it could be.

She swung her backpack onto her shoulders and walked out of the room without looking in my direction, ignoring me completely. I flew out of bed and followed her down the hall, whispering after her so this didn't become a scene to everyone asleep around us.

"Please, at least wait until morning. It isn't safe to walk home alone right now." Despite my cautionary efforts, her hand reached for the door and turned the handle. Cold air rushed in, filling each corner of the room, taking me over.

"I think I can manage." She shut the door and disappeared from my sight.

I ran out the door and followed her, dying to beg her to stay, to dump all my truths on her and ask her to help me fix this.

Things I should have done months before.

I had never seen her like this. She was always sweet and quiet and loving – now she was fierce and dark. The girl that was like sunshine in any room, sweeter than candy, could suddenly make hell itself freeze over with one guarded look and words like bullets.

43. Jordan

Jake, Ryan, and Camilla walked into my room the next morning as I scrolled through my phone, hugging a pillow in front of me, my eyes red and swollen. I didn't look up as they sat on my bed and desk chair.

"How'd you get home?" Jake was stern, not shy to break the silent tension in the room.

"I walked."

"You walked?" He enunciated each word. "What do you mean you walked? Why didn't you wake me up?"

"I was upset and wanted to leave. I was going to wake you both, but I didn't see Camilla on the couch, so I figured you would know where I was this morning, anyway."

Camilla spoke before Jake could scold me more. "Are you going to talk to him?"

I scoffed. "I have nothing more to say to him. He wasn't honest when that's all I've ever been with him. I can't deal with waiting for an alcoholic to change for me my entire life, let alone hoping a heroin user might."

Jake's eyes went wide with my words.

Camilla sighed, defeated. "I know. But don't act so innocent either. We have all done things we aren't proud of," she mumbled.

I stayed silent. She was right. I had done plenty of things I wasn't proud of, but not goddamn heroin. Just anything else that made me numb from the pain I was yet to face.

I was being so hard on Adrian because of the scars my mom had left on me. All the horrible times had become marks on me, wounds that I was afraid of reopening. Wounds that I was confident the depth of Adrian's addiction would rip wide open.

I too was using various substances to distract myself from the memories that floated around my head, the endless hope, and disappointment, and frustration, and insecurity my mother's self-sabotage had been causing me. The feeling of not being enough to get her to stop killing herself slowly.

Being with Adrian every waking hour I could be was another substance used for distraction. Before Adrian, I had used Alec to fill the voids in my heart, though all he really did was make them larger, while making my self-worth smaller. I had justified my insufficient coping mechanisms by believing I wasn't as bad as others around me.

"What happened anyway? Why did you leave? Adrian was already surfing when we woke up this morning, so I couldn't ask. Are you okay?" Camilla spoke softly.

I took a deep breath to stop tears from forming.

"I'm sure you have an idea."

"He told you, didn't he?" Camilla looked at me sympathetically. Even in a messy bun and no sleep, she was still strikingly beautiful.

"Yeah. I didn't leave because he uses. I would have been willing to help him work through that. I care that he hid it from me, and made me look clueless with everyone else around me knowing. Him leaving me alone while he was fucking doing heroin at Analyn's house was the cherry on top. I'm done. "

"I didn't know until last night if it makes you feel any better."

"But he still told you before he told me. Jake, why didn't you say anything?"

He was scrolling through his phone as the words left my mouth. His eyes crept towards mine.

"Why didn't *I* say anything? I tried to warn you when you first met him, Jordan, and I didn't think you would be into him. Once you were in so deep, he needed to tell you, not me. And he knew that."

A sigh left my body in defeat. He had warned me, and I damned him for that, rather than seeking an explanation.

"Ryan, you fucking knew! You were *there!*" I stood up and rushed over to him, shoving him away from me. "How dare you!" I screamed, pushing against his hard chest repeatedly without a budge. His arms wrapped around me, restricting me from moving any more.

"I know you're mad, Jo."

"I'm fucking furious with you!"

Sobs broke out from my chest as I gave into his hold.

My heart and head were conflicted.

I wanted Adrian.

I loved him, and now I wanted to believe he loved me.

But why had he waited until I was leaving to tell me?

Why didn't he do what it took to keep me in the first place, rather than trying to win me back once I was gone?

My biggest fear was being hurt and let down by yet another person I loved. That was why I built up walls to be torn down before letting anyone into my heart. It was so much easier to have never loved at all, than to have loved and lost – especially when you lost a part of yourself with it.

Ryan's hand stroked my head, his chest heavy with each breath. "Shhh. It's okay, Jo. I'm sorry."

Alec's car pulled into the alley, and I snuck out the garage before anyone could realize what I was doing, and who I was doing it with. I hopped into the front seat and quickly shut the door, hiding behind his tinted windows.

"Hey babe, you good?"

I kept my eyes fixed out the window. "Yes. Just go, please."

"What's wrong?" One eyebrow raised as he shifted his car into drive, without looking away from me.

"Nothing, it's a long story. I just need to get out of that house for a little bit."

I knew this was a mistake that I would regret later, but I didn't care. All I wanted was to hurt Adrian as bad as he had hurt me. I wanted him to feel the betrayal and confusion I felt after trusting someone and having them blatantly go against your wishes, saying fuck what you felt.

If he had even cared at all.

Alec chuckled, tapping his fingers on his steering wheel. "I knew you'd come running back to me. You always do."

44. Jordan

I snuck in the front door of a silent house. Besides the light from the living room TV, it was nearly pitch black inside as I kicked my shoes off by the front door.

I rounded the corner into view of the living room, Jake sleeping on the couch with his mouth ajar.

Ever since the whirlwind with Adrian had begun, we had barely spent any time together. I missed him so fucking much. We had always been each other's number ones, and now I had never felt so distant from him.

I threw a blanket over him and shut off the TV, making my way upstairs to my room. I flicked my light on, jumping when I saw Ryan laying across my bed on top of the covers.

"Ryan, go home." I said through a deep breath, throwing my purse onto my desk. He blinked rapidly as he woke, rubbing his eyes to adjust to the new light.

"Jesus Jo, took you long enough."

"I don't want to talk to you right now."

"I know." He said flatly, sitting up on my mattress to look at me. "Which is exactly why we're going to talk about this."

"You don't just get to choose when you're a decent friend to me. I'm sick of everyone only having my back half of the time."

"Where were you?" Ryan leaned back onto his elbows, his eyebrows scrunched together.

"With Alec."

"Did you fuck him?"

"Does it matter?" I snapped, pulling my hoodie over my head and throwing it into my hamper.

"Kinda."

"My sex life isn't anyone's business but my own. But no, I didn't. You can go now."

"Just because you're hurt doesn't mean you should make it worse for yourself. Being around him is self-sabotage, and you fucking know it."

"Oh, so now you care about me? Nice to know what a selective friend you are."

He took a deep breath, rubbing his hand along the stubble on his cheek. "Just because I fucked up this time doesn't mean that I'm a shitty friend."

"You knew everything! You've been hiding shit from me since the day you warned me about him. It's not fair for you to keep me in the dark about everything! You're supposed to be my friend too!"

I squeezed my eyes together, pressing the tips of my fingers between my brows. "This is too much for me to handle. I didn't ask for any of this."

"I am your friend too." Ryan muttered.

"It doesn't feel like it sometimes. You have been absent from my life lately. I know you're figuring out things between you and Kaylee, which is fine, I get it, but all I'm asking is for you to have my back."

"Me and Kaylee are," exhale, "complicated, to say the least. But that doesn't mean I'm any less of a friend to you. I'm sorry I made it seem like that."

"This is just difficult to get a grip on. I don't know how things got like this."

"Come here." He patted the bed next to him, and I sunk into the mattress. "I'm sorry, Jo."

"Me too." I whispered, twisting my ring around my finger.

"I can't believe that I let him do this to me. I'm so fucking stupid."

"Hey," he whispered, moving my hair behind my shoulder. "This isn't your fault. You'll be okay."

"I just hate feeling like this."

"I hate seeing you like this. It's not fair to you, and I should have stopped it before it began. I knew he couldn't change who he was, but I didn't want to believe it."

I looked at him with heavy eyes, studying his sharp jaw.

Jake, Ryan, Camilla, and Kaylee.

They had always been the only ones I could count on. I don't know why I had tried to extend that circle farther, especially when they had warned me not to.

Ryan's hand found my face, his fingers tracing lightly on my jawbone. My eyes shut right as his lips met mine, and I fell into his kiss.

If I was going to go down, I was going to go down in flames.

He grabbed my hips, pulling me on top of him without breaking our kiss. My legs fell on either side of his waist as he laid back, bringing my wrists into his grasp and placing them against his chest.

Lips parting, his tongue traced my bottom one, and I opened slightly to let him in. Our tongues slid against each other, deepening our kiss. Our mouths continued to dance together, his cock hardening beneath his sweats. He lifted his hips, bringing his hand to the back of my neck and pulling me closer to him.

I let myself melt into him, taking advantage of the temporary distraction. Of the beating in my broken heart that his affection made me feel.

We continued to move against one another, lost in lips that should have never been touching. Ones that had lingered in the back of my mind, somewhere I refused to turn the light on and look at for years.

I waited, waited for the electricity to spark, for him to fill the gaps in my heart as our hips greedily continued to grind against each other. For him to give me everything that had been taken from me and more.

Thin fabrics separated him from slipping inside of me, ones that could have easily been removed. I felt as his cock pressed against my entrance, both of us ready to rid each other of the minimal barrier and get what we needed. What we both so desperately needed from each other.

His fingers slipped below the waistband of my sweats, running the fabric of my thong between them. Slowly, his fingers found my clit, rubbing it carefully.

I moaned into his mouth, his breath husky as our bodies sunk together. Somewhere between wrong and right, we allowed peace to sneak into the gaps of our souls.

"Fuck, Jo Jo," he groaned, grabbing the back of my neck and pulling me into him.

No space was between an inch of our bodies. How could a single molecule find its way between the invisible barrier that forced our bodies together?

My hips rode him, grinding against his swollen length as his fingers reminded me of what desire was. A desire that ached to be answered.

But he hadn't been able to fill the gaps that Adrian was meant to. Ryan was meant to fill the gaps that he had for my entire life, and nothing more.

It was too calm.

Not rough enough.

Not passionate enough.

Not world stopping or breathtaking or insanely   addictive.

It wasn't… him.

I pulled my lips from his, staring into his hooded caramel eyes. "We can't do this, Ryan."

"Fuck, I know." He pulled my face back to his, pressing a desperate kiss against my lips. I gave into him once more, letting him cloud the dark hell of my mind.

"Kaylee will never forgive me if we do."

Breathlessness lined our words, almost taking them completely. We met each other's lips, trying to tame the battle between desire and morals.

"We won't," he whispered, bringing another closed mouth kiss to mine. Plush lips pressing against my skin. "But you can't with Alec either. Promise me you won't, Jo. You're better than him."

"I won't."

His fingers slid to my hip, holding me tenderly. If only he could give me all the love I needed and more to piece together my shattered soul. He kissed me again, fisting my hair as we enjoyed our last intimate moments together. The unspoken ones.

"I love him," I said between pants, staring at him with begging eyes.

Give me some fucking clarity.

I didn't have to say who.

He knew.

He always fucking knew.

"I know, babe."

"How do I stop?"

"Fuck, I don't know, Jo. I really fucking don't. But you need to give it time. You can do this, I promise."

Ryan pressed one last soft kiss against my lips, running his hands along my scalp as loose strands of my hair fell beside my face. "Let's get some sleep."

I rolled off of him and he lifted his arm behind my head as I snuggled into his side. Silent tears fell into the black fabric of his shirt as he wrapped his arms around me, hugging me into the safety of his being.

My closed eyes continued to cry, though the heart-wrenching weeps never came. If they dried before I slept, I never knew, as I dozed off in the safety of Ryan's arms.

45. Jordan

"What if things are changing between us?"

I stared into Ryan's eyes, his face relaxed.
Stress free.

Calm.

The exact opposite of how I was feeling.
Storms were brewing constantly in my chest,
unwilling to give me a moment of calmness.

Music pounded through the house as I
watched the flashing lights shine against Ryan's skin.
We had steered clear of Hansen's since the last time
that I saw Adrian weeks ago. Ryan's house had
become the new stomping grounds, where we could
avoid conflict to the best of our ability.

*Though I was the only one apprehensive
about going anywhere else.*

Nevertheless, everyone silently abided and
planned to meet up anywhere besides the
unspeakable bar. They bent over backwards without
me even asking.

Leaning against the hallway door as I waited
for the bathroom door to open, I was running off
fucking fumes, emptiness, and a need to keep going
no matter how badly I didn't want to. No matter how
badly I wanted to give up, and let myself fall victim
to my surroundings.

Just as my mother had.

"Relax, Jo. Nothing is changing between us. You're overthinking everything fucking possible lately."

"I know, but I don't know. Ever since... you know, I just can't stop thinking, what if I lose you, Ryan? I can't afford to lose anyone else. I really fucking can't-"

"Hey," he interrupted me, putting a stop to the thoughts that fell from my mouth in a panic. "Nothing is fucking changing between us. Got it? *I* don't want shit to change between us. I love us. So just relax, Jo. We're the same that we always have been."

I took a deep breath, my heart beating against my ribs – painfully beating.

"I know, I'm sorry. I just love you and I can't... I can't imagine not having you with me."

"You don't have to imagine that because it will never happen." He pulled me into his chest, his arm around my shoulders. "I'm worried about you, but we'll all get through this. We've been too strong for too long not to."

Wrapping my arms around his back, Ryan placed a long kiss on my lips, followed by a few short ones.

He had become my safe place, even more than before. Where Jake couldn't be, Ryan could.

It was different with him.

No obligations.

No judgment or shaming or hiding things. Just *us*.

"I fucking knew it." Adrian's voice boomed as Ryan dropped his arms from around me. "I fucking knew there was something between you. There always has been."

Ryan threw his hands up to his shoulder, innocently holding his palms towards Adrian. "What the fuck are you talking about?"

"Don't act like you didn't just kiss my fucking girl."

Ryan scoffed, chuckling mockingly at Adrian. "Dre. Chill the fuck out. We're all sick of this shit, including her."

"So you want to tell me you've never kissed my girl before right now?" Adrian stepped closer to Ryan, inches away from his face, as fires raged behind his eyes, darkness circling beneath his sockets. He looked like he hadn't slept in a week, maybe longer.

"I'm not your girl, Adrian." Calmness laced my voice, contrary to what I was feeling inside.

His eyes snapped to me, green contrasting against white that had been stained with red. Whatever he was on, whatever he had been doing since I had seen him weeks ago, I didn't want to fucking know. The evidence on his face was more than enough to remind me I needed to stay away.

I held my breath, eyes darting between the two of them as Adrian approached me, putting his hands on the wall beside me, caging me in.

He leaned down to my height, his nose brushing against mine lightly. "So you want to tell me you've never kissed him? Done anything sexually together? Amuse me. Tell me you didn't."

"I'm not going to tell you that," I gulped, my eyes falling to his plush lips. Heartbeat sounded in my throat as I focused on my breathing.

In and out.

In and out.

"Good. I would hope that none of you are stupid enough to lie to me, mija. Admit it. You fucked him. I can see it."

"What?" I breathed, my eyes darting between his. "We barely kissed. It's not a big deal, so quit making it one."

"Dre, back the fuck up," Ryan warned from besides me. I kept my eyes fixed on Adrian as I spoke.

"You invited him?"

"I invited Analyn," Ryan replied. "Apparently, she took it upon herself to bring a guest."

Adrian nodded, laughing to himself as his head bowed down, hanging between his wide shoulders. "Leave it to my best friend to go after my girl right when he gets the fucking chance. Is anyone surprised?"

"What?" Kaylee appeared through a now open bathroom door, the lights still on behind her. "Jordan, what? Is that true?"

Adrian's arms dropped to his side, staring at me with a blank expression. The only emotion behind his eyes was despair. The same horrible, heart-wrenching despair I had been feeling for weeks.

Except he was the one who caused it – for both of us.

"Don't bother trying to get them to admit it, it's true," he said to Kaylee, his eyes fixed on mine. "But neither of us will ever know how fucking far it actually went." Adrian turned and walked back towards the living room, his shoulder rigid with disgust.

"Kaylee, I'm sorry-"

"Don't." She held her hand up to me, not looking in my direction with eyes that were now filled with tears. "You guys deserve each other, really. I'm sorry about what happened to you, Jo. I really am. But that isn't an excuse for you to treat me like shit. I've done nothing to you."

Ryan pinched the bridge of his nose, his eyes squeezed shut. "Kaylee, this isn't her fault. I came on to her, and she stopped it. If you're going to blame anyone, blame me."

She scoffed, her watery brown eyes finding him.

"Oh believe me, I already did blame you. I just don't want anything to do with either of you ever again."

She sniffed lightly, rushing away from us and down the hall, Ryan chasing after her.

I threw my head back, closing my eyes and trying to calm the sinking feeling in the pit of my stomach.

How had I fucked things up even worse?

I hadn't thought that was fucking possible.

Adrian had lied to me. Betrayed me. Hid everything under the fucking sun from me, gotten between me and my family, me and my friends.

Yet I was the one in the fucking dog house.

Goddamn, he was good. Really fucking good.

He always got his way, no matter what.

I took a deep breath, making my way to sit next to Camilla on the couch. I rubbed my eyes with my fingertips, bringing my hands to my forehead and resting my elbows on my knees.

"You okay?" Camilla's hand found my back, her voice sweet with understanding.

"I don't think I've been okay for a while." I chuckled, lifting my head and wiping tears from my cheek.

I'm so sick of fucking crying.

My eyes met with Adrian's right as he leaned down and held a rolled up hundred-dollar bill to his nose. Snorting a line of cocaine off the kitchen counter, his green, bloodshot eyes never left mine.

Analyn had her hand on his back the entire time, swooning over him as he snorted up poison.

My stomach twisted, ready to send vomit right back up my throat.

"I need to leave," I breathed to Camilla, standing up and walking past Adrian.

"Jo-" Camilla started, uncertainty in her voice.

"No." Adrian interrupted her, his voice thick with anger. "Let her fucking go. We all know that would be better."

"Shut the fuck up, Adrian!" Camilla yelled, fed up with everything. With her friends ripping each other apart in front of her eyes.

"You're fucking high! You're always fucking high! Quit being so goddamn pissed off all the time! Or better yet, quit doing the drugs that make you so pissed off all the fucking time! You're so fucking lucky Jake isn't here," she breathed, following me. "Quit acting like all of this isn't your fucking fault, Adrian," she stated coldly, before slamming the front door behind us and walking down Ocean Blvd beside me.

46. Jordan

This was stupid.

I knew it was stupid.

Everyone knew it was stupid.

Yet the stupidity wouldn't stop me.

I lazily ran my eyes over the surrounding crowd, my breathing labored with alcohol and heartbreak.

Was it the alcohol or the heartbreak that made me feel like I was going to die?

Could anything kill me if I was already dead inside?

Alec's arm wrapped around my back as I watched Jake throw a match onto the wood, letting the flames invade the empty fire pit. Towering towards the sky, Jake poured gasoline in every direction, angering the already furious fire. The sun had just set, leaving a pale blue begging to stay behind, before blackness took over both the sky and the ocean in front of us.

Jake wouldn't look at me.

When Ryan did, there was disappointment laced in his gaze.

Camilla was the only one who offered me a smile.

If only it wasn't one that had been based on sympathy and biting her tongue.

When I was with Adrian, everyone was cautious.

They were unsure about me being with him, but they learned to accept it. To give him a chance and trust my judgment, even if it went against their own.

With Alec, everyone looked at me like I was plain fucking stupid.

And I was.

I was plain fucking stupid.

The thing was, when your heart was broken and all you felt was despair, you'd take any feeling as a distraction.

Even if it was shame.

Or judgment.

Or both.

Alec's arm dropped from around my waist as I gulped down my mixed drink, letting the vodka and lemonade bite my tongue. Hands grabbed my shoulders, and I leaned into the familiar figure, my eyes resting on the waves as they melted into the sand.

"If you ever let him touch you again, I'll fucking kill him." Breath laced with whiskey trailed down my neck, bringing goosebumps to my skin. A voice that I hadn't heard in weeks. *One that I had been trying to forget.*

I turned my head slightly, Adrian's face coming into view out of the corner of my eye as he gripped my shoulders tighter.

"Probably should have thought about that when your opinion still mattered to me," I sneered between gritted teeth. Pulling out of his grip, I began moving across the sand, away from him and towards Ryan. Our eyes locked as Adrian grabbed my wrist, whipping me around.

"I'm not just letting you fucking walk away from me."

His permanently bloodshot eyes darted around my face, begging silently.

Angrily.

Eyes laced with a pain that was hidden behind every type of drug that you could name.

"Then I guess it's a good thing that I'm not asking for your permission."

"Jordan. I'm sorry. Please give me one more fucking chance. I promise I won't fuck it up." His voice strained as he brought his hand to my cheek, tempting me to rest on his palm.

I missed him.

I missed him so fucking much.

I missed his kisses and his laugh and the way he got lost in explaining things he was passionate about as I stared up at him from his chest.

I missed tracing his tattoos with my fingers before we fell asleep.

I missed watching his smile grow when he learned something new about me.

I missed the way that he felt like home.

But my eyes still glanced at his elbow, searching for track marks – and that's when I was reminded why it would never work.

I turned my head away from him, locking my eyes with Ryan and Jake, Ryan full speed ahead towards me.

"I can't do this, Adrian. We can't do this anymore."

Tears pricked at the corners of my eyes as I looked at him behind the water, his jaw going slack. Hope drained from his face right in front of me. Ryan rushed up to him, putting his hand on his shoulder.

"This isn't the fucking time, Dre."

Adrian kept his hand wrapped around my wrist, running his thumb softly along my skin. He looked from me to Ryan and back again, desperation dying out. "Ryan, please."

Ryan looked at me for confirmation, my head shaking before we made eye contact. Tears streamed down my face slowly and I swiped them away before they could reach my cheek, keeping my gaze fixed on the sky above.

Black, without a star to be seen.

"I need to go."

Adrian dropped my hand, and the world moved slowly for a moment as I shifted through the sand.

So slowly.

I couldn't have been more than an inch away from them before Ryan spoke again.

"Just let her go, bro."

"I can't," Adrian breathed. I could feel his eyes pinned to the back of my head as I took another step.

Just take another fucking step, Jordan.

"You have to," Ryan replied calmly, sympathy lacing his words.

"When did you turn into such a fucking traitor?" Adrian sneered, his eyes burning into the back of my head.

I was so grateful not to be Ryan at this moment – even more thankful that he was taking Adrian's wrath for me.

"Dre, just calm down." Ryan kept his cool, trying to talk Adrian down.

He didn't give a shit that he was causing a scene. He would disrupt the world if it meant being able to fix everything between us.

But it wouldn't.

That's what I kept reminding myself, pleading to myself to remember the reality of what we were.

One foot in front of the other, I let my heart get ripped out of my chest once again, as I made my way towards Jake. He pulled me into his chest as I let silent sobs escape my lungs, staining his white T-shirt with tears.

Memories flooded my mind.

So long ago, we sat around this same fire pit, silently drawn to one another in ways we didn't know.

Was it so long ago?

How many days had gone by?

Years it felt like.

I could have sworn that was a different lifetime ago.

Lifting my head from Jake's chest, I wiped my cheeks and looked towards Alec. He tilted his head sympathetically.

Could he see how much he had hurt me?

Or did he think he was my savior after what Adrian had done?

He wasn't the one to save me. How could he fix something that he had made the first crack in? People who purposely break delicate china don't deserve to be the ones to fix them and enjoy their beauty.

As he took another step towards me, only feet away, Adrian's fist connected with his cheek. He stumbled to the side, keeping his balance and looking back at Adrian with rage in his eyes.

Rage that could never match Adrian's.

No one knew the fire that burned inside of Adrian's chest, waiting to be released.

Before Alec could redeem himself, Adrian's knuckles collided with his face once again. His palm gripped the collar of Alec's shirt, fabric stretching as he held him upright.

"If you put another fucking hand on her in front of me again, I'll throw you in that fire before you can fucking blink. Hell will sound *nice* compared to what I'll do to you."

Adrian stared down at Alec, his eyes wild and breathing labored. An animalistic side of him I had only seen glimpses of before, it now made its full appearance.

Jake made his way towards Adrian as he held Alec over the fire pit, leaning against the cement ring. Without a care in the world, Jake walked up to Adrian and didn't say a word. He stared at him silently, shaking his head so slowly that surely no one noticed it besides me and Adrian.

"Let's go, Jo." Ryan swooped me up like a baby, his arms under my knees and around my back. I waited for the tears to come. For something to come.

Silent with shock, I stared at the street as Ryan trudged through the sand.

Why?

Why did God look at me and decide that I needed to deal with all of this?

Why did he make all the people who I loved the most, the biggest disappointments of all?

Why did he betray me in the biggest way possible?

Why did they?

A sob broke loose from my chest as I buried my head in Ryan's neck. "Why do they always fucking betray me?"

He didn't try to explain, didn't argue with me. He just squeezed my shoulder, running his thumb softly over my skin. "I know, Jo, I know."

"Wait!" Camilla yelled from behind us, running as quickly as she could through the thick sand. "Jake's coming," she said between pants as she slowed her pace to match Ryan's.

We all remained silent as we made our way towards Ocean Blvd, walking along the boardwalk towards our house.

Cars passed slowly, some couples on bikes and teenagers on long boards as they made their way home from the beach. I counted the headlights that passed as I rested my head on Ryan's chest.

Why was he always the one to pick me up when I was down? Jake did so silently, as he had my entire life. Where Ryan was physically, Jake was mentally. My rocks. My other halves. The ones that found me in this lifetime, as they had surely been in the one before.

Why hadn't Adrian ever done the same for me?

Done anything?

My chest caved in the entire ten-minute walk home, and by the time we walked up the steps to our porch, I allowed the defeat to overtake me.

There was no coming back from this.

He was never coming back from this.

Trying to fight it was a futile effort. I had slowly accepted the truth over the last few weeks until he walked right back into my life and smacked me in the face with it once again.

"I can't believe he would act like that," I whispered, taking my sandals off by the front door.

"Me neither." Camilla matched my volume level, mimicking my actions. I held onto Ryan's shoulder as I slipped my slippers on. Through all the commotion, I had forgotten how drunk I had been.

Was I drunk?

Maybe heartbreak was enough to intoxicate you on its own.

"He was so fucking high," I said to no one, focusing on keeping my balance as I placed my foot back on the ground.

Jake confirmed what I already knew, but didn't ever want to believe. "Yeah. He was."

47. Adrian

11/4/19.   2:02 A.M.
We really need to talk.
               5:33 A.M.
Goddamnit, Jordan. Why are you always so

 fuckking difficult.

11/7/19.   7:58 P.M.
**I'm sorry for flipping out. Over text, at Ryan's,
the bonfire. I'm sorry for it all. I'll always be here
for you if you need me.**

11/18/21   4:25 A.M.
**Hopefully Ryan is giving you everything you
fucking ned. Or Alec. Or whoever the fuck took
my spot from my handds.**
               4:29 A.M.
No ome will ever love you like i do.

11/27/19   3:48 A.M.
I love you.

And that's when my messages stopped delivering.

48. Adrian

Weeks passed with no word from Jordan. The only reason I knew she was still alive were various Instagram and Snapchat stories people posted.

Her at the beach with Camilla.

Jumping off the boat with Ryan.

Catching a fish with Anthony, wearing the lonely ghost hoodie I loved on her. Her blue eyes twinkled in the sunset, matching the ocean that surrounded her.

I blocked them all before deleting my Instagram.

Each day I felt the miniscule fucking desire that I had to live dwindling slowly.

I reached out time and time again, each of my texts and calls left ignored. Every time I wandered the beach back to my car after surfing, my eyes scanned the sand and the sea, hoping to be in the right place at the right time and to run into her. I did the same at grocery stores, gas stations, parties, but I never was. It was always the wrong place at the wrong fucking time since she had left me.

Thanksgiving came quickly. My mom couldn't afford a ticket out, so we used FaceTime so we could have dinner together. The rest of the night was spent alone with a couple of benzos, some opiates, and a bottle of gin. With no one left in my life who I cared about anymore, I used the company of some whiskey and comedy shows to celebrate the holiday.

I had stuck to my vow of never doing heroin again, no matter how badly the desire to escape my new reality without Jordan was.

I had thought I needed a mental block of my current situation before – little did I know how heaven-like it seemed compared to my new one.

This time of the year was always harder than most, though this time it hit me like a fucking bus.

Everyone was preoccupied with spending time with their families. All of my friends had loving homes to celebrate in, while I had an empty apartment and an addiction. I popped open another fifth and sunk into the couch, watching everyone's snapchat stories of their traditional Thanksgiving meals, in their traditional family homes, with their traditional loved ones.

My mouth watered at the sight of endless perfectly baked turkeys and homemade meals so delicious, I had almost forgotten what they tasted like.

I envied the couple photos with cheesy captions, a reminder of what I had lost. What I had single-handedly fucked up beyond repair.

It didn't matter how much hatred I had for my addiction; it was a part of me I couldn't rid myself of

– though if it had been as simple as removing a limb, I would have cut it off with no pain meds.

It was still hard to admit to myself the reality of what my fixation was – an addiction – but deep down, I now knew the truth. When I tried to enjoy it, I couldn't control it, and when I tried to control it, I couldn't enjoy it.

Jordan had called all my bullshit out, said it so confidently it was like reading a headline on a newspaper. As much as I wanted to take the easy way out and deny it to myself and anyone else who would listen, I knew that wouldn't change the reality of the situation.

I was an addict.

The lines of cocaine that I was snorting off my coffee table, the football game playing dully in the background, proved exactly that.

People can judge addicts all they want.

Well, if they truly loved me, they would stop.

The ugly truth about addiction was that our love for others was the only reason we kept going at all.

If it was simple enough to stop because your love for others had overpowered any need to feed those cravings, addicts wouldn't exist.

The fact that we *couldn't* stop for the ones we loved only fueled our guilt and hatred for ourselves, which then strengthened our need to escape. Now that I had lost the only thing in my life that was bigger than myself, there was no reason to fight my inner demons. Giving into them came so naturally – so easily.

My heart ached for Jordan, though it ached for myself more.

How dare she define me by my weakness?

But then again, how dare I allow my weakness to define my life?

My heart ached that she couldn't be what saved me. And if she couldn't be that, nothing could be. She was the reason my heart beat, anyway.

My grasp on reality must have left me slowly, leading to a few more benzos than I could handle that Thanksgiving afternoon.

I woke up on the bathroom floor, next to a toilet full of vomit, Trevor violently shaking me while he yelled my name.

"Bro, what the fuck Adrian? What did you take?"

The sound rang out distantly.

The world shifted and tilted in every direction as I tried to get my eyes to focus on him. It felt like I was looking at him from under water, like he was trying to yell at me, but the sound couldn't travel through the liquid correctly.

Like when we were kids and we would try to guess what the other was saying while speaking underwater in his pool.

Was that the game we were playing now?

Some invisible wall separated me from him, making me an observer of the room, rather than a participant within it.

I stared at him as he shook me over and over, my eyes struggling to stay open, before closing again only seconds later.

Heartbeats slowly sounded in my ears as my shirt clung to my sweat soaked skin. Trevor was begging me to come to, though I couldn't respond.

Unable to move.

Unable to breathe.

My heart unable to fucking beat.

My breaths were long and slow, each one harder to drag in and out of my lungs than the last.

I had lost control of my body and after an endless struggle, I finally gave up trying to gain it back.

Trevor's face spun steadily above me against the blinding white ceiling until he faded completely into the darkness for one last time.

The silence of the water swallowed me whole, my lungs struggling to breathe liquid instead of air.

The weightlessness and freedom I craved to discover had been attained.

Floating, I calmly drifted out into the sea.

I was in the tranquil eye of the storm.

Serenity had been found.

Before We Drowned Book Two:

Swimming Lessons

Coming In Summer 2022

Acknowledgements

Wow! As I sit here, having read through Before We Drowned for the billionth time, I can't believe I'll actually be hitting print here in a few hours. Talk about a WTF moment. I started this book for fun many years ago, never thinking it would see the light of day, but here we are.

I would like to thank, first and foremost, anyone who has read this book from front to back, or even opened the cover. Addiction is a hard thing to talk about, and doing so in a way that is raw and real is even harder. At times, I wanted to punch all of these characters in the face (and still do), but going about this novel in a way that felt authentic and realistic was always my main priority. I hope that I stuck true to that!

If you or anyone that you know is struggling with addiction, I hope that this book gave you somewhat of a voice. Addiction looks different for everyone, and loving someone while hating their addiction is one of the most conflicting feelings, whether that person is yourself or someone else. By changing the stigma and talking openly about addiction, hopefully we can allow others to feel safe and get the help that they may need.

To Dominic, thank you for listening to me cry, complain, laugh, and go through all the feels, and for not getting mad when I ignored you for hours on end while writing. You are my muse through and through, and I love you.

Mom, you have believed in me and supported me everyday of my life, and I would be lost without you. Hopefully this novel will re-spark your love for reading!

I have to thank you Amanda, for listening to me and keeping my feet on the ground and calling me twenty times per day. You and me against the world forever, baby!

Everyone needs a cheerleader, and Bailey you are my biggest one. No matter what I do, you help me remember that I am amazing and will strive in whatever I try. Thanks for always lifting me up and never putting me down. You help me see the good in me and everyone else.

Tesia and Meg, thanks for inspiring me with your wild stories. You both keep me young and I wouldn't have it any other way. Adding this novel to the never-ending lists I will continue to send you!

Chase and Cade, you are the perfect contrast of sweet and harsh, and somewhere in the middle, Jake was born – though a little more harsh than either of you. Love you guys.

To my Grandpa Jim, who passed away on Christmas, three months before I finally finished this book. He always had a book in his hand as he sat on his front patio. I thank him for my love of reading and love of life.

To my dad, who always pushes me to be better and helps me see the light. You remind me to keep my life fun in any way that I can.

I would like to thank my editor, Roxana, and Kaley, Maddy, and Valeria for all of their insight, and for helping me to find the flaws and highlights of this crazy story. You helped me see my words come to life on the page.

And thank you to everyone who has listened to Adrian and Jordan's story. They give a voice to those who may need one the most.

Until next time.

Just keep swimming.

Made in the USA
Las Vegas, NV
30 August 2022